To H[...]

Good luck with your design
business and keep
living a creative life!

Angels and Avalon

Book One

Catherine Milos

For my husband, who helped me to let go of the past and build a brighter future.

Part 1

1

RUN. HER FEET STRUGGLED to comply with the command her mind bellowed. Run! Heavy foot falls echoed behind her and encouraged her forward. She darted into a side street and hoped it would not dead-end. She had no idea where she was going. The new sensations in her feet as they hit cobblestone caused her legs to jolt and jar uncomfortably. She turned left and dodged a few people walking in the morning air. Not that there was any air left in this retched place. She sped around another corner and paused to listen for the steps of the guards over her pounding heart. A faint echo from behind told her they were coming. The softer their foot falls, the closer her mother's guards were to catching their prey.

She ducked into an alley and curled up in the shadows. She prayed, hoping against all odds that they would not find her. Soon the foot falls grew silent and she feared the worst. She had heard from the other prisoners in her mother's dungeon that the guards whispered your name before sealing your fate with a swift blade, if they were feeling merciful. She wondered what it was they would whisper to her. She had no name. Would they be merciful and swift or would they end her short existence slowly?

She hoped her inner-light, as her mother had called it, would not betray her hiding place. She tried to rub soot all over her exposed skin. The dark green dress her lady in waiting had stolen for her covered most of her, but her neck, face, arms, and feet lay bare. Her skin was pale like moonlight, glowing white with subtle, swirling pinks, greens and blues just beneath the surface. Her hair could not make up its mind, changing with the weather, her mood, or the light – flowing from chestnut to auburn, auburn to the colors of fire, and fire to the color of straw and back again. It was not her fault she was so bright. She would change if she could. She would be like the others with their dark hair, grayed skin, and dark eyes. But she was not and could not be like them.

Towers of smoke billowed from homes. Soot fell, coating the bitter cold ground. If there was ever any color in this world, surely the smoke and soot would have choked it out quickly. The crumbling church steeple teetered like a gaping maw, ready to swallow up all the light and joy in the world and spew darkness from its blackened depths. She had heard other children talking about it as they sat outside the dungeon walls to try and get a glimpse of her, the freakish daughter of the Queen.

The girl turned away from the sight of the church and curled up closer to the wall. Her mother, had no other heir, but would not pass on her throne to someone like her daughter. She was too soft, too loving, too bright to rule over the type of court the Queen had built and maintained: a court of darkness and pain. Six years in the darkness and shadows of the dungeon, facing the demons, sorcerers and criminals her mother sent down there had not chased the light from her eyes. She closed her eyes tightly to hide their dancing colors. In the interest of her kingdom the Queen declared an alternative heir, a distant male relative, and ordered her nameless daughter killed so she could not try to claim the throne for herself. Fearing for her life, she had escaped from the dungeons and now cowered in the corner of a frigid dead-end.

It wasn't long until the little nameless girl lost all sensation from the cold. She may have cried, but her tears had dried up long ago. Instead, she fell into a fitful, exhausted sleep hidden by soot and darkness. She drifted in the bright world of dreams. The only place she had ever felt she had belonged.

A growing light surrounded her and pulled her from her dreams. Her imaginings of trees and blue sky flew past her. Beyond her dreams was a blinding white light. She drifted there unable to move or speak. Terror flashed through her, but it was chased away by a sense of warmth and safety. For the first time in her life, the unfortunate girl felt safe enough to let go and sleep deeply.

2

WHEN GODDESS FIRST STEPPED into the space that would become Avalon it was half formed: a dead space in between all worlds. She shaped the space until it reflected the beauty of her own being. She created plants and stone, breathed life into the sea, and painted a sun in the sky. It was bright and beautiful. Too bright. She birthed a moon to chase the sun, dividing the day in half, and tossed stars into the sky to illuminate the night. Goddess had built many worlds before this, with the help of the Others. But this place, this paradise, belonged only to her.

On Avalon she built herself a temple, her gateway between this world and the Others. Here in a temple of darkness and silence, Goddess could think, rest, and dream. Here she hid from the Others. Goddess stepped out of the temple, walked down the stone steps at its entrance, and exhaled calmly. Her breath caressed Avalon with an eternal breeze that soothed and calmed.

Goddess smiled at her creation and with her smile Avalon became populated with friends. Birds sang the song of Goddess's joy, flitting about and chasing each other through the trees. Smaller creatures chattered within the forest and burrowed underground, busying themselves with building homes and families. Larger animals lazily grazed and ambled across the meadows.

To pass the time, Goddess spun a river from one end of the land and wove it through to the other to empty into the sea. Fish with rainbow scales swam through the crystal clear water. The vast ocean filled what once was the nothingness surrounding her paradise. Cradling the golden-green isle, the ocean caressed white and pink sandy beaches.

There came a time when Goddess could no longer visit her temple on Avalon as often as she liked. The Others began to demand more of her. To sustain the creatures, the waters, and Avalon itself, Goddess left a piece of her heart deep in the foundations of the island. Her heart pumped life, energy and power into the plants, soil, air, creatures, and water. To keep the sun shining, and so she could always look upon Avalon, she left a piece of her eye at its center. Finally, Goddess left a tiny piece of her spirit in the middle of the moon, to make sure night always quietly fell each day.

Because the Others must not find her secret world, for they would surely take it away from her if they did, Goddess built a misty, concealing barrier around Avalon. The Others, especially God, her consort, were jealous of her capability to create thriving worlds on her own and so They had forbidden Goddess to create without Them. They claimed that anything created by Goddess alone would be a half-creation, lacking all the elements necessary for complete existence in the realms. All Goddess wanted was a place to call her own. Was it so terrible to want a place no one else could touch or twist or take from her?

The Others did have one good reason. A very long time ago, when Goddess and God first wished to create, they created children without the Others. They called these children Angels. Each Angel was unique, just a little bit, for Goddess had put a sense of self within each of her children. They served as messengers, and, when Goddess or God could not watch over a world, as guides and guardians of the many worlds that were created.

Misfits, Angels had no world or place to call their own. Ethereal in origination, they used the ether to move about; not like Goddess and God who were already everywhere and nowhere. The Angels followed the will and wishes of their creators, for they had no freewill. As they grew older, not all the Angels agreed with following God or Goddesses desires.

Angels were powerful, but they were far from gods. The Angels could not create the elements out of nothing as their makers and the Others could. However, there was a consequence God and Goddess had not foreseen. Because the Others were not a part of the Angels, the Angels were not bound by the Others. It was an Angel's duty to control their self and ensure the Others were obeyed and considered, but not all Angels heeded this responsibility. Some Angels rebelled and wanted to make themselves gods. Because of the rebellion lead by Lucifer, the Others decreed that all – the Fates, Time, Balance, Death, Birth, Darkness, Light, Justice, Hope, Agony, and God and Goddess – must be equal parts of the creation of any living thing or world. As a result, the Others forbade God and Goddess from creating any further Angels. There was no way They would let Goddess create beings on her own, surely the result would turn out worse than the Angels.

Although Earth had not yet been formed, many other worlds had been created, were dying, or had already ceased to exist. It was the responsibility of the Angels, Goddess, and God to watch over worlds formed, and destroy worlds that threatened Balance. The darkness of the nameless girl's world had grown and the planet, unable to sustain life, had slowly curled into itself, dying. The desperate heap was to be cleansed of all life and given an opportunity to heal, start over. If it was unable to recover, the mass of planet would be ended too.

Goddess put a little fragment of herself into each creation and each cleansing took a toll on her, destroying that fragment. It was in a desolate world, in the nameless girl, that Goddess saw a piece of herself gathered whole again. The last of what was left of her in that dying world. Goddess nurtured this treasured part of herself and held fast to it and nestle it safely away.

Goddess brought the young girl to Avalon where she laid her down on the side of a hill. The girl's world slipped away under an army of Angels as she slept. Avalon was her home now. Here Goddess could watch over the girl and provide her with everything she would ever need, including a name.

Adamina, Goddess whispered, *Adamina, wake up child.*

Lightning snapped through the sky and thunder shook Adamina awake. The rain poured down over the green hills. Fear and adrenaline filled her as she clambered to her feet. She had to keep running. She ran down the hill and into a plain covered in grass and clover slick with rain drops. Adamina's eyes darted wildly, searching for the inevitable arrival of … what. She couldn't remember what she was running from. The scent of lavender and lemon thyme filled her lungs, causing her fear to ebb and her racing heart to slow slightly. A forest on the other side of a plain came in view and Adamina jogged towards it. She tripped over a tree root and fell.

Soil! Fresh soil? No soil was left in her mother's kingdom as far as she had known. Before she had been given to the dungeons, the little nameless girl rode out on a little brown pony in search of a patch of soil and seeds. Stories of trees and forests, wildlife and plants beyond those few harvested in the soot-covered fields ignited her curiosity. Digging in the ground all she had found was sand and soot. The trees and flowers she had dreamed about would never be. And yet, here they were in front of her very eyes.

Adamina pulled herself up off the ground and looked around slowly. Trees clouded her vision. The rhythm of rain drops sliding and bursting on leaves above her were the only sounds she could hear. Her mouth gaped at the scene and she had to blink and rub her eyes several times before she began to believe. Adamina realized that she was not cold. She had always been cold. The new warmth caused her limbs to ache. The tempo of the rain began to slow and she walked unhurriedly, taking in the forest, mentally mapping exits and clearings as she came across them.

When the sun began to peek through the clouds and the rain stopped, Adamina found herself in a large clearing. The path that led her there had been made of fine reddish and grey sand that clung to her feet. A small circular space was framed by two stone benches. Adamina had never before seen so much sun, so much color and life. She gaped in awe as her gaze stretch up and up over smooth stone.

A temple reached high above with pillars taller than trees and four stone steps each nearly as tall as she was. Humming began to fill her blood and urge her into the darkness past the doorway of the temple. A small voice inside her heart answering her unspoken question told her this place was called Avalon.

She remembered temples. Gods lived in temples. She climbed the large stone steps until she faced the entrance. Inside was pitch black and silent. Adamina stepped into the darkness. At first nothing happened, so Adamina kept moving forward. Then she fell. Images began to flash before her eyes and Adamina became aware of other places.

She hovered at the entrance to a desert road lined with a gypsy fortune teller, shadows, and a book on a pedestal at the end of the road. Chills skated down her and Adamina tried to turn away. The world tugged at her. Goddess, seeing this through the sun of Avalon, reached out and caught the young girl, pulling her away from the shadowy realm.

Hello Adamina, Goddess said.

"H-hello," Adamina stuttered back into complete darkness.

The sound of her own voice startled her.

Do not be afraid. I am Goddess. I have taken you away from a world of darkness and pain and brought you here to Avalon. If you need anything, you shall have it. I will teach you how to live well and you will be well here. Remember, Adamina, Goddess soothed, *I am always with you.*

Adamina, remembering that only priests and priestesses could talk to the gods, asked, "Am I your priestess, Goddess?"

Goddess laughed with a soft joy and replied, *Yes, child you will be my first priestess,* for Goddess had no other. *But do not worship me like those gods of your painful world were worshiped. Love me as a child loves their mother. Perform no sacrifices for me. Honor me with respect for all of Avalon. Learn the beat of my heart which sustains the land. Know that you are safe as I watch over you from the great light in the sky. You are loved my child. Now live, priestess of Avalon, Adamina.* Goddess poured her love into Adamina and everything became silent.

I AM WEARY, MOTHER, the Angel mourned.

Goddess sighed softly in understanding and heartache,

My child, I understand. What is it you have come to ask of me?

Is there no place I can go and retire to where Father cannot find me? I am done fighting his wars and cleaning up my kindred's messes. The devastation I have seen, the lives I have taken.

The Angel mourned, holding reverence for life, for mortality, that few of his kind possessed. Goddess smiled and saw herself reflected in the amber-gold Angel. Yes, there was a place where God could not see.

My sweet child, there is a place, but you must keep it a secret at all costs.

If it grants me peace, then secret it shall stay.

It is called Avalon and exists between the realms. Where once there was nothing, now there is my paradise. I have a treasure there. Keep it safe and well for me and you may stay there in peace.

As you will it.

She held the veil open for him and he journeyed through.

ADAMINA BLINKED, THE LIGHT from the sun almost blinding her. She was standing in the entrance to the temple looking out over Avalon. Her dress was soaked from the rain and weighed heavy on her shoulders. Awareness of the near-silence, the peaceful stillness around her, unnerved her at first. She focused on the breeze and the sounds of flowing water. Caked in soot and grime, Adamina steered herself towards the whispers of the water.

The river rushed passed her as she approached the bank. The current was too strong here. Walking further down the shoreline, Adamina found a sheltered beach framed by forest. Across the river, on a high bank, a doe munched on lush greens eyeing her uncertainly. Adamina peeled off her dress and asked a tree if she could hang the dress on its branches. The tree's leaves gently rustled an affirmation and Adamina hung the dress to dry. She slid into the river and was nearly brought to tears by the joyous sensation. Relief flooded through her. She breathed.

The water washed away the mud, sweat, and the last of her pain and fear. Adamina sighed happily and lifted her face to the sun; its warmth chased the deep chill of despair from her bones. A flash of memory floated to the surface. Darkness, a dungeon, pain and fear. Adamina resisted the memory, pushed it down and out of her, letting Avalon erase her past. She vowed she would never look back. It did not matter where she came from. She had been given a second chance. Adamina took a deep breath and then exhaled. Something gently nudged and slid past her leg in the water. She looked down and a small rainbow scaled fish looked up at her. A laugh of delight escaped her mouth and startled the fish away, for it had never heard a noise quite like that before.

"Oh, it is alright," Adamina said softly.

After a moment, a school of the fish slowly swam out from behind water weeds and lilies. Adamina smiled, and the fish darted around and jumped in the air, competing for her attention. Eventually, they grew used to her company and swam off upstream, leaving Adamina to her thoughts. Closing her eyes she hummed softly. The tune channeled through her of its own accord, the beat of Avalon laying the foundation. The trees and wind swayed in time, soft and gentle.

When she had finished bathing away the past, Adamina realized she was without functional clothing and without shelter. What she had arrived in was in tatters.

She climbed out of the river and was assailed with uncertainties of where she would sleep, where to seek protection, and how to clothe herself. Aside from the animals and Goddess, Adamina had seen nor heard anything that indicated any of her kind resided near.

Goddess heard her fears and whispered, *I will provide for you Adamina. Follow my voice.*

Adamina headed in the direction of bleating and baying. Sheep with brown faces and brown wool bounded and grazed in an open field. Adamina became aware of how to cut the sheep's wool with a sharp stone, to build a wheel, spin wool into thread, dye wool, and how to fashion clothing for herself. Until she could provide herself with a new dress, Adamina learned to void herself of shame for her body. She was after all, alone here and sheep and the birds did not care for her state of dress. She lived as she was made.

The weather of Avalon stayed agreeable and so she required little shelter than what the entrance to the temple and the forest provided. She wove baskets and collected herbs and berries, but that was not enough to sustain her body for long.

Goddess presented her with a bow and arrows and instructed her to cover herself in mud and clay dyed green with wilted leaves.

Hunt the stag.

Adamina held the bow and arrow in her hands with uncertainty. Avalon sung the call of the hunt, the ground vibrating, pulsing. It overwhelmed Adamina and carried her through the forest on swift and silent legs. The song clouded her mind and intoxicated her. Silently, Adamina moved through the trees until he came into view. He was majestic and gentle: tan, muscled, and proud.

The stag lowered his head, his antlers telling his age. He had no herd or mate to watch over any longer. He too heard the call of the hunt. It was his death called for.

He lifted his head, ears twitching at the sound of a branch breaking. He would not out run her in this forest. The trees were too close together, too many low branches. He accepted his fate, but would taste freedom one last time before surrendering to the cycle of life.

Adamina approached slowly. He caught her scent on the wind and startled, darting as fast as he could through the network of bark and leaves. The trees whispered, urging the prey and the hunter on. Adamina's slender body slid through the forest like a snake through water. She stopped, raised her bow, drew the arrow, and Avalon held its breath. He stopped running, looked at her. She released the arrow. It flew through the air and hit true. He fell. The call of the hunt died away and Adamina ran to the animal. Dropping to her knees beside the creature, she looked the stag in the eyes as he drew his last breath and the light of life left him. The reality of taking a life settled upon her heart and her chest heaved with sobs.

She faced the lengthy task of skinning and preparing the body. A reverence for life, the stag's and her own, compelled her into action. Determination and adrenaline propelled her forward to the completion of the gruesome task. When she was finally done preparing the meat, hide, and sinew she would need for herself, she dug a pit and pushed the remains into it. She did not cover it as the wolves and ravens waited nearby. Nothing would go to waste.

Adamina rushed to the brook and washed off the blood. It had not been a clean job. She shook and shivered and felt sick to her stomach, but once the blood was washed away, she calmed. Adamina stumbled out of the forest with her prize wrapped in hide. It still needed to be cured by the sun. She found her refuge on the steps of the temple where she slept, tear stained, as the deer's muscle dried against the stone.

When she awoke, Goddess showed her how to grow food from the seeds of plants. Avalon provided the perfect climate for fast growing and plentiful harvests. The joy of creating life had dulled the sorrow of the previous day's kill. The feel of soil beneath her hands, the joyous fascination as she watched worms wriggle about and the green of a seedling sprout and grow. She would not have to journey far to feed her hunger, and more delightedly she would not be required to hunt so often. Her heart still pained her at the thought of the stag. She silently held vigil for the life taken for her own to thrive, kneeling before her garden in sorrowful reverence.

LOOKING DOWN UPON THE land, he adjusted his wings to catch the up-drafts. Silent in every move, he waited. A slight movement on the ground caught his eye. He aimed, pulled his wings close to his body and plummeted towards the ground. His talons reached out and snapped up the mouse. He found a hidden perch within the edge of the forest and feasted on his catch. When his meal was finished and his feathers preened, the owl had an order to follow. He was to guide the daughter of Avalon in the ways of wisdom and silence. He stretched his wings fully and launched into the air. He found her in the garden, sitting down, hands covered in soil. He sat himself on a branch of the tree overhanging the far edge of the garden and waited. He called for her gaze in the silence.

ADAMINA FELT EVERYTHING AROUND her still. It was as if time had stopped. Her gaze rose, drawn by a call unheard. Her eyes met large black orbs rimmed in yellow as bright as the rising sun. She took a breath as the knowledge and comfort of silence filled her. With her heart, she extended gratitude to the owl and to Goddess for this lesson. With her mind she whispered to the owl, *If I have need of your guidance, what shall I call you?* Adamina could have sworn she felt the owl smile. The answer came in silence.

She searched for an hour, having stumbled across a cabin on her afternoon explorations, but found no one in the surrounding area so Adamina filled the holes between the logs with mud and grass from the river banks and meadow. She hung the hide of the stag in the doorway and built herself a bed with herbs and grasses in one corner. Adamina paused to caress the hide door, remembering the hunt and the stag's gaze. She swallowed back the emotions that threatened her peace and settled to sleep in the bed. Avalon rained and stormed heavily for several days, only letting up to allow Adamina a trip each day to find food. When the rains stopped, she would move her garden nearer this place so she would not have to journey so far. Each night she closed her eyes, she knew her safety in the owl's silent gaze from the trees above.

HE WATCHED HER AS she slept, invisible in the dark and silent. *Treasure Mother? Your treasure is sleeping beneath the roof I built for myself.* He chuckled softly to himself. She tossed in her sleep and he reached out to calm her dreams. His step forward was not as silent as he would have liked. Grass crunched softly beneath his boot. She stirred and he burst into golden flecks that disappeared in the breeze.

STARTLED AWAKE, ADAMINA BOLTED out of bed and looked around. Her vision, blurred by golden specks from a heavy sleep, took a while to adjust. Finding herself in no danger, the ebb of panic calmed and was replaced by a sense of urgency and loneliness. She had been certain someone else had been there. Someone of her own kind. Someone like the fish and birds and deer had. There were so many of them all roaming or swimming or flying across the skies, together. She had sworn she felt that community for herself just now. She had been filled with the excitement of it, as much as the fear. Disappointment choked in her throat as a void rent open inside of her, drawing tears to her eyes. She dashed out of the log cabin and to the temple. Kneeling in the darkness, silent tears ran down her face.

"Goddess," Adamina begged in whispers, "I see all the animals have their own kind. I would like the company of my own kind as they have."

There was no answer and she fell asleep draped on the stairs of the temple, waiting.

IN SILENCE, THE OWL landed on the cuff upon his arm. He murmured and caressed the soft feathers and the owl responded with a short whistle.

Show me her wishes and needs wise one.

With large yellow eyes the owl spoke in silence. Images, emotions coursed through the Angel's mind, when they stopped, the owl took flight. The Angel would abate the sorrow in Adamina's heart through warm furs and meat. The rest, he could not give. He would give what he could and no more. He promised to care for the treasure, not sacrifice himself.

Her heart was gentle and ached with each kill, but her body would need the nourishment. He could ease that part of her soul, and take the kill upon himself. As he had promised Mother, he watched over her and provided so she would never again need the hunt. Her heart would not ache so and tug at his own. *If Angels had hearts*, he scoffed. Drifting through the trees, his gaze reached to the stars as the sun began to chase away the moon again. The Angel allowed himself a deep and dreamless sleep he did not know he needed.

HER EYES DARTED AROUND trying to find the source of the gifts, the meat and furs piled at her feet, but all she saw was Avalon. Her stomach alerted her to its hunger and ravenously tore into the dried meat with gratitude in her heart. When she finished, she gathered up the rest of the aids and returned to the cabin. Her heart and the chill upon the air told her the next season would begin soon. Autumn would be cooler; the trees would begin to fall asleep. Avalon would be painted in reds, yellows, oranges and browns. The owl would stay until spring awakened everything again. She knew about cold and winter with icy rains. Even Avalon needed rest.

She was thankful that she could make clothing now. The wool dress, deep green, sheltered her from the cool breeze. As often as the weather and terrain allowed, which was often, Adamina went barefoot. Her bare feet made her feel more connected to the nature around her, more grounded, as if she needed to be in contact with Avalon to keep from floating away or losing herself. She would have to start making warmer garments before the chill and rains of winter set in. Adamina dreaded the barrier to the land her feet coverings would provide.

She arrived at the little cabin and found the small hearth ablaze. She placed the folded fur on the mattress and sought out her basket of wool and fabric. She found it close to the hearth, empty. She did not have the time to prepare more before Avalon's cold season, and her mind began to work. She would have to go to Goddess again for help.

A burst of color caught her attention out of the corner of her eye. She whirled around. Folded in a pile on the small table at the opposite end of the room were garments. She unfolded and inspected each piece. They were thick and beautiful, crafted with unbelievable skill. A wool dress the color of the lapis she had found spattered about the island, and as soft as the coat of a rabbit. A cloak, heavy and thick was dyed the color of the forever-green trees lined in the fur of an animal she could not identify. And there were hide coverings for her feet adorned with lapis.

One item she had to consider for a long time. She slipped her feet into the two holes and pulling the trousers up and laughed. These were much more useful than a dress for the cold days. The last of the work in the garden would need to be completed today.

Adamina drew back the hide; she paused and turned to face the horizon.

"Thank you," she whispered softly to Goddess.

Throughout the winter, Adamina found a fresh basket of dried meat and bread each sunrise. She would learn to make the honey-sweet staple as soon as she could return to the temple and ask Goddess, for it had become her favorite. Adamina never had to search for

wood or light the hearth as it seemed to burn steady until the winter rains ceased and the sun warmed the soil
again. As Adamina worked, preparing wool into yarn on
a spinning wheel she hummed and sang. Once, she could
have sworn a low voice had accompanied her song. It
must have been the wind.

GODDESS CONSIDERED ADAMINA'S WISH for a long
time. Adamina's people had been gone for centuries now.
Goddess could not re-create another of Adamina's race
without the Others. But They would not be pleased with
Avalon or Adamina. Avalon had to remain a secret. To
fulfill Adamina's request, Goddess would remove someone from another world and bring them to Avalon.

She followed a desire, a hope for a new home and the
call for a past to be washed away to a ship that travelled
alone across the waters. Goddess covered the ship in a
mist and lifted the veil between the worlds. The massive
boat swiftly sailed onto Avalon's sea, Goddess guiding it
toward the southern shore. Shouts and tugs of rope, flaps
of sails and men darting across the deck ensured the ship
docked securely. The woman aboard fulfilled Adamina's
prayer, and, Avalon answered hers.

Pagan took a deep breath. The air was not heavy ocean
air as she expected it to be. No, there was something different about the air here. She had risen early that morning; the men were taking advantage of what seemed to
be a danger-free island and sleeping in. The lack of danger
did not ease the men's superstitions about the island and
some slept uneasily. Stories of fantastic creatures inhabit-
ing the island had circled the campfires last night. Who
had begun those whispers she couldn't guess. They were

a superstitious lot. The men were content to stick to the beaches and avoided going further than the need for firewood required, but Pagan felt drawn to the heart of the island. She never invested much in superstition.

She stood on the beach and looked inland. A meadow began at the edge of the beach and stretched backward over hills. To the east the coast inclined upward wedging itself into a small mountain range. The west was dotted with a forest that appeared to snake behind the hills and out of site. The forest took up at least half the visible part of the island. That was where Pagan decided to begin her exploration. After all, some of the closer trees had a unique fruit that looked delicious. Pagan was hungry for something other than rations.

3

h OOTS AND A WHISTLE echoed from the trees and drew her gaze to search for the owl. She could not make out her friend's form, but he was there none the less. Adamina let her mind drift. Nearly a full season's turn since her pleas for company of her own kind had passed. Silence, as she fondly called him, had become a constant companion, watching from trees and the sky above. She smiled and waved at where she knew he perched. In a way, he was an answer to her wishes. She was content enough, even if her heart panged when she dreamed of others like her. Goddess had been absent and silent for a long time, unable to answer her questions. Too long, Adamina decided and turned her direction to the temple. She didn't get very far before the island had a different idea.

Against her intentions, Avalon hummed and called her to the shore. Never one to deny the call of the island, Adamina's legs carried her swiftly down through the forest. At its edge, Adamina peered out over the beach. Bless Goddess! There were so many of them all intermingled among the camps they had set up. Strange fabrics pulled over wooden frames functioned as shelters. She needed to know more, but caution and apprehension held her back. One man was putting food in metal containers and putting them over fires. Adamina stared, puzzled and awed. So many were here and so many things they brought with them. Hands seized her shoulders and spun her around. Adamina's heart sped up, screaming at her to run, but curiosity and joy froze her in place.

"Who are you?" Pagan demanded.

Pagan's blonde hair caught a beam of sunlight piercing through the trees. Adamina had never seen that color before and stared gaping in awe. Pagan repeated her question.

"A-Adamina," she stuttered out. Adamina had not spoken out loud in quite some time and her voice was raw. Gaining more courage and her voice, Adamina demanded back, "And who are you?"

"My name is Pagan. Is there anyone else on the island? Where are your parents?"

Adamina stared at Pagan, her mind working. Finally, Adamina responded, "I am the Priestess of Goddess. There are many on this island, but no others like me, except all of them," she motioned to the shore, "and you now, Pagan."

Pagan stared in disbelief. This was a child, barely entering womanhood. She needed guidance and family.

"So there is no one else but you here? No other people?"

Adamina shook her head no. Pagan studied the girl in front of her. She was tall. Pagan would guess Adamina was about thirteen years old. Her hair shifted in the light and her eyes swirled with vibrant color. An innocent strength, awe and determination, as well as a glittering joy showed in the glint of her eye, the angle of her lips, and her tensed fists. Well, Pagan had wanted an island with as few people as possible to settle down on. One marooned girl was few enough. She just hoped there was a practical living space available. At least she would have another female to talk to. After months on a ship full of men, Pagan appreciated female company.

"Show me where you live," Pagan demanded.

Adamina led her through the forest and cut across meadow to a small cabin. Pagan immediately assumed the cabin had been left here by someone before Adamina. There was no way this one slight girl could have built it.

"This won't do," Pagan mused to herself.

Pagan had been used to a luxurious life style. The cabin that lay in front of her yielded no such comforts. But this was what she had wanted, right? Adamina shared everything she could with Pagan about the tale of killing the stag whose hide hung in the door way, eyes welling with tears, and her garden which brought pride into her features and chased away the sorrow of a kill. Adamina prattled excitedly about Goddess, and how she had wished for family and Goddess had brought Pagan to her. Furs, soft and exotic were piled in a corner. Adamina careened on about the sheep that offered wool, the fish Pagan had to meet, but she didn't tell Pagan of the owl. The owl, she felt, was better kept in silence. Pagan's heart ached. Adamina reminded her of someone she once knew. Someone she had loved dearly. Finally, Adamina took Pagan to the temple of Goddess. The stone structure was flawless and looked like it had been built by a master stonemason.

"Who built this?" Pagan asked Adamina.

"Goddess. It was here before she brought me here," Adamina responded.

Pagan gazed at Adamina in disbelief, and then studied the outside of the temple. She had long given up on gods, but this craftsmanship, the stone was too eerily perfect to have been built by any human master mason or builder. The stone was perfectly smooth, the entrance protruding from the side of a mountain. Inside the temple was pitch black, Pagan could not even see the temple floor, but she was never one to hesitate and stepped forward anyway. The sensation of not knowing where to put her feet unnerved her, as did this *Goddess* Adamina had gone on about. Pagan looked behind her to find the entrance and panicked a little when she could not locate it. Perhaps she was dreaming this all. Gods did not exist. This must be a dream.

Hello Pagan, Goddess whispered.

Pagan started and looked around her, but all she saw was darkness. She tried to run in one direction, then another until she tripped and fell to her knees. She felt arms wrap around her and hold her, then lift her to her feet. Safety and warmth filled her and she swallowed back her fear.

"Who are you?" Pagan demanded.

I am Goddess. Welcome to Avalon. I would tell you not to fear me, but you have always been a fearless one. Haven't you, Pagan? I have brought you here because Adamina needs her own kind. Avalon can offer you what you seek. My request is for you to stay. Teach Adamina the ways of people, but do not let the ways of people make her forget my ways. I also ask, Pagan, that you become one of my own priestesses. Worship me as you would worship a mother. Perform no sacrifices for me. Honor me by honoring Avalon. Adamina will teach you my ways and you shall teach her yours. You came seeking a land where you could peacefully retire. Avalon offers you that resting place.

Will you do this for me?

Pagan was hesitant at first. She had never conversed with gods before. She turned around to face the direction she thought the entrance of the temple was. She was blinded as the light of day filtered through. When her eyes adjusted, she peered out over Avalon. The island offered her a home, one that met her wishes, her needs.

She weighed her options and chose a new life for herself. She looked at Adamina. The young girl sat on the steps patiently, waiting for Pagan. So, Goddess thought Adamina needed Pagan. Did Goddess know? Surely Goddess would not thrust a life into her hands if she knew.

For a moment, Pagan saw the little sister she had lost on that faraway place sitting on the steps instead of Adamina. The pain of that loss welled up and she fought it away. Perhaps Goddess did know. Those from her kingdom that spoke of gods had mentioned second chances. This could be a second chance for her. That was what she was seeking after all.

"Alright, I agree," Pagan spoke into the darkness. "But I can't do it and live in that cabin of hers. I need a few comforts of society. And, I want your promise that when I leave this world behind that I will not be judged for my crime."

Goddess smiled at Pagan's bravery, but she had no idea of the consequences of such a request. Her request for comfort meant exposing Avalon to a steady stream of ships carrying supplies. A small port village would have to be built so trades people could create shops and live there to provide these comforts of society as Pagan called them. But Goddess would give all she could to Adamina, to Pagan, to her priestesses. Goddess needed someone to watch over Adamina. There were limits to what a god could teach a mortal. Pagan could make up for some of that.

Granted, brave Pagan, Goddess replied, *I thank you.*

Pagan left the temple and shared with Adamina the discussion with Goddess. Filled with joy, Adamina embraced Pagan. Both separated quickly and awkwardly. The sensation of a hug was odd. Pagan had not shared a familial embrace for a very long time.

Adamina… Goddess called Adamina to enter the temple.

Adamina, I cannot return to Avalon for a while. God is

looking. Pagan will guide you and offer you the friendship and family you wished for.

But Goddess, why must you go? I need you!

Adamina, there are things that a god cannot teach a mortal. Life must be experienced through your own eyes, not mine. Oh child, do not weep, Adamina wiped at her tears and continued listening to Goddess' words, *I have something you must remember. Angels will come to Avalon and with them, Avalon will fall. Beware of them and keep your distance child.*

What are Angels, Goddess?

They are my children, mine and God's, but they were made to assist in the destruction of worlds. Avalon, was not to be made. It was meant to be a secret refuge of mine, but it has grown and whispers of this land extend to other worlds. And like this world, you should not be.

At her unspoken question, Goddess offered the truth, *I have hid from you much of your past. It was a dark world you came from and that world no longer exists. It has been dead for a very long time. In you a seed had been planted, a seed of moonlight and creation, planted by a wish of mine. I was irresponsible and when I felt you call, I knew what I had done and had to fix it. I wished for a daughter, a selfish wish, a daughter and a world of my own, away from the Others. Avalon was that for a long time for us Adamina. I could not keep you isolated forever here, it would starve your spirit. Pagan will bring great joy to you and Avalon will grow and flourish, but because of those that will come here, Adamina, Avalon will change. I will watch over from the sun and the moon, but I cannot return for a long while for the devastation that will come at the hands of the Others, should they follow me here, will be far greater than any change Angels will bring. Beware them and keep your distance, perhaps it will change what will come to pass if you do. Keep Avalon safe, Priestess.*

Adamina nodded and left the temple with a heavy

heart. Pagan settled on the steps, taking in the sensations of life around her. She noted the brightness of the sun and the sounds of birds. The feel of a gentle breeze on her skin. Yes, Pagan could make this place home. Adamina stepped out of the darkness and sat down beside Pagan. They sat in silence for a long while, just taking in Avalon and their new friendship, before either of them spoke.

"I will need a house built by the men I came with," Pagan explained.

She warned Adamina to stay near her cabin while this was happening, and, to stay away from the men. Sailors were not exactly gentlemen, Pagan cautioned. She returned to the captain and expressed her desires. Pagan had gold to pay them all handsomely enough to earn their loyalty until the job was finished. A team of seven men, two carpenters, a black smith, and a few other volunteers stayed to begin building the house she requested using some of the materials from the ship. The captain and his crew embarked the following day to retrieve additional supplies, after they delivered the remaining cargo to its destination. None of the men were to go beyond the site of the house. Their obedience bought by gold and secured by sailors' superstitions, and maintained their camps on the beaches.

Pagan held camp a little further down the beach away from the men until her house was finished, but visited Adamina regularly. She told Adamina countless tales of the world she came from: of carriages and tools and vehicles. Pagan taught Adamina about people and culture and how different it could be from village to town to farm. Pagan introduced Adamina to the many crafts someone may apprentice to like metal smithing or the bardic arts. From Adamina, Pagan learned too. She learned to love again, to open her heart to family. She learned to live full and leave her past where it remained.

THE SUDDEN INFLUX OF men gave him the opportunity to build his own house and maintain physical form for longer periods of time. The owl flew off his arm as he stepped out of the forest and slipped back into the camp. Since Adamina had required the use of the cabin he had built, Archangel Gabriel had needed to construct another shelter for his physical existence. There were things a body could learn and experience that ethereal form lacked. Although his power would be significantly limited in physical form, he still had enough of it to do what was needed. His coming and goings would go unquestioned by the men and the opportunity to perform physical labor suited him.

Although Adamina would no longer need the necessities he had been providing for her, now that they were more easily provided by this harbor town, Gabriel still had sworn to Goddess to watch over her. A fierce protectiveness driven by his sense of duty kept his eyes on the men. Ones that got curious enough to think about wandering away where they may run into Adamina found their minds dissuaded from such actions. Gabriel also supplemented the magic of Avalon with his own wards until he was sure no one who may harm Adamina would wander past them. Then, with the house built and the wards in place, Gabriel felt he could take a much needed vacation and tour the worlds he had been meaning to see. Adamina would be safe.

4

THE WHISPERS OF THIS paradise called Avalon piqued his interest. It was difficult not to notice when more than one world developed the same stories about a land, shrouded in mists, surrounded by water, where creatures that no longer lived strolled about. A land of plenty and peace, he had heard. A land that he had not made or permitted. God sent out messengers and spies to locate this fabled paradise, to bring him any information about its location. Forty Angels were sent, and among them, his most beloved Archangels. Or at least the ones he could find. Gabriel seemed to be missing in action. For a while no new information of the world in between worlds graced his ears. Not one Angel could uncover its location. He recalled all but ten of his best. He sent them to live in physical form until they could uncover the hiding place of this mysterious world, however long it took. There was no need to concern the Others with this matter. He would resolve it himself and maybe, just maybe, their meddling would end.

THE HOUSE STOOD THREE stories tall with its main entrance facing south towards the harbor. The gable was steep and littered with small windows allowing light and room for an attic library. Simple in construction and style, the house would have passed for any public building back in the city Pagan came from. Four pillars accented a shallow veranda at the front entrance where double doors were accented by two windows on either side. The remaining sides of the building had five windows each face allowing light to pour in abundantly no matter which room you were in.

The kitchen had a dirt floor and stretched the width of the house and half its length. A door on the far left of the hearth entered into the windowless cold room. The open hearth was large enough to fit a cooking cauldron the size of a pony. There was a crude wooden door with large black iron hinges that creaked loudly when it was moved so it was left open to the upstairs.

The main entrance gaped into a long hall which stretched all the way to the back of the house. The floors were made of unpolished wood planks. At the back of the house was nestled a dining room dominated by a table that could comfortably seat twenty. To the right, a large sitting room with a second massive hearth. To the left of the entrance were stairs reaching towards the second floor.

The second floor was characterized by thirteen simple bedrooms, with each a small garderobe channeled to empty into the ocean. A third set of stairs snaked into the attic. The attic held Pagan's treasured volumes and was furnished with padded benches and chaises to lounge on. The collection of books and scrolls grew larger each season until they overflowed the shelves in the walls and spilled onto benches and stacks on the floor.

Avalon became a stop on many supply routes. Within a few months' time, the port of Avalon had become well established. An inn, a black smith, a potter, a carpenter and a few retired soldiers and sailors set up homes. Rumors of the sirens dwelling in the heart of the island kept all but the brave and desperate away from the priestess house. Now and again, a child or a woman would venture past the port, up to the house, drawn by the whispers of Avalon. Soon the priestesses of Avalon were thirteen, not including the children.

Pagan and Adamina guided the women, teaching them practical crafts, the ways of Goddess magic, and warned them of the Angels. Each woman, and child, brought a blessing to the community. A skill or knowledge useful to improve their way of life. Some even brought means to increase trade with the harbor town and merchants. None were turned away. But Pagan and Adamina did not share everything with the priestesses.

Many nights Pagan and Adamina secreted away in the attic, sitting together, pouring over books. As Adamina was taught to read, she became enamored with the tomes and her hunger for more stories, more information almost outweighed Pagan's. Books were everywhere, piled to the sky and invading corners. Adamina had once asked why symbols made different sounds and some were so strangely drawn on the pages or scrolls. Pagan had explained that many places had different languages, but on Avalon, it seemed that it didn't matter who you were talking to, or what language you were saying it in, everyone could understand everyone else.

Pagan often returned from the harbor with a new volume, scroll, or scribbling. Sometimes they would read about happenings in other lands. They would read poetry or plays aloud, acting like the characters and falling down in laughter at the sight of themselves. Adamina's favorite, though, were the dreaming stories of pretend places and people. She had read many different ones set in castles or farms, or large gardens. She wondered what those other worlds would be like to experience and sometimes her dreams would carry her to them on the owl's wings.

One evening as the moon stretched above the sky, they read plays by candle light. Pagan had acquired a whole shipment of them. The merchant had said they came from a great library that had been attacked and burned.

"How did the golden rain get her pregnant?" Adamina asked.

"Oh dear," Pagan replied, "Well you see, the person who wrote this. Well he was a very angry man. And the world he came from believes in the power of a philandering god."

Adamina stared at Pagan blankly.

"Maybe we'll try this one instead."

Pagan handed Adamina a different scroll. "Pallas Athena," Adamina's eyes darted over the characters on the parchment as she read aloud. Pagan interjected a few times to correct her pronunciation. After a few moments, Adamina stopped to comment.

"I like this one much better than the one with the woman locked in a dungeon with golden rain."

"Yes. You should read Medusa and Medea next. Then maybe we can work on some more with Zeus later."

"Are all gods like him?"

"I don't know."

"I'd hate to think Goddess had a counterpart like that."

"You'll have to ask her someday when she comes back, won't you?"

Adamina nodded and resumed her reciting. Sometimes Pagan told stories from memory about kings and faraway lands. Sometimes they created their own stories or changed the endings or characters as they walked about Avalon talking and laughing at how foolish some people could be. It was hard to believe that people could act so peculiarly.

"Believe me, Adamina. Real life is filled with a great many oddities."

HIS PHYSICAL FORM WAS tall, compared to those busying themselves in the harbor. His long black hair was tied in a leather thong at the base of his neck. His body was muscled like that of a soldier. He was outfitted as a sailor. Compared to his brothers, he was very young. The last of the Archangels to come into being. Avalon could only be accessed by ship in the world he had been placed on, and it took him several seasons to find a captain who knew the way. The air was filled with shouts as the men secured the vessel before turning their eyes towards the island. He commended his mother for the place, if this was indeed Avalon.

It was lush and unbearably green beyond the busy harbor. The salt was subtle on the gentle breeze as he inhaled. It was a paradise. He had acquired a small house at the outskirts of the port that reeked of Gabriel, though his brother was nowhere on the island. He had wondered where the old man had gotten to in his retirement. A hidden paradise wasn't a bad retirement spot. The thought brought a grin at the displeasure the knowledge of Gabriel's abandonment of duties would bring Father. Curiosity compelled a venturing through Avalon. He had rumors of long dead sirens to investigate and Father would need a thorough report.

ADAMINA STOOD UP AND looked to the sunlit sky. She smiled, closed her eyes and took a deep breath. The song of Avalon pulsed through her veins. Her body was lean. Her muscles were hardened from the labor of helping Pagan run the priestess' house. Her cabin in the woods had long been neglected. Adamina's hands were covered in dirt. She pulled at a bushel of pink carrots until it lifted from the earth. She placed the carrots in the basket beside her and lifted the load of food onto her hip. Her fingers were stained and her face smeared with dirt. Smells of stew permeated from the kitchen and rumbled Adamina's stomach.

The large cellar kitchen revealed itself as she walked down stone steps to deliver her spoils. She smiled at the other women in the kitchen and left her basket on the stone slab in the middle of the kitchen. A young girl scooped up the basket, plunked it in a basin of water along a side counter, and began scrubbing. A massive cauldron, a gift from the blacksmith who had recently married one of the priestesses, sat over the hearth. Smoke from the fire billowed out of a chimney above the large building. Pregnant, the blacksmith's wife stirred the pot with a large spoon the carpenter had carved: another wedding present. Nevara had told her of the terrible hunger pangs that came with her baby and could be constantly found by food. Adamina smiled and nodded at the priestess.

A few men knew of the priestesses now, but they only ventured up to the house when escorted. Nevara had met the blacksmith when she had wondered into port, looking for someone to re-attach a handle to a pot. He had been just her type, the silent type, sending butterflies fluttering in her stomach. Nevara had thought it to be an ailment and went to the witchdoctor who laughed so loudly, the whole house had gathered to hear the truth of Nevara's feelings revealed. Nevara attended to the kitchen each day, returning to the blacksmith's house in the port each evening.

Adamina ascended to the attic to check on Pagan. Pagan was lounging on a chaise reading.

"Adamina!" Pagan said softly and rested the book she had been immersed in on a pile of other books beside the chaise.

"Pagan," Adamina bent down to hug her friend.

Adamina paused before gently embracing Pagan. Her heart whispered a terrible prediction. Pagan had been ill for a long while. She tried to hide it from Adamina, but it was difficult to hide when she was half her weight and had lost all color in her skin.

"Adamina, I have a story I would like to tell you," Pagan stated softly and patted the space beside her.

"Am I not a little old for stories friend?"

"You are never too old for stories. The only thing that changes are the stories you tell yourself," Pagan smiled as Adamina settled on the floor in front of her.

Pagan began, "A great many seasons ago there was a princess named Pagan."

Adamina's head shot up and her eyes met Pagans, but she did not interrupt, "Pagan had golden hair and piercing eyes. She grew up in the lap of luxury, wanting for nothing, or at least that's what everyone in the kingdom said about her. She had an older brother named Boone whom she loved dearly, but saw rarely for he was often on conquests and learning how to one day be a king. On her tenth birthday, her mother had another child, a second daughter named Hyssop.

"Hyssop was everything bright and cheery in the older princess' world. They played together, took lessons together, and Pagan became fiercely protective of her sister. As they came of age, suitors were presented, but both girls refused to marry for anything short of love. Not a notion practical for princesses. One day, Pagan found Hyssop in the gardens with their literature tutor. Unfortunately, Pagan was not the only one to discover them. Their father, the king, found the two together at exactly the same time. The king had never been soft and seasons of ruling and war made his heart calloused and frozen. Refusing to be shamed by Hyssop and the tutor, the king had both executed the next morning.

"Pagan had been haunted for moons by anger and hate for the father she had never learned to love. Devastated by the loss of her sister. Her beautiful, innocent sister full of light and love smothered by the arrogance of a man who fathered her. The pain and anger inside of Pagan grew and grew until it burst. Enraged by her grief, late one night as the king slept Pagan crept into his chambers with a dagger and took his life as terribly as he had taken Hyssop's. Revenge offered nothing but numbness in her heart. Knowing the punishment for her crime, Pagan fled the palace and her life, leaving her brother to take over their father's throne. There was nothing left for her with Hyssop gone.

Pagan had reached the docks before her mother's guards and her brother's fleet captain found her. She thought she was going to die as their footsteps drew near. They grabbed hold of her. Pagan held her head high, drawing every breath as if it was her last. The guards released her and guided her onto a ship, a large satchel of gold placed in her hands. They had been sent not to make her answer for her crimes, but to protect her and ensure she ended up somewhere where her brother would never have to carry out the punishment for the treason she committed. She sailed away from her home and found a paradise with a friend not too different from her own Hyssop and lived a peaceful life."

So here was the story Pagan had hidden amongst all those others all her life, Adamina mused. If she had been home-sick, Pagan never once showed it. For all her strength, Pagan now looked frail. Paleness had taken her over. She was prone to chills, and was always tired. Adamina drew a blanket, made by one of the priestesses, up and around her. Pagan smiled and hugged Adamina.

"You are my friend, Adamina, my sister priestess. You are the first priestess of Goddess and you do not need me or anyone to help you run this place or live your life. The others can manage well, but they look to you to guide them now."

Pagan began to cough and had to sit back. She did not stop coughing for too long a time.

"I'll go get you some water."

Adamina rushed out of the room and down the stairs until she reached the cellar. She ladled water into a glass from the drinking basin in the kitchen cellar and carried it back up to the attic library. Adamina rounded the pile of books to hand Pagan her glass of water. "Pagan?" Pagan was ashen white; her eyes were closed and she was unbearably still. Pagan was wearing her best outfit, one reserved for special occasions like festival celebrations. Pagan had known that she would die today.

Adamina brought her hand to her heart in horror, dropping the glass of water on the floor. The vessel shattered into millions of irreparable pieces. She sobbed and fell to her knees, clutching Pagan's body, shaking and calling out Pagan's name over and over. One of the other priestesses, Gwen, came rushing in. Gwen, observing the cause for the broken glass and Adamina's cries, covered her mouth as tears began to slide down her face. Adamina looked up to see the girl. She spoke as calmly as she could and ordered the girl to notify the others to prepare for the ceremony of passing. Only two deaths had occurred on Avalon before this. A young child who had arrived to the priestesses too ill to cure, and an elderly woman, Matilda, who had taught them medicine and midwifery, had died last month. Gwen did not move, frozen in place by terror and sorrow.

Adamina stood up, lifting her head high and ordered the girl more firmly, "Go."

Gwen blinked and rushed out of the room, alerting the others. It had been a cool morning and Adamina had the cape she had been wearing still wrapped around her shoulders. She unfastened it and covered Pagan's body, whispering, "May your spirit rest in Avalon, and be reborn when you have washed away the heaviness of this life, sister."

An older woman, Diane, entered the room. Her dress swished with each step toward Adamina.

"Adamina," she said softly. "Pagan had ordered three of us to build the funeral pyre earlier. It is almost completed."

Adamina swallowed, they had known too.

"Have the new initiate and the other priestesses dress in their solstice wear. The young children..." Adamina's voice cracked.

"Have been taken care of, Priestess."

The older woman smiled slightly, offering reassurance than left to finish preparations. Minutes passed like hours as Adamina fought against weeping. Two priestesses brought up Adamina her solstice robe, an emerald green with spirals of gold and brown, and dressed Adamina as she stared in a daze. When her belt was fastened around her waist, silver and rainbow fabric, Adamina inhaled. A few of the women tried to lift Pagan. Adamina pushed them away.

"I will do it," Adamina said.

She lifted Pagan and nearly sobbed at how light her friend's body was. She walked in a daze, floating to the funeral pyre on the cliffs behind the temple of Goddess.

The ocean crashed against the rocks violently. A procession of women followed the priestess of Avalon, their hooded cloaks of black covering them from head to foot. Clouds covered the sun and sky, and a shadow fell over the isle. Even the birds paused in their gaiety to pay homage. The owl let out a mournful cry.

Adamina placed Pagan's body gently on the funeral pyre, arranging her cloak to cover Pagan. Someone draped her shoulders with Pagan's hood and fastened the silver cloak around Adamina. A sea breeze blew past them as Adamina raised her hands to the cloudy sky.

"Goddess!" Adamina cried. To her own surprise her voice did not crack with the emotion choking her, "Your child Pagan returns to you. Birth her into a new life fitting for her spirit."

Adamina stepped back and two other priestesses lit the pyre. Flames cracked the wood and devoured their way to her friend's body. It took all of Adamina's will not to pull the body away from the finality of the flames. Instead, Adamina sung a melancholy funeral dirge in a strange, ancient language. The voice of Avalon rose up, flowing from Adamina in a song of mourning carried on the wind. When the song had ended, and the flames had consumed her friend's body, Adamina left the others to mourn.

She ran. Filled with fear, despair, and sorrow. She ran through trees until she reached the riverbank. The bank was steep and high. Collapsing to her knees, she stared into the water below her. She could not cry, so she sang. In response to her song of grief, the current slowed, the wind whispered more softly, and the forests went silent. She sang and sang the funeral song until her voice gave out and she could only stare in silence at the water flowing past her and wished she could fly away. The owl, perched high in the trees, closed its eyes in sorrow.

5

H E TRUDGED THROUGH THE forest. Relying on instinct, he headed in a north-west direction. He had been in this forest nearly all day and it was getting close to sunset. The land felt strange, warding him off from certain directions, making him uncomfortable. He felt lost, but would never admit that to anyone. He decided to go against the discomfort, pushing past Avalon's resistance. Perhaps those rumors of strange creatures were really just stories. The forest around him stilled and went silent. Almost inaudible, he heard a heartbeat. The ground, he realized, the heart beat came from beneath him. Then he heard it. The soft melody of an Angelic voice.

Could one of his own kind be here already? He had not sensed another Angel on the island, but it was possible they were masking their location. At first he considered it could have been Gabriel, he had been inclined towards female forms before, but the voice did not match one of Gabriel's forms. He adjusted his course toward the direction of the song. As he got closer he could make out the words. A loss voiced in an ancient language of a race that had been long extinct. His steps became painfully heavy, as if the song was casting a spell over him. Perhaps those tales of sirens were correct after all, he mused at the recognition of the language as one that should not be alive, laced with magic and agony.

The trees thinned, leading him to the bank of a river that seemed to snake through all of Avalon. She was kneeling on the edge. No, she was not an Angel. She was assuredly a mortal. Her long hair was tangled and neglected. The sight of slightly pointed ears peeking through strands of auburn silk intrigued him. He stepped forward, snapping a twig and her head swiveled around, startled. Her race was supposed to have been eradicated over two centuries ago. They had become dark and destructive, killing anything and everything until there was nothing left but a few hundred for his army to cleanse. There was no doubt in his mind Goddess had disobeyed the Others and saved this creature. Mother was fickle like that. This was Avalon, the mysterious world created by a rogue god. He had found what he was looking for, and his mother was at the heart of it all.

A TWIG SNAPPED AND she whipped around. A sailor stood behind her. They weren't supposed to be here. The magic of Avalon should not have permitted them to explore beyond the harbor. She stood up quickly, about to demand he return to the harbor, but the bank collapsed under her. She plummeted into the river. Adamina struggled with Pagan's cape as it threatened to strangle her, pulling her deeper, weighing her down. She managed to unclasp it and fought against the current, trying to reach the surface. Her hand broke the surface, but the undercurrent grabbed her and threw her back down.

Adamina struggled, feeling the effects of the lack of air. The current grabbed at her again and pushed. She slammed into the riverbed, her head smashing against a large rounded rock. Everything went black.

This was the first time he had required wings while in corporeal form and he wasn't sure he liked it. Flying on feathers and bones required a little more finesse than ethereal flight. He gazed down the river, saw her hand break the surface and dove after her. In a matter of three wing beats, he had carried himself to where she had been tossed further downstream. Reaching into the icy water, he snatched at the woman's clothing. He got a fist full of dress and tugged. The dress tore and he cursed as she plummeted out of reach.

He could hear rapids ahead of them and soared upward to gain momentum, then sped forward. He cursed his mortal form for the pain shooting through him and to expedite circumstances, whispered to the water to surrender her body to the surface.

The water pushed upward against the woman's body. It had not meant to hurt her, it whispered back. The water was simply excited as it rushed through Avalon, hurrying to empty into the sea. Just before the rapids could take her, he snatched her up. He followed the stream, flying low, until he reached a side shore. Placing the limp woman's body on the shore, he rasped in Angelic tongue to the water in her lungs, *Return to the river*. The water bubbled up and out of her mouth, then slid down the shore and back into the river. She coughed and gasped, but did not wake up. Tucking his wings together against his back, he reabsorbed them into his body. He was getting the hang of this shifting thing. No wonder some of the others would shift from one form to the next. There was a lot of use in growing wings. His body pumped full of hormones that made him feel elation. He would have to try it again sometime soon. He hurried through the trees, carrying the woman, until he reached his lodgings.

He placed the woman down on the bed and listened. She was breathing. He had time. He lit the fire in his small hearth and set some water to boil. He grabbed a dagger and cut at the woman's destroyed clothing. Her body was covered in bruises and a few gashes, nothing grave. He placed his hands on her forehead and noticed the bruising there. Closing his eyes, he pulled at his power, willing bruising and cuts to mend. He couldn't help but stare at the supple form of her flesh. A hunger ignited inside of him. She could rest now, but he had questions for the woman when she awoke. Using her body would get him no answers. He went out to the village to locate some meat and vegetables for the boiling water. He was starved and couldn't think on an empty stomach. Being corporeal had its downsides.

CONCERNED, THE PRIESTESSES HAD sent one of the novices, Palla, in search of Adamina since she had not returned and night was rising. The young woman followed the signs of the forest: a broken branch, trampled ground, until she nearly reached the river embankment. She saw a man standing behind and off to one side of Adamina. The men should not have been able to cross the harbor wards unescorted! He was tall, taller than others Palla had seen. His hair was impossibly dark and tied at the back of his neck. His jaw was angular set with anger and impatience. She could not make out his face from this distance, but when he turned the glimmer in his eye shocked her at its brilliance.

Palla got the distinct sense he was not to be trusted. Movement directed her gaze back to Adamina. Adamina stood up, startled by the man. The man said something in an odd accent that Palla couldn't quite make out and the riverbank fell. Blindingly white wings stretched out from the stranger's back. Her eyes grew wide, the Angels had come! Goddess had warned them before her great silence that Angels could look like anything. She had seen no man with wings before and the impossibility of it could only mean one thing. The Angel lifted off into the air, hesitating to help Adamina as he flapped his wings awkwardly.

Palla froze. Palla owed Adamina her life, as did many of the priestesses, women, and children living at the house. She and Pagan had forgiven every past, healed every transgression, and had offered many women and children safe refuge refusing no one. But an Angel was powerful, an Angel she knew she could not face alone. Palla watched helplessly as the Angel dived after Adamina and out of sight. The young novice priestess ran back to the temple to alert the others. Angels had arrived on Avalon and one of them had Adamina.

THE SUN HAD NEARLY finished its decent. It was dark at first, than her eyes adjusted to the dimly lit room. The bed she was lying on was hard and uncomfortable. She sat up in a panic. This was a sailor's cabin. Pagan had warned her all about unscrupulous sailors. Adamina realized she was unclothed and felt shame and fear fill her against her better judgment. A large cloak hung by the door. Her own clothes were lying in a torn heap on the ground beside her.

She bolted up, grabbed the cloak and donned it, the large size completely covering her. Adamina grabbed the bundle of her ruined robes and raced back to the priestess house through the forest. She was thankful the occupant was not home. Adamina longed for the safety of the house, for warmth and protection, for her family. When the house came into view she almost cried out like a child for its mother. She heard voices cry out in frenzy.

Palla rushed out the door, quickly followed by several more women. With inquisitive concern, the women ushered Adamina into the house. Supper would be ready in a while they told her. She needed the food. Thankfully, they knew better than to ask any questions of her right now. The women escorted Adamina to the bathing room and quickly removed the stranger's cloak from her shoulders. The tattered robes were pried out of her clutching arms and tossed aside, then scooped up by a set of arms and rushed out of the room. Three of the women ushered her into a bath. The water, mixed with witch-hazel and mint, warmed her and the shock of the bucket being dumped on her head grounded her in reality. The door Adamina had been ushered through was outlined by garlic garland. It was a test.

When Adamina was ready, the room was filled with women who washed and dried and dressed her as she told her story to those assembled. As she finished, the women explained Palla's version of events. The man was an Angel.

Panic rose up in her. An Angel. They would take her precious world away from her, from the others. She closed her eyes and chased away the terror inside of her. She centered herself and looked ahead to the predicted destruction of Avalon with the arrival of Angels. She was the first priestess of Avalon, its defender and its voice. She steeled herself, a warrior for the others. A hush fell as they looked at her expectantly. Adamina took a deep breath and opened her mouth to address the women.

Gwen burst through the door to announce, "The Angel is at our door step. He wants to speak with Adamina."

How did he find her? The high priestess of Avalon looked towards the messenger, "Show him in, but do not let him see too much. No one is to speak with him."

She would hear his words and send him off the island. Perhaps she could save Avalon if she could drive this Angel away.

HE WAS LEAD THROUGH the entrance way into a room that was furnished with pieces from many worlds. A table, a hand-woven rug, a chest, these were objects made each in a different world to which Uriel had been. Two, the table and chest, were from worlds he had been sent to as a messenger. The hand-woven rug had been from a place that Uriel had spent a short, unscheduled visit on during his search for Avalon. He recognized the pattern and material. Hands that wove similar rugs had belonged to a woman he had met during that visit.

A rocking chair and a bench were grouped to one side of a hearth. Uriel recognized the carpenter of the harbor's craftsmanship. The house smelled of mortal flesh, female flesh. The woman leading him stopped and motioned for him to sit in the room. He said he preferred to stand. The woman smelled of lavender and was young, barely a woman. Need rose in him like a fire consuming everything in its power. Uriel tried to compel the woman to speak with him, but she turned to leave. He grabbed her arm and held her there, pulling her close and whispered for her to meet him at the edge of the forest. Through his touch, Uriel forced his need into her body, a temporary outlet for these physical urges. He could hear her pulse race and her breathing grow ragged with his desire.

She pulled away, shook her head as if to clear away a

haze, and quickly left in silence. It was clear he was an intruder here. He could smell garlic above him. One of the foulest smelling plants that had ever existed. Why garlic or similar vegetables had ever caught on with the mortals was beyond him. His stomach growled again, his meal postponed as a result of the woman that was no longer where he left her.

"Who are you?"

Uriel swiveled around to face the woman he had saved earlier, now adorned in a simple brown robe with a purple belt. She must be a person of considerable influence in this community of women, Uriel judged by her dress, and her speech. No one else would acknowledge him. He guessed that had been at her order. She asked the question again.

"Who are you?"

"My name is Uriel, I am a sailor. I heard about the sirens of the island and came to…"

"We know what you are. Goddess warned us about your kind," Adamina stared him down.

Startled, Uriel reacted, "I saved your life!"

Adamina motioned and one of the other women brought his cloak folded up and handed it to Adamina. The woman who brought the cloak quickly skittered out of visual range. He tried not to think of himself a man at a buffet.

Adamina held the black bundle in front of her, "Thank you for your assistance."

"Goddess warned you?" Uriel questioned.

Adamina backed him into the entrance way, "Goddess warned us the arrival of Angels would threaten Avalon. Now please leave."

She thrust the cloak into his arms and he caught it, however Uriel refused to budge any further.

"I could have let you drown in that river. I saved your life. The least you could do is offer to share with me whatever it is you are cooking. It smells delicious"

Adamina paused. She would fulfill her debt and send him on his way, immediately, "Very well, one meal."

6

ONE MEAL TURNED INTO three moons of visits and discussions, which Adamina tolerated and eventually came to expect. However, she decided that his visits should now come to an end. She would confront him, damn this fear of him returning to God, which he took every opportunity to hold over her head. His voice pierced her thoughts most unwelcomingly.

"You intrigue me. Did you know your race no longer exists? The place you come from is gone?" Uriel offered.

"I do not care where I came from or what my race, as you call it, is. I am a priestess of Avalon. I am of Goddess. I have had enough of you. Why have you not told God of us?"

Uriel considered her. On several occasions, he had tried to use his powers of persuasion on her. They had never worked. It frustrated him that he could not sway this woman. Resisting Angels was good enough reason to eradicate a race to him. Then a terrible idea sparked in his mind, a means to an end. A race strong enough to resist Angels could be bent to his purpose, could produce what he desired. It did not hurt that she was a fine sight to look at and he longed for her. Perhaps, he could make her his for a time, perhaps permanently. He had just the deal to make her give in.

She was strong, perhaps a little ridged for his liking, but everything else suited. She would make a good mother for his son. The one he could teach the ways of the Angels, one that would be undyingly loyal to him. Someone he could trust. A terrible grin slid across his face. Eventually, he must tell God of Avalon. When that should happen had not been specified. He could work around the order, as long as he intended to fulfill God's command.

"I have a proposition for you," Uriel began. She froze, jaw twitching at his negation of her question, "Become my wife and I will never tell my Father of this place."

Adamina nearly choked. She took a deep breath and stopped to consider the proposal. As priestess, Avalon was to come first. This would protect Avalon from destruction. It could keep them all safe. Most of all, accepting his proposal would keep Goddess safe from the wrath of the Others Uriel had told her about. Then Adamina considered herself. He was not unattractive in his physical form. He was a suitable mate, she assumed. No other man had ever demonstrated that type of interest in her. She may not ever get another chance to experience a family, children, like Nevara. She remembered the look on Nevara's face, pure bliss after the toll of birthing, as Adamina had cleared away the after birth. Accepting his proposal would keep them all safe.

Adamina took a deep breath, ignored the twisting of her stomach and said, "I agree to your proposal."

He smirked at her, "That was fast."

"I weighed the decision carefully. There was nothing hasty about it."

"Very well then, ask your priestesses to have a hand fasting ceremony ready in three moons. I have some guests to gather."

After issuing his orders Uriel slipped out of sight and

toward the harbor. Adamina inhaled and prepared herself for the impending conflict with the women of the house. She called for Palla who was in the gardens a few meters away from where Adamina stood and asked that the novice round up all the women for a meeting in the attic library. Adamina steeled herself.

It took several minutes for all the women to settle. They gathered in a circle. Children played in and around the women's feet. One little girl rushed past Adamina as she entered the attic library and skittered behind her adoptive mother. The women looked at their Priestess expectantly. *I am too young for them to rely so greatly on me.* Adamina sighed, *They will all be safe, and Avalon and Goddess will be made safe by this.*

"I have an announcement. The Angel has made an offer. He will keep Avalon safe from destruction, if I become his wife."

Gasps and noises ranging from relief to terror could be heard from the women. Chattering surrounding approvals and disapprovals of the proposal began to swell. Adamina raised her hands to hush the crowd.

"I have accepted his offer."

One of the priestesses stormed past Adamina, the scent of lavender lingered in the air than dissipated. Adamina made a mental note to locate the priestess and ask her the reason for leaving so abruptly. Adamina hushed the women again.

"I do this for Avalon. I will not ask him to live here. The temple and the house will strictly be for the priestesses and children only."

Adamina called the woman named Diane to her and asked softly, "Diane, I ask you to be the Matron of the house. Would you be comfortable taking on the necessary responsibilities of running the priestess house in my absences?" The woman nodded gratefully and hugged Adamina.

"If you have any concerns or needs, please ask Diane when I am unavailable. I am asking you all to continue to go on as if nothing has changed. We are a community, the priestesses of Goddess. I do this to keep Avalon safe; all of you and Avalon will always be my greatest concern. Uriel has asked that the ceremony be held in three moons. Please prepare for it."

The women exchanged blessings and congratulations to Adamina. A few brave women raised their concerns with the marriage. Gwen lingered last.

"Adamina, I don't trust him. I have heard whisperings…"

Adamina cut the young priestess off, "I know, Gwen. I know they are dangerous. Goddess warned us. There is no other way to keep Avalon safe." Gwen gave Adamina a weak smile. "Could you locate Raven, Gwen? She stormed out during the gathering. I am concerned about her."

Gwen nodded and Adamina thanked her. Alone, Adamina slowly wandered to her room. The bed was covered in gray colored cloth, Pagan's cloak folded neatly on top. Palla had returned to the river several times in search of the cloak until she had finally located it lying in a heap on one of the smaller beach shores. The clasp had been torn off, but Palla had mended it. Adamina sat on the bed and whispered to the cloak, "Pagan, I had to. For Avalon. Please let it be the right decision." Then she curled up on the bed and fell asleep, tears running down her face, clutching at the cloak.

IT WAS VERY EARLY morning. The sun rising just over the horizon. Birds chirped and fluttered around the priestess house. Excitement and peace filled the atmosphere. Further north, the forest was still with unease. Adamina took a few measured breaths as she walked and tried to imagine all her worries seeping away for Avalon to recycle. She had slept fitfully and her stomach was knotted. The walk helped, but only a little. She had heard about love from the stories in the library. Pagan had warned her that love and marriage never worked out. Love rarely existed in the hearts of people.

"Choose wisely, and live well," Pagan's voice haunted Adamina's memories.

Please let me have made the right choice, Pagan, Adamina prayed silently.

Adamina became aware of a thrumming from the land beneath her feet. It became warm, soothing, comfortable, and vibrantly excited. The breeze swished and swayed the long grass. The trees, moved by the breeze, creaked and groaned in rhythm with the whispering wind. She stopped walking and took in her surroundings. Her gaze fell on the cabin. Smoke billowed out from a rudimentary chimney. Someone had added a room to it.

Someone had changed her secret, sacred space, making it larger, and, Adamina had to admit with resentment, much improved. She rushed forward towards the building and walked inside to confront whoever it was. The cabin was empty, but a fire blazed in a hearth as something in a pot boiled. A well-built bed, a table and two chairs, a chest, and a rug adorned the room. How long had somcone been living here? Adamina moved towards the boiling stew to investigate its ingredients. It smelled wonderful.

"Hello."

Adamina startled, grabbing the log poking stick leaning against the hearth and spun around, holding it out in front of her. The man who had addressed her jumped back so quickly she barely discerned the movement. He was only slightly taller than her. He had well-defined muscles, etched into his body from hard-labor. He had brown hair and honey-amber eyes. A smirk played on his lips. His hands hung loosely at his sides. It was impossible to tell his age. There was something familiar in his features and form. Perhaps he had assisted with the building of Pagan's house. Yes, that must be where she remembered him from. He stared her down, amusement glinting in his eyes as he surveyed her.

"Who are you?" Adamina demanded.

He restrained a chuckle, "I am no threat to you."

"Who are you?" She repeated.

He stood in silence, waiting to see what she would do next. He was intrigued. She had grown into a woman in his absence.

She looked at him wearily, squinting her eyes. Had she blinked, she would have missed the movements he made to knock the stick from her grasp. He held her arm gently, then pulled her close to him. She gasped slightly as she stared him down. He held on to her, arm around her waist. She did not like the way he made her feel. It was uncomfortable, knots in her stomach, a haze around her vision, and light-headed. She was most uncomfortable. The warmth from his embrace made the sensations all the more unnerving.

"If I wanted to harm you," he said softly in a satin-smooth voice, "I could have already done so."

He released her and she took a step back. The distance from him made her feel suddenly cold and empty. She swallowed and took a deep breath to calm herself. She struggled to think straight and clung on to anger and fear, letting the emotions drive her questions and preparing her to flee if need be.

"Who are you?" she demanded again.

"Persistent," he smirked at her. "I am Gabriel," he made a slight bow, "You must be Adamina."

Gabriel sat down in one of the chairs leisurely, clearly

at home, though not faulting her entirely for the occupancy of his home. He had, after all, allowed her to use it when she was in need.

"How do you know my name?" She eyed the stick again and made a quick movement towards it, almost as quick as him.

He snatched it out of her reach.

"Let's put this away before someone gets hurt," he said and placed it back by the fire.

This man was insufferable, "What are you doing in my cabin?"

"Your cabin? You built this? Well, I have to say I am impressed. As you can see, I made a few improvements to it."

"Improvements! You... you... uh!" she took a deep breath, checking her rage, infuriated further by his smirk. "How long have you been living here?"

"A few moons, maybe more. I did have a place by the port, but it seems my brother, Uriel, has commandeered it for the time being," he shrugged and turned to retrieve a bowl for stew, "Would you like some?"

She froze and swallowed back the knots in her stomach, "Uriel's your brother?"

She sat down on a stool and wrestled with a sorrow and agony she did not understand. He ladled stew into two bowls and set them on the small table, motioning her to follow. She followed his command easily. Tears welled up in her eyes. He had lied to her, Avalon was not safe.

"An Angel? More Angels? He said he would protect Avalon! He..."

Gabriel held a finger to her soft lips to silence her, "Avalon's secrets are safe, Adamina. I have long been retired from my duties and am loyal to no one but myself. Your precious isle is safe, I promise. Please, eat with me."

She gave into her stomach and slid back in the chair, silently ladling food into her mouth, staring at him with more questions in her eyes. She was hungry. She had not had supper last night, or breakfast this morning. She had been so out of sorts since the proposal. She attacked the soup until she was full enough to continue conversation in between bites. It made her feel almost herself again.

"Why are you here?"

He sighed in frustration and said quickly, "I am here because I want a place to retire to for a while. I do not see eye-to-eye with my father and disapprove of many of his actions. I am tired of being a messenger. I do not look like Uriel because although in spirit we are brothers, my body is of my own making. And thank you, my hair does look pretty good in this light, doesn't it?"

Adamina's mouth hung open at his answers to her unanswered questions and she blinked, "How did you…"

"Know what you were thinking?" He finished her sentence for her and answered, "Because all Angels can hear thoughts. It's how we communicate over long distances with each other. I am surprised you did not know this. Uriel did not tell you?"

"No, I barely know anything about Uriel," Adamina went back to shoveling food into her mouth.

Gabriel almost choked on his food. He swallowed and reprimanded himself for being so liberal with her and assuming his brother would have told her anything. He felt guilty for using his abilities so unwisely. There was just something about her that let him drop his guard.

"I apologize for intruding on your thoughts. Why did you agree to the union if you know nothing about my brother?" Gabriel looked at her puzzled that anyone would handfast to someone they knew nothing about.

"To save Avalon. Keep it a secret," she said in between mouthfuls.

"I see," Gabriel had suddenly lost his appetite. Uriel had lied. The only reason Gabriel could be here, living as if he had freewill, was because Goddess had mercifully ordered him to do so. Uriel had no such order. He would be obligated to tell God eventually. The best Uriel could do was postpone the inevitable. And he would do that now to get what he desired. Her.

Her hunger satisfied, Adamina sat back and watched him in silence for a very long time. The uncomfortable feeling of needing to leave filled her.

"The stew was delicious, thank you" she said to break the silence.

Gabriel only nodded, lost in thought. Adamina sat for a few more minutes in silence before sliding off her chair and heading for the door. He did not stop her.

7

Pit. Pit. Pit. Whish. Pit. Pit. Pit. Whish. Thunk! She shot awake. The sunlight streamed into the window. It was very early morning. The sun had just barely climbed into the sky. Thunk! *What in the name of...* Adamina slid out of her small bed. Bare feet touched the cold wooden floorboards and her sleepiness was chased out by the morning chill. Adamina donned a dress and cloak, slipped into shoes. The house was silent as she passed by rooms.

Someone's door was still open. Inside, one of the priestesses, had fallen asleep in a rocking chair with a dozing child in her arms. Adamina smiled at the scene and headed down the stairs and out the back door, stopping in the kitchen for a piece of bread. The noises slowly got louder as she walked east, away from the priestess house. Not even the birds were awake this early. Thunk! A murmur of voices, deep voices accompanied the noise.

She wandered away from the priestess house toward the noises some distance before she felt she was nearing its source. Finally, Adamina stepped into a clearing filled with men, planks of wood, straw and thatching, and tools. The only man she recognized was Gabriel on top of the roof, thatching straw to the framed structure of a roof. His gazed met her own. The morning sunrise caught the highlights of dawn in her hair. It appeared that she truly was born of the isle itself, not plucked from a world of darkness as she had been. He smiled gently at her and Adamina found herself smiling back.

"Gabriel! What are you doing? What is all of this?"

Gabriel smirked at her and replied, "Ask your betrothed, lady."

"Where can I find…," Adamina was interrupted when one of the men accidentally knocked her over as he walked past carrying timber.

Gabriel jumped off the roof and came to her side, helping her up.

"Are you alright?" Gabriel looked her over for any injuries.

"Yes, thank you," she smiled to reassure him.

"Adamina!" Uriel came around from behind the house somewhere. He pushed Gabriel aside, looking her over in a panic, "What happened?"

"Peace Uriel, I was knocked over, it was an accident," Adamina responded.

"Who was it?" Uriel demanded.

"I don't…" Adamina tried to explain, but Uriel cut her off before she had a chance to continue.

"Anyone who hurts you will pay, tell me who it was. Was it Gabriel?" Uriel shot a look towards his brother.

Gabriel was about to refute the accusation when Adamina said, "No, Gabriel was helping me up."

Uriel's gaze darkened and Gabriel rolled his eyes at Uriel, their exchange of expressions interrupted by Adamina's inquiry, "What is going on, Uriel? Why are you building a house here? Who are these people?"

"Why, silly Adamina, this house is for us. You will come to live with me here after the hand fasting. Anything you want, anything at all, let me know."

"A house?" Adamina stared around in disbelief.

"You didn't think we could raise a family in that priestess' house, did you?" Uriel laughed.

"A family…Well, no, but I…" Adamina struggled to find the words.

"Gabriel, introduce Adamina to everyone here and show her around will you? I have some important things to attend to," without waiting for an answer, Uriel left his future wife in his brother's care.

Adamina stood there stunned, able only to blink as she processed everything that was about to happen. Gabriel pitied Adamina and fought against a knot of dread within his gut. Uriel was off constructing his own little world again, and Adamina was helplessly caught up in it. Gabriel wrapped an arm around Adamina's shoulders. Adamina's body relaxed into his and she blinked away the confusion, turning her head to look at him. He smiled at her reassuringly.

"Let's introduce you to everyone here shall we?"

Gabriel steered her around the building, introducing her to about a dozen men. Some she recognized from the small port village, but most became a blurring of faces and names she tried to grapple with. Gabriel's voice interrupted her thoughts.

"There is one more person whose company I believe you may enjoy. Now where the heck is she. Jophiel?!"

He turned his head in the direction of the rustling of straw that was piled up for thatching. A blonde head of hair popped up and Jophiel grinned and waved at them. She instructed a man to finish thatching the roof, then began walking towards them. Jophiel was small in stature and dressed in blue garments: a tunic adorned with a golden belt, legs clad in flowing pants.

Gabriel embraced her and said, "Jophiel, this is Adamina. Adamina, this is my sister Jophiel."

Jophiel stepped forward and warmly embraced Adamina.

Turning back to Gabriel she said, "You're right, this one's way too good for our brother, Gabriel."

Adamina looked at Gabriel questioningly.

"Well, I am famished! What about you?" Gabriel turned to Adamina who replied with a nod.

He ushered her into the house through a backdoor and Jophiel returned to her work. The house was almost finished. She entered into a large kitchen, not incredibly unlike the one in the priestess' house, but definitely more ornate. Wooden carvings accented cupboards and counters. Running her fingers along the carvings in adoration, Adamina took in the room.

"Do you like it?" Gabriel asked softly.

"It is breath-taking Gabriel, who carved all of these?"

"I did," he said with a slight shrug.

Adamina's stomach fluttered and turned and she became aware of the aroma of stew. At the back of the room a large hearth, only slightly smaller than the one in the priestess' house, blazed bright. Adamina closed her eyes and inhaled slowly.

"You made the stew as well."

Gabriel smirked, "I am impressed. How could you tell?"

"The combination of herbs is the same as the stew you fed me when we first met."

"There is nothing wrong with being predictable, especially when it produces excellent cooking."

He spooned stew into a set of wooden bowls he had retrieved from the cupboards and set them down on the polished stone slab that sat in the middle of the kitchen. Silently, they ate, lost in their own thoughts. When they finished, Gabriel removed the bowl from in front of her, she watched him carry it to a basin and wash out the dishes.

"What?" He asked at the expression on her face.

She smirked at him, "Nothing, I've just never seen a man clean up before."

"Well, you are the honored bride. Can't have you getting your hands dirty can we?"

Adamina scolded him for teasing her. "I should return home, I have a lot I need to prepare before tomorrow." She headed toward the backdoor of the house.

"Adamina!" Gabriel called to her and she stopped and turned around.

"Yes?"

"You haven't seen the rest of the house."

"If you had a hand in it, I am sure it is just as beautiful as this room is."

She left him and returned to the priestess house. Faces smiled at her, but thankfully no one spoke to her. She quietly closed the door to her quarters and sat on the bed. She took a few deep breaths trying to calm herself, worry and fear welling up inside her. A small pebble flew into her open window and clattered to the floor, interrupting her swirling thoughts. Adamina peered out over the window-ledge. Uriel, clad in a white tunic and leather breeches gazed up at her.

"Hey! What were you thinking? You could have hit me with that pebble!" Adamina shouted down to him.

"Sweet maiden fair," Uriel bowed, "I come bearing gifts for my wife-to-be!"

Adamina sighed softly and rested her head on her hands and her elbows on the window sill, "What gifts do you bear, sir?" She tried not to blush. Perhaps she would have her own happily-ever-after after all.

Someone knocked on the door to her room then Gwen and Palla entered, arms full: a bouquet of wild flowers, a poppet in the shape of a rabbit, and a large bundle of cloth. She smiled and rushed to the window, but Uriel had disappeared from her sight. Adamina thanked the women and opened the bundle of cloth. A pale blue dress adorned with delicate spirals of darker blue emerged from the bundle. It took her breath away.

Ink and parchment spelled out a message of blessing from Jophiel, who had made the dress, and a wish from Uriel that she wear it for the ceremony tomorrow. She barely had a moment to consider the dress before priestesses whisked her about to finalize this or help with that. The day flew by as the hand fasting creeped nearer. The night would not surrender sleep for Adamina.

WHEN THE SUN BEGAN to rise, Adamina gave up wishing for rest. She flew out of bed and donned the blue dress. She snuck out of the priestess house and ran towards the temple, her heart calling for the comfort of her mother-Goddess. But the stone was silent, Goddess was nowhere. *Goddess is everywhere*, Adamina corrected herself. She closed her eyes, inhaled and listened with all of her being for a sign. Silence enveloped her for what felt like ages. When she felt like it was going to smother her, the silence gave way to something she had never heard before, a melody not sung by any voice. She ran towards the noise, guiding her to a grove.

A stringed apparatus was held up by male hands. Hands lead to arms, a torso, and a face. His hair was black, his eyes were a piercing blue, his nose and lips were thin and had the constant impression of mischief upon them.

"Adamina I presume?" the man set down the instrument and her eyes followed it.

"I have never seen anything like that before. What is it?" She questioned.

"It's a harp," he held it up to her and she took it. It was heavy in her hands, she turned it over, scrutinized it. Adamina plucked a few strings and startled at the sounds it made.

"My name is Michael. I am Uriel's oldest brother."

"But you look younger than him. How many brothers does Uriel have?" Adamina returned the harp to Michael.

Michael paused for a moment to consider the question. "Thousands."

Adamina choked, "Thousands? There are going to be thousands of Angels on Avalon?" Adamina nearly fainted.

Michael burst out a boisterous laugh, "No! No," he got a hold on himself and explained that only Jophiel and the five, maybe six of them would be on Avalon for the celebrations today.

"Five? I have only met Gabriel and yourself."

"Raphael, Tyrryal, and Lucifer should be attending the hand fasting. If they can find their way here."

"I see."

"I get the sense you don't care for Angels."

"I was told they will be the end of Avalon."

Michael solemnly considered her statement. "So this is the paradise we searched for then. Mind you, it is nothing in comparison to my birth place."

"And where might that be?"

"I was born somewhere very, very far from here."

A twig snapped in the woods. Someone was heading toward them. Leaves on a shrub rustled as Gabriel brushed passed them. "Michael, Uriel needs... oh, hello Adamina!"

Adamina nodded and smiled at Gabriel.

"Shouldn't you be getting some beauty sleep honored one?" Gabriel teased her.

"I was unable to sleep. I came out here and heard your brother playing the harp."

"I am surprised you didn't turn around and run from the atrocious noise!"

"Hey! I am an accomplished musician Gabriel," Michael defended himself.

"Uriel needs to speak with you, Michael," Gabriel said without taking his eyes off Adamina.

Michael looked back and forth at them and smirked, "Okay, I will see you at the hand fasting then."

Michael left in the direction Gabriel had come from.

"You shouldn't let Uriel see you dressed like that. I have heard it is unlucky for a bridegroom to see his bride before the ceremony."

"What nonsense!" Adamina shot back and stormed off.

"I apologize if I offended you," Gabriel chased after Adamina.

She sighed, "No, I am sorry. I was unable to rest last night."

"There are still a few hours before the ceremony, why don't you use the cabin to try to sleep a bit. I will wake you so you will not miss the ceremony."

Adamina half-smiled and nodded, "Thank you."

Gabriel sat outside the cabin as Adamina slept. The sun shone more brightly than he could stand at the moment. He closed his eyes and leaned his head back. His lungs struggled to fill with breath. He was nervous. He laughed at himself. After all, it was not he who was getting married today. That young woman sleeping in his bed should be filled with apprehension and butterflies, not him. Part of him secretly hoped she was dreading the day as much as he was.

A ripple of energy notified him that Tyrryal had arrived on the island. He hoped the brute of an Angel washed up before he attended the wedding. Why Tyrryal couldn't grasp basic grooming habits while in mortal form was beyond him. Mind, so was Tyrryal's trust of Uriel. Brothers they may be, but he and Uriel could not be more different. Uriel grated on his nerves and Gabriel could see little that warranted trust, let alone like. Tolerance was all he could muster, especially since Gabriel had had to clean up Uriel's messes more than once.

His thoughts returned to Adamina. How could someone so beautiful, so innocent, so breath-taking ever want to bind themselves to Uriel?

The more he thought on it, the more his blood boiled He would never interfere with Adamina's choice, but the rage at the way his brother had trapped this poor woman threatened his composure. There was nothing he could do about it. At least Lucifer had had the smarts not to show his face around here. The fact that Uriel had invited the fiend made Gabriel question his sanity and loyalties deeply. If Lucifer did show his face here, Gabriel would see that Lucifer met the fate he should have. Father's leniency still irked him. Gabriel let out a sigh, noting the sun's position.

I guess I should wake her, Gabriel mused, dread weighing him down. Dread he did not understand. He pushed away at it until it disappeared from his psyche.

Gabriel stood up and stretched his stiff muscles. He stepped inside to wake her. Adamina lay peacefully asleep. It was dark in the cabin, there was no fire in the hearth as the day was warm. Gabriel could see Adamina clearly. He had decent vision in the dark, but the clarity of her form was not due to his vision. Adamina's skin was glowing, as if the moon was shining out through her skin. It took every last ounce of will power to restrain himself from reaching out and caressing her skin in awe. Instead, Gabriel swallowed down the dry lump in his throat and spoke her name.

She roused and opened her eyes, blinked to clear her vision and smiled at him.

"Hello," she spoke softly.

"Hello," he replied.

It was that look that undid him. Those innocent eyes that caused his heart to scream at him to tell her she was doing the wrong thing. Telling him to spout nonsensical promises and wishes, anything to keep her from Uriel's grasp.

He shook off his feelings. He would honor her decision,

"It is almost time for the ceremony."

She shot out of bed, "I almost forgot!"

Her legs were numb from sleep and she almost plummeted to the ground. Gabriel caught her and set her up right.

"Relax. You still have some time," he comforted.

Adamina blushed. After a moment she pulled away from him. Without speaking, she nodded and walked past Gabriel into the clearing. Sunlight burned her eyes and she closed them for a moment. When she opened them again a meadow filled with wildflowers bloomed in her vision, then suddenly became a clearing with two figures huddled in a corner, then fire, hot and painful on her skin, turning everything to ash. Her heart raced and her lips uttered repeatedly, "No, no, no," she panicked.

"Adamina!" Gabriel shook her. "Adamina!" She had screamed and was staring in shock at something. He couldn't tell what it was. He looked into her eyes and slid his way into her thoughts. The vision flashed through his mind, but did not take hold of him as it had Adamina. He gently nudged the vision to the back of her mind, bringing her back to reality. "Adamina, are you alright?"

She blinked away tears and focused on him, "Yes, I saw," her voice was raw, "I saw."

Gabriel interrupted her, "It was a vision. Have you ever had such visions before?"

Adamina shook her head and swallowed against the burning in her throat. She began to focus on her breathing to calm herself. When she had regained her composure she pulled away from Gabriel's grasp, assured him she was okay, and headed towards the priestess house. Gabriel resisted the urge to follow her and instead headed out to find Raphael.

Gabriel called out to him, *Raphael, I have something I need to discuss with you urgently. Where are you?*

The quiet and gentle voice of his brother responded, *I*

am in the kitchen of the house of priestesses. They have commandeered my cooking skills for this wedding so they can attend to other things.

Gabriel ran after Adamina. They walked in tense silence back to the priestess house. Thankfully, Adamina took the route through the kitchen, sparing him asking her for directions. Not often was the priestess house kitchen orchestrated by a man, except when they had been asked to tend to a pot, a counter top, or a water pump. Even less often was it empty of children and women. Raphael was met with immediate suspicion from Adamina. He was tall and gently built. Grace filled his every movement. After introductions were made, Adamina's suspicion ebbed. She would have no problem calling him brother or trusting her life to him. Raphael was preparing quite a feast.

"Making a mess of things I see, Gabriel," Raphael's voice was as gentle and graceful as he appeared to be, but it held a warning, filled with dangerous possibilities of what he was capable of if crossed. His hand moved with unhurried precision as it sliced vegetables.

Gabriel responded with an eye-roll and an irritated shake of his head.

"If you will excuse me," Adamina hurried out of the room, grateful to put some distance between her and the ever growing amount of Angels.

She found a wash basin and splashed water onto her face and righted her appearance. She did not pinch color into her cheeks or dye her lips as some of the other women did. She left her skin pale, her lips a natural pink-near-mauve. She fussed a little over her hair and then took a deep breath steeling herself before she headed towards the ceremony site.

Down in the kitchen, Gabriel expressed his concerns about the vision Adamina had.

"I think our presence here is causing worse damage

than we may have considered, Raphael."

"Our purpose was to seek out Avalon, Gabriel, nothing more. Although, for such a place to be damaged would be unfortunate. It is very beautiful here, reminds me of Mother."

"Your purpose," Gabriel corrected. "Mother is not here anymore, but I can hear her heart beat inside Avalon, inside Adamina, and her eye disguises itself in the sun so she knows all that is happening here. Her life force is how this island came into existence. It is her life force that keeps everything alive. I do not know how, but Mother is communicating with Adamina."

"Ask yourself, Gabriel, when do we tell Father about this place? Father is going to find out about this one way or another. After all, Uriel is wedding a girl stolen from a world that Father destroyed. Do you really think Uriel will take the blame for keeping her alive? Do you really think he will not end this world? The Others will wish it."

Gabriel was filled with anger and it took all his will not to express it. "I know what our brother is like, Raphael. I do not need a lecture on the probable outcomes of this. Mother has warned Adamina through a vision about the consequences of our presence. Adamina cannot bind herself to Uriel."

Raphael ceased his chopping, stared into his brothers eyes with warning, "Because of the consequences of Angelic presence on Avalon, because of Uriel and his known pattern of behavior, or because you want her for yourself, Gabriel?"

"That is absurd Raphael," Gabriel snapped.

"If it is so absurd, then why are you watching over and following her like a lost puppy dog?"

"I am doing no such thing! I admit that I do not want to see her destroyed by Uriel, but I do not want her or anyone for myself, Raphael. I am a retired man. I chose here to retire. I want all of you off this island to leave me in peace!" Gabriel was glowing with rage.

"I suggest, Gabriel, you leave this place before you destroy this island with your own anger," Raphael returned to cutting the vegetables, letting Gabriel deal with his turmoil.

Gabriel turned on his heels and fled out the door. He caught the next ship off that island and swore he would never return.

BUTTERFLIES DANCED INSIDE A stomach, somewhere, but not inside Adamina. Inside, she felt numb. She thought she should feel something. Excitement, resolve, dread, fear, hope, joy, but nothing was all she could feel. Someone had pulled her into a looking glass and her reflection now stared back at her. She was unable to stop this day from happening. The looking glass showed a blank expression not even she could read.

She felt abandoned by Goddess and by Pagan. How dare they leave her here! But even her feelings of abandonment were swallowed up quickly by the great nothingness inside of her. One of the priestesses came to tell her it was time for the ceremony to begin. Soon, she was in position, hiding behind a volley of trees, wanting to run, but frozen in place. Adamina looked at a young woman's face who passed by and saw no features, just a blur of flesh colored light.

Michael joined her. He said something about escorting her to the ceremony and she nodded and took his arm. The walk to the altar in the meadow seemed to take forever. Michael joked with Adamina, suggested he could sweep her off her feet and whisk her away from here. She stopped walking abruptly for a moment, staring at

Michael and considering, somewhere deep inside her being, his offer.

She could not speak. He laughed off the suggestion. The desperation in her eyes unsettled him, He wondered what Uriel had done to reel this one in. He had hoped his brother had gone and gained some sense this time.

A cluster of people blocked the view of the altar and her soon-to-be-husband. They parted to reveal Jophiel, Uriel and the altar. A terrifying vision of her lying chained to the altar with Uriel standing over her, dagger in hand, laughing caused her to stumble. She felt Michael hold her steady. Adamina did not know how she came to stand in front of that ominous stone. It was not until it was too late, when the cord was tying her to this man she barely knew, sealing her fate that she wanted to cut it. She wanted to call out to Michael, Raphael, Gabriel, and the priestesses.

She lifted her head, gaining the courage, opening her mouth to beg for freedom, but before she could, firm lips assaulted hers. Her eyes searched for Michael, his face held a smile as his hands joined the chorus of applause. Her eyes darted around searching for Gabriel, but she could not locate him. Someone untied the cord so they each had one free hand and Uriel led her through the crowd of people. He stopped to shake a hand here or there. At one of these stops she turned to Palla and quickly asked about Gabriel.

Palla blinked, confused and said, "He left just before the ceremony, after speaking to Raphael. Took a ship off the island. Didn't you know?"

Before she could answer, Uriel tugged her away and swept her towards their new home. He carried her past the threshold, up the stairs, and into a bedroom adorned with a massive bed. Adamina noticed the intricate carvings along the bedposts and boards and she was filled with a choking despair. Uriel placed her on the bed and caressed her skin eagerly, even a little harshly. She stared at the doorway. He untied his wrist from the cord, got up, slammed the door shut and locked it. Adamina started and finally looked at her husband, this stranger.

"I am not well," she managed to whisper.

He reassured her she would feel better soon and climbed on top of her. Adamina felt nothing, drifting away into a world of her own, losing herself in the twists and turns of the carvings until exhaustion sucked her into darkness.

8

HE SUN WARMED HER hands as she worked, squatting in the dirt, pulling weeds, harvesting the few herbs and berries that were ready. Her body was heavy and she struggled to stand up. Her belly was round with the child inside. The sensation of having life grow inside her was thrilling and terrifying. She could feel the child turn and summersault, swimming around inside of her, ready to come out soon, she knew.

She picked up the basket and brought it into the kitchen. There was a basin full of water already. She looked around and, finding no one, smiled. Raphael must have filled it for her this morning. She went about washing the vegetables and hanging herbs. As she worked, Adamina's mind wandered. She had watched the seasons pass from summer, to winter to summer again since she had wed Uriel and moved into the house, *his* house.

Raphael had become a constant companion Adamina was grateful for. He stayed on Avalon, teaching the priestesses about medicine and magic and helping Adamina in little ways. Her baby kicked her and Adamina smiled at the strange sensation, rubbing her hands over her belly to soothe the infant.

"What are you doing?" Uriel's agitated voice uttered behind her.

She sighed softly and her shoulders sunk slightly. She did not turn to face him, "I am washing vegetables, Uriel. There is no harm to me or the child in doing that."

Adamina picked up the now empty basket and headed back to the garden, if only to get away from his nagging. She knelt down and began pulling weeds furiously, stuffing them into her basket.

"Adamina!" Uriel called after her, "Get inside at once. Leave that work to someone else. You need to be resting!"

Adamina stood up, basket posed against her hip, "I am pregnant Uriel, not an invalid. And besides, I had a wonderful rest last night, thank you for asking."

Chuckling and snickering followed Adamina's words and she turned to face a group of Angels. She hid her smile and scolded them playfully.

"Ramiel, Tyrryal, and Michael, you should be ashamed of yourselves for laughing at a pregnant woman!"

"My dear Adamina," Michael began, "We would not dream of laughing at you. We were, in fact, laughing at my brother for hen-pecking you!" The three broke into a raucous laughter.

Uriel's face turned red, "Shut up, all of you and wipe those stupid grins off your faces. We have work to do."

He stormed towards them, ushering them away from the house to discuss whatever business it is that Angels discuss. Adamina was grateful for the reprieve. While she appreciated the men's presence, they could be a loud bunch. It had been far too long since she had a reprieve of silence. She sought out the owl that was always present in the trees. She knew he was there, even if she could not see him.

Only Raphael knew of her fears, her concerns surrounding Uriel and this pregnancy. Adamina was no fool and had heard of the risks child birth brought. If it wasn't for Raphael's kind words and support, she was sure she would have lost her sanity by now. Tears came to her eyes. She had been crying a great deal, but Raphael had assured her it was due to the baby's effects on her body, that it was nothing to worry about. She still did not enjoy the lack of control over her emotions.

She walked around the house to a large pile of weeds and dumped her basket out over it. Her hands were filthy so she waddled her way out towards a small, clear pond and slid into the water. She scrubbed away the dirt and dust and hummed softly. A strange sensation seized her. Adamina clutched her belly, but the sensation subsided quickly and she relaxed herself, breathing deeply. She had cramping days ago, but Raphael assured her they were just her body preparing for labor still a while away. She dismissed the concerns that rose in her and finished scrubbing off the dirt. Her belly was seized again with cramping and heaving several moments later.

"The baby is coming," she gasped, half pleading for help to anyone who may hear. Her call for help turned into a cry of pain and fear.

The spasms increased in frequency quickly and she was unable to climb out of the pond.

"Someone, please…" she cried out hoarsely. *"Someone, please help me…"* she called to anyone who would hear her.

"Ah!" Her belly heaved and contracted beneath her hands and she nearly doubled over in pain.

It took all her strength to stay upright. She stood there, muscles straining, fighting against the pain for what felt like ages as the spasms quickened and she cried tears of despair.

"Adamina!" A voice from the woods, "Adamina! There you are, don't worry dear."

"Raphael!" Adamina let out a sob at the sight of him and three of the priestesses.

"Shush, relax as best as you can," he said and climbed into the water. He stroked her hair to soothe her. The baby was coming too fast, "There is no time to move you from here."

Adamina nodded and concentrated on her breathing, trying to meditate. Raphael ushered her to a mound of earth beneath the water which functioned as a seat. "May I touch you Adamina…?" Raphael asked, communicating the entirety of the nature of his touch with thoughts.

She knew what a birthing entailed and irrational anger rode the waves of contractions.

Adamina nodded furiously and said, "Just get the baby out!"

Raphael instructed two of the women that had come with him to hold her head above the water. They sunk into the water on either side of her and Adamina grasped their shoulders as they supported her weight. The third priestess was sent for lots of hot water, one of Raphael's medicine kits, and warm towels and blankets. Adamina whimpered in pain, but kept herself as calm as possible, Raphael's whisperings urging her to relax. Her breathing slowed and she relaxed in spite of the spasms.

"Don't worry Adamina, it won't be long. I can feel the baby's head already," Raphael smiled at her.

He was careful to hide his thoughts and concerns. Not many mortal women survived the birthing of Angelic babies, especially if they were born with wings. He prayed Adamina's experience would be different, thankful her race was strong. Raphael began to sing softly. He wound magic into his melody to sooth and relax Adamina further, his words caressing her and intoxicating her enough to free her from the awareness of her pain for a few moments. The third priestess returned with another, both arms full of what Raphael had asked for. He instructed them to lay the objects nearby. He knew she had been in labour since this morning, and cursed himself for letting her out of his sight for a moment. This labour had not been causing her too much difficulty and he had judged it would take a great while before the babe made its way into the world. He misjudged. The baby would come quickly.

"Okay Adamina, it's time to push."

Adamina began to flex her muscles, pushing the child out of her. She felt like she was on fire, but the water lapped at her, cooling her.

"Once more Adamina," Raphael pleaded.

Ribbons of crimson snaked through the water.

Adamina took in a small breath and pushed, hard. She screamed out.

The baby slipped out of his hands and it tried to swim to the surface of the water. He secured the child and lifted it out. Raphael cut and tied the umbilical cord. The child screamed. He handed the child to the priestess not holding Adamina, to be toweled off and wrapped in a warm blanket. Adamina was shaking, but the worst was over. Raphael coached her through the after birth then gently lifted Adamina out of the water. The priestesses cleaned her with the hot water and toweled her off, wrapping her in blankets. They handed her the child. Raphael magically healed the tearing left by the child then applied ointment from his kit. Thankfully, the child did not have wings. Raphael relaxed. Adamina smiled at her baby.

"My little water child, my little Nerina," Adamina cooed to her daughter.

One of the priestesses was behind her, supporting her so Adamina could sit up. Their heads all swivelled in the direction of snapping leaves and twigs and what sounded like a small army running through the forest. Uriel, followed by Tyrryal, Michael, and Ramiel rushed out of the trees.

"Congratulations brother, you're a father," Raphael

said to Uriel without meeting his eyes.

"What is it?" Uriel demanded.

"A girl," Raphael said softly.

Adamina smiled at him, "Her name is Nerina."

"A girl?" The joy in Uriel's eyes died away.

The others froze at the distaste in his voice.

"Adamina, the others and I will be gone for a while. We have something to take care of. Have some of the women come to stay with you while we are gone."

"Uriel, don't you want to see your child?" Adamina asked.

"I am sure she is beautiful," Uriel called over his shoulder as he walked away. He left Adamina and his daughter to Raphael and the priestesses.

"Don't worry, I will be here to help you," Raphael soothed.

When she was able, Adamina was taken back to the house and settled into bed to rest. The priestesses all filtered into the house to cluck and coo over the blue-eyed little girl. Adamina stared at the ceiling. She knew Uriel had hoped for a son. Her daughter will never be short on love, Adamina vowed as she listened to the women below her room fretting over her little water girl. Adamina closed her eyes to sleep.

9

U RIEL WAS AWAY FOR several months. By the time he returned, Nerina was almost one. Uriel burst through the door, picked up the little girl who giggled and embraced her. He returned the child to the floor where she resumed chewing the corner of a blanket. Adamina stood up from the rocking chair she had been in.

"Uriel!"

"My wife, don't just stand there. Embrace your husband," he grinned and opened his arms wide.

She closed the distance between them and hugged him. She had missed his companionship. Few of the priestesses ventured to the house he had built them. Only Palla had remained to support Adamina and to deliver Adamina's wishes to the others when Adamina was unable to. Adamina had become unwell and was unable to leave her bed for many days following Nerina's birth. The ague seemed to linger unendingly. Palla had been Adamina's unfailing support.

"Palla!" Uriel addressed the priestess, "please watch the child while my wife and I get reacquainted."

Palla looked to Adamina who nodded slowly in response just before Uriel swept her up the stairs to their bedroom. Adamina swallowed as her throat began to tense. A young male servant carrying a decanter and two goblets appeared in the door way. Where had he found a servant? Adamina would have to talk with him about releasing the poor boy. She believed no one should own another living creature.

"Ah! My dear," Uriel said as he removed the goblets and decanter from the grasp of the young man and sent him away, "You must try this wine!"

She took the cup he handed her and sniffed the liquid slightly and took a sip.

Uriel continued, "It was given to me by a merchant. It is herbed and blessed by a mystic to ensure the conception of a son."

Adamina stopped in mid sip and swallowed the suddenly heavy liquid. "What do you mean ensure the conception of a son?"

"Exactly what I said Adamina. I must, after all, have a son to carry on my legacy," Uriel placed his goblet on the bedside table and scooped Adamina's out of her hand.

Adamina blinked as the room began to spin, "Uriel I don't feel…"

"Hush love…"

Lights danced around the ceiling as Adamina found herself lying in bed. Uriel was speaking to her, but she could not understand him. She felt his hand brush her hair. Uriel nuzzled her neck. Adamina tried to blink away the dizziness and lights. She was far away, floating through glistening orbs until she landed in darkness. Her limbs became heavy and her mind gave in to sleep.

✳

THEY WERE DANCING AMONGST the stars. A gown flowed around her. Music graced her ears, making her weep at the beauty and the sadness of it. They swirled and dipped and swooped. Dancing? No, they were soaring. She let out a laugh of great joy that echoed about them. Adamina looked up at the man that embraced her and found not her husband's eyes, but amber-honey eyes of comfort and passion. Fire glinted from Gabriel's gaze. She thought she should pull away and protest. Gabriel was not her husband. What she felt and did, however, was a very different matter.

"Gabriel," Adamina whispered.

"Sh, my love it is alright. I am here. Nothing can hurt you. He cannot separate us…"

"Who?" Adamina became enveloped in confusion and fear.

"Sh…"

Adamina shot awake and was assaulted by the sun's bright light. She attempted to slide off the bed and the reality of the world set in. Her hand shot to her swollen belly. Eight months ago, Uriel had given her the strange concoction in hopes of impregnating her with a son. The pregnant part had been achieved; however, Adamina was filled with doubt that the child was a son. Nerina's giggles echoed down the hall as she raced into Adamina's bedroom.

"Mommy, mommy, I made a dolly!" the little girl with golden hair and blue eyes gleefully held out a straw poppet.

The priestesses were making them for Mabon bonfires to celebrate the harvest. A small section of the land had been cultivated and farmed this season to provide food for the priestesses. Food had become scarce earlier in the season. Famine had reached much of the lands from where the ships sailed and the starving had nearly depleted their small garden. The women had decided to extend their gardens to offer food for the ships to take back and the harvest had been bountiful.

"That's wonderful Nerina!"

"Is that my wife I hear awakened from her heavy slumber?"

Uriel's footsteps echoed down the hall towards her until his figure filled the doorway. Adamina had come to appreciate Uriel's presence over the past eight months. He had barely left her side. The three of them, Uriel, Adamina and Nerina, had become quite an attractive family. She beamed at her husband. If only this pregnancy did not leave her so weak.

"Good morning," Adamina said softly.

"Morning?" Uriel laughed, "Why it is practically dinner time! The mid-day stew is almost ready!"

Adamina's paled cheeks flushed in embarrassment and Uriel hugged and kissed Nerina on the head, "Run along back to your fun my dear girl and I will be there shortly."

"Okay, bye daddy," Nerina slid out of her mother's arms and scampered out of the room and down the hall, playing with her poppet, flying it through the air.

Adamina smiled softly and slid out of bed, upon standing she was seized with pain not yet due. The pains of labor are hard forgotten.

"Uriel!" Adamina gasped. "The baby, it's too early, the baby…"

Uriel bolted out of the room screaming for Raphael who appeared an instant later. Raphael carried Adamina back into the bed. Uriel paced loudly and made inquiries seconds apart.

"Uriel, I need you out of this room. Go and fetch three of the women, I need hot water, clean linens and my kit. This baby is coming early, and it is coming fast," Raphael demanded. He had been afraid of this.

Uriel looked as if he was to protest, but then left the room to fulfill his brother's requests. In a matter of hours the baby had been delivered. She was small and a moon too early, but healthy. She had black hair like her father, and her mother's piercing green eyes squinted at the bright world. Uriel had not entered the room to inquire about the child. One of the priestesses who had brought the fresh linens had found him to tell him the baby girl's name, Artemesia. Before the priestess could tell of the baby's or the mother's health, Uriel had sent her away.

Artemesia was taken to a wet nurse at the priestess' manor. Too weak from the ordeal, Adamina was unable to feed the child. Her skin was so pale, it was almost translucent. Raphael repaired what damage he could and left her to sleep in peace. He closed the door behind him and leaned his head against it. He pinched the bridge of his nose sucking in breath and trying to calm his fears for his dear friend. It broke his heart to see her suffer so much at the hands of his brother. He had to do something fast if she was ever going to survive this.

"YOU CANNOT!"

"Do not tell me what I can or cannot do, Raphael! She is my wife, not yours," Uriel's voice boomed.

Raphael sighed knowing this was a futile argument, but he had to try.

"Uriel, Adamina needs time to heal before another pregnancy. This birthing almost killed her!" Raphael's voice raised in concern.

"Adamina's race is strong. She can handle it. I will have my son."

"And what of the two beautiful daughters you have? Will you forget them for a son? Daughters have equal merit to a son, Uriel. You have not told Adamina or Nerina of the special gifts that our children can manifest. Nerina is already showing signs of her connection to the water. The other day, she was talking to the river and it responded to her! It threw her ball out of the waters and onto the shore toward her!"

Raphael's concern was not unmerited. If Nerina's power was left unchecked, it would cause great harm. Nerina's promise with the element of water was getting stronger each day. Something had to be done about it.

"Do you see any female Arch's Raphael? I don't want just any green-Angel to take my place when I retire! I must have a son to train to take my place. You teach Nerina if it is so important to you. Besides, it is just water," Uriel said unconcerned and bit into an apple.

His appetite had sky rocked in the past few months – all of his appetites. Over five years in physical form was beginning to take its toll on him.

"Just water!" Raphael sighed and gave up the argument. He didn't think mentioning Father would never accept a half-bred amongst his army any remedy to the situation either.

Uriel dug into the fifth meat pie in an hour and Raphael's concern was directed to another matter.

"When was the last time you returned to ethereal form?" Raphael demanded.

Uriel shrugged and continued eating.

"Are you going to disregard every rule we are to follow?!"

"I am fine, Raphael. You are dismissed."

Raphael very rarely raged, but inside he was seething with anger. Out of all of the Archangels, he was the most calm, the least subject to emotion and physical desires in physical form. He was a healer and he considered his body's wisdom as much as any ethereal wisdom. Doing the best he could to calm himself, Raphael nodded to his superior and left the kitchen. The walk through the forest did nothing to calm his nerves so at the edge of the island where the rock face dove into the sea, Raphael let go of the substance of his body, dissolving into light blue wisps. Returning to ethereal form was the only way to ensure his calling was heard by the intended brother and hidden from the others.

Gabriel, your concerns regarding Uriel were well found-ed. You must return to Avalon.

ALTHOUGH NOT UNEXPECTED, RAPHAEL'S call was a hindrance. He had been floating amongst the mist of a sea, watching a sunrise in his ethereal form when he had received Raphael's call. Gabriel had watched Uriel become more and more unpredictable throughout his incarnation. He was prone to outbursts of rage and swings of excessive emotion. Worse, Uriel refused to do anything about it. Gabriel had chalked it up at first to the proud demeanor of a youngest sibling, but the nagging feeling had not gone away. He knew better than to deny his intuition. Gabriel had consulted God about it and God had made it clear that he was unconcerned and had larger matters to attend to. Unable to shake a premonitory dread regarding the matter, Gabriel had asked Raphael to keep an eye on their brother before he had left Avalon. Before he had left Adamina there to seal her fate.

It was her decision and he scolded himself for his criticism of it. Though she had chosen to hand fast to a man she had barely known he had no place in the matter. Gabriel just wished the dread would ease up and stop telling him he was wrong. He wished the tendrils of light wouldn't tug so tightly, guiding him back there. That weight in his heart should have lifted by now. A small voice at the back of his being whispered about the casualties Uriel left behind.

Too many women, children, villages, even worlds had become casualties of Uriel's mood swings. Uriel's wives and mistresses were no exception. Gabriel cringed at how Uriel had played with their mortal souls to try and be the first to create a new Angel. He believed a son would be the key to his glory and God would grant Uriel freewill in return. Some had passed naturally into the Otherworld, forgotten and left to build new lives, but most were not so lucky.

How could he have been so blind? How could he have forgotten what Uriel could be like? How could he have just left her like that? Cursing himself, Gabriel physically manifested in an empty house on one of the worlds that still held voyages to Avalon. It took him a while, but he finally found a ship sailing that way. He boarded the ship and began the long voyage to Avalon. It would take him a fortnight to reach there, but he valued the time to think over what to do.

10

*I*T WAS WISE OF *you to come to me brother*, a voice hissed from the shadows.

The room was dark. Light from a hole in the ceiling illuminated a circular pattern on the floor where Uriel now stood. He had no idea how many of his brethren sat at the massive half-moon table before him. Or how many creatures of the dark sat there watching him from soulless hungry eyes. If God knew where he was, surely God would remove him from his place of respect; but, Uriel didn't give a damn about God and his wishes right now.

Why don't you stop skulking in the shadows Luc? Uriel demanded, *And get rid of anyone else sitting at that infernal table. This is between us.*

Lucifer appeared at his side, a smile sitting on his long face. Lucifer was much bigger in stature then Uriel, for he had a taste for grandeur when it came to presentation. Grey eyes billowed like smoke and pierced like glass the gaze of any who dared look into them. Black hair, razor straight framed Lucifer's angular, arrow-like features. His thin lips slid into a sympathetic pout.

Please, tell me of your sorrows dear Uriel. I will do what

I can.

Uriel relaxed slightly and they walked out of the council room into what must have been Lucifer's personal living quarters. In dusk and candle light, Uriel could see that Lucifer had adorned himself with a tailored suit, no doubt the best he could find on the planet. Uriel did not understand Lucifer's desire for physically created, expensive clothing. Manifesting what he needed suited Uriel much better. Uriel did not have the patience to wait for something to be created by mortal hands. They sat down in the middle of the room and Uriel began to share his reasons for coming.

I have a wife…

Just one? Lucifer joked.

Luc…

I apologize, please go on.

Uriel began explaining about Avalon, Adamina, and his lack of a male heir.

Yes, that is troubling brother isn't it? I had realized that Avalon and Adamina were in your life now. Michael filled me in as he bayed on about returning and repenting to Father and all that. He extended me an invitation to your wedding. So sorry I was unable to attend, I had matters to deal with here.

Lucifer stood up indicating they should walk, and held open the door to the building.

Oh dear, can't have you going out there like that, Lucifer mused and waved his hand in between himself and Uriel.

Uriel's attire altered to match something similar to Lucifer's. Uriel immediately wished for his cotton shirt and trousers again. The tuxedo chaffed. They stepped out into the 1920s, New York, New York, Earth.

Lucifer, when suspended from duties for challenging his Father's will, decided he fit best in budding corporate America where he could influence as much of the world order as possible. Not to mention it offered privacy for his plans and excellent parties. The fashions weren't atrocious either.

Lucifer continued after several minutes walking beside his brother in thought, *An heir is what you seek. Have you tried with other women to conceive an heir?*

I have born many sons and daughters, Lucifer, with other women. None of them are Adamina. None of them have the power or control of a world like she does.

She controls Avalon you say? Lucifer's interest was ensnared.

She is the only one who can get a response from the ever-growing island. It appears that her needs, and hers alone, are what the island listens to. If she needs food, the gardens she touches or envision grow. I have tried to grow food from the seed of other plants on the island. They will not flourish even though the soil is ripe.

Come now brother, you never were any good at growing anything but a desire, Lucifer chuckled, *Let us nurture that creativity in you.*

They turned the corner and Lucifer led them to an unmarked building. He was greeted at the door by the porter who led them in, closed, and locked the door behind them. He whistled and a moment later, a scantily clad woman in a corset and petticoat, stockings and braids appeared to lead them into a basement. Uriel felt his body respond eagerly to the woman's allure. The urge to possess her nearly overwhelmed him.

The burst of noise from the gentlemen's club assaulted Uriel's ears when the door at the bottom of the stairs was opened. Shouted bets, cat calls, and music pounded and pulsed. Women danced and gyrated to carnival music or sauntered around the room with trays. Some women sat on men's laps, others led men into the private, red curtained booths.

Uriel cocked an eyebrow, *A man could get used to this.*

Lucifer burst out laughing. Uriel had been in physical

form too long if he was referring to himself as a man.

He motioned to their guide. She perked an ear towards Lucifer and he cooed to her, "Prepare the next largest room to mine upstairs for my brother. Oh, and send him Jezebel, and any other woman he wishes, would you dear?" He slapped her ass with his hand and she ambled off to fulfill his orders. "Anyone else you desire, Uriel? Take your pick. I'll have them sent to you."

Uriel's eyes darted like a hungry wolf across the room.

"Don't worry about Adamina brother. Keep trying. She will conceive your heir sooner or later," Lucifer hissed into Uriel's ear.

URIEL PEERED OUT OF the window of the cabin he had rented for his voyage back to Avalon. The young escort from the club slept amongst the white sheets as he pondered his return. He would take Adamina to bed that night, but he had to leave in the morning to attend to something for Lucifer. Acquiring some ancient human relic from a dusty weather storm of a place somewhere on Earth was not his idea of fun, but Lucifer had asked rather nicely. Uriel's gaze darted to his prize for the agreement. Resisting another romp, more out of boredom than anything, Uriel pulled on his trousers and shirt and headed on deck.

The open sky stretched endlessly in bright blue glory. The gulls called out and floated on updrafts. Uriel sucked in a breath of fresh air and smiled to himself. He would make a son and be gone with the leaving of this ship at dawn tomorrow.

11

P ALLA PACED, CLUTCHING AT the broom. She couldn't just sit here while her Priestess died. She had to do something. She looked around at the others. Some had busied themselves with mending or weaving, others were gardening, watching children, or sweeping. The rhythmic movements of routine life caught Palla in a trance. A sweep forward to clear a space of old, and one sweep backward, welcoming in the new. Forward, and backward, the sweeping of a circle. Beneath her, she felt Avalon shiver.

"Sh," Palla petitioned the others.

They all stopped what they were doing. Avalon had grown still, waiting, as if holding its breath. Not a single breeze nor bird call. Palla swallowed and in her stomach energy grew. She must do something.

"Quickly, a circle," Palla rushed everyone out of the house except the few priestesses that were required to watch the children.

Night was falling slowly. The great sun was sinking into the horizon. It would be some hours before the moon revealed her luminescent face. The women had gathered in a circle, just as at every festival, full-moon, or as need required. Need required now. Palla took Adamina's place, doubts and fears welled up inside of her and she pushed them away.

"Here we gather," Palla spoke softly, "in perfect love and trust of Goddess. In perfect love and trust of ourselves. And for Adamina."

The priestesses drew the circle as they joined hands. Voices called for Goddess.

"I call to the land of Avalon, the soil and the foundation of all."

"I call to the Sun, the fire of the hearth, and the passion in the heart."

"I call to the moon, she who watches over the night."

"I call to the wind that whispers its song."

"I call to the waters, the blood of our home."

"Hear us as we cast this falling night. Our voices take flight."

"The first Priestess wanes. Bring to her aid."

"The power, and keep her alive."

GABRIEL RETURNED TO AVALON all too late. When he reached out to find her, he found her life force fading. For the last leg of the journey, his heart had raced in terror for what he might find, or rather, might not find when he arrived. Adamina was round with another of his brother's babies, and, as Raphael had warned, she was near death because of it. The scoundrel of his brother was nowhere to be seen.

He knocked at the door. While waiting for an answer, he ran his hand along the frame and the detail of the door. His work not some five seasons ago. Such love and care he had put into it, imagining her face when she saw it. She had been the inspiration for all of the careful details he had carved.

A beautiful little girl with straw hair ran to him giggling and chasing fluffs of seeds floating through the air. She flowed to a halt in front of him.

"Hello," Gabriel spoke softly and crouched down to her level.

Hello, she replied.

Gabriel blinked and tried to mask his surprise at her chosen mode of communication. He had not even sensed her enter his mind.

How old are you little one?

Gabriel recognized the little girl's vibrant blue dress. It was made of the same fabric that was used in Adamina's wedding gown. His stomach twisted at the memory.

Five, the little girl replied as her eyes darted back to the floating seeds.

You must be Nerina. Where is your mother, Nerina?

Mommy's not well. She's up the stairs with Raphael. I have to go now, my sister needs me.

Alright sweetheart, I won't keep you much longer, Gabriel took the little girl's hand, *my name is Gabriel and I am a friend of your mother's and Raphael's. If you ever need me, you call out for me, just like this, and I will be there as fast as I can. Understand?*

Nerina nodded her head and darted away towards the priestess house. Gabriel pushed the door open and stepped inside. The wood groaned underneath his foot and the door creaked shut. They would need repairs and adjustments. The furniture in the sitting room to his right had a layer of dust. It had been months since anyone had used or cared for the bench or chairs he had carved. The hearth lay empty, the swirls and notches of the mantle covered by soot and more dust. Gabriel swallowed back the emotions he felt growing inside of him and turned for the stairs. One step was completely sunken and the wood was snapped in two, probably by his brother's careless foot. Gabriel noted to replace it later. Raphael swung his torso out of a room.

"Gabriel, thank God you're here!"

"He had nothing to do with it."

Gabriel followed Raphael as he disappeared into Adamina's bedchamber. Raphael did not even roll his eyes at Gabriel's remark. Adamina must be faring terribly for Raphael never passed up a good eye-roll at his brothers. What Gabriel saw nearly stopped his heart as it sucked all the air out of his lungs. Adamina lay there so pale you could nearly see through her. Her inner light, that joyous vibrant light, had all but faded away. Her chest barely lifted with breath and her hands weakly rested on her round belly, as if protecting the child within.

"There is nothing more I can do for her or the children, Gabriel," Raphael lamented.

"Children?" Gabriel was not sure he had heard correctly.

"Twins, both with wings in the womb," Raphael's voice was thick with despair.

"We have to cut them out," Gabriel said instantly, "Are they aged enough to do it?"

"I cannot keep Adamina alive and tend to the children."

"Are they aged enough to do it?" Gabriel demanded fighting against a torrent of emotion that threatened to choke him.

"Yes," Raphael said softly and nodded, "But..."

"I will keep Adamina alive. Lock the doors to this house and bring me a chair."

Gabriel began rolling up his sleeve and Raphael stopped his exit mid-stride.

"You aren't..."

"Of course I am!"

"Gabriel, you will tie yourself to her for eternity if you do this. She has no way of accepting or rejecting this bond."

"Yes she does, I asked her in a dream and she agreed if something like this ever happened, that she would accept it."

"You've been visiting her in dreams… Oh Gabriel…."

"Get the chair and lock the doors," Gabriel cut-off his brother and set about his work.

Raphael sighed, but said no more and left the room. He had no time to worry, protest or argue. His dear friend was fading fast.

Gabriel gently lifted one of Adamina's arms and laid it by her side, palm facing up. He tore her sleeve and peeled it back. Finding a vein wasn't difficult. He could see it through her thin, strained skin. Hate for his brother welled up. He wanted to tear the world down until he found the rat hole Uriel was hiding in. Then he wanted to break the bastard's neck with his bare hands. Taking a deep breath, Gabriel harnessed his emotions to pour them into what he had to do.

Raphael returned with a chair and placed it at the head of the bed behind Gabriel. Raphael's eyes spoke the concerns and warnings.

"Don't," Gabriel ordered and sat in the chair.

"Fine but if you melt into a puddle or burst into pixie dust, I am not cleaning up the mess," Raphael smirked at his brother who visibly relaxed a little. Not the laugh he had hoped for, but it would do.

Raphael busied himself preparing for the procedure. Gabriel closed his eyes and shut out the world, everything but Adamina. He heard her breath as it echoed in silence, heard her heart struggle to pump thin blood through her veins. It skipped a beat and Gabriel felt her energy seep away, absorbed hungrily by the babes within. He cursed his kind for causing this. As an Angel, he was responsible to fix this. It was not a matter of his feelings for Adamina, he told himself, but a matter of honor.

From his own arm, he manifested a tendril of light, pulling from his essence the lifeblood of an Angel. *Forgive me.* He forced the tendril into her arm, sliding past the skin, into a vein, into her heart, into her soul. Adamina's body jerked and Gabriel sent a flood of calm and blocked her body's sense of pain. Her body relaxed. Gabriel's heart pumped for them both, the lifeblood trickling into Adamina, keeping her heart pumping, forcing her lungs to take breath. As Raphael went about his work, Gabriel heard a distant cry of one child, then another.

Gabriel pushed more of the lifeblood into her, as much as she needed, but slowly. He didn't want her to wake up too quickly. He slid his consciousness through the connection and began repairing the damage, healing the infections, chasing away the cold from her bones. He whispered muscle closed and skin sealed free from scarring. He whispered veins whole and blood clean. Finally, he poured more lifeblood into her heart and lungs. He would give all of it and end his existence as an Angel if he had to. As much as she needed. Thankfully she did not need it all, or would not let him give everything, Gabriel wasn't certain when he ran into the wall where she would take no more. Satisfied she would live, he slumped in the chair, returning to himself and pulling back the tendril of light into him. His eyes slid closed against his will.

EYES SNAPPED OPEN AS the light of dawn streamed through open shutters. He blinked away the blurriness and realized he was still attached to a body. His body groaned and spasmed from being slumped over in that chair for three days. His mind cursed the brother he knew was lurking for not moving him. A punishment for the disagreeable and dangerous act he had performed, Gabriel was sure of it. Damn brothers were good for nothing but making life more difficult. He let out a moan of pain as he uncurled his body. His vision slid over to her.

Adamina slept peacefully beside him. Her skin was pale, but no longer translucent, and her breathing even and strong. He sighed with relief and leaned back in the chair, stretching out his legs. Slowly, he stretched out his body and stood up. There was no sign of Raphael or the babies, but a strong smell came from the kitchen and his stomach bellowed at him for food. If he didn't enjoy food so much, he may have been inclined to entirely despise the physical body's undignified way of indicating the need for nourishment. The first few steps sent sharp needles through his legs and back, but gradually, step-by-step, Gabriel's body finally awoke and relaxed. Never, in all his incarnation, had he felt so worn out. Then again, he had never given his Angelic lifeblood to a mortal. A smile slid across his face. Not quite mortal now was she? There was Goddess and Angel in her now. He managed to make his way to the kitchen nestled at the back of the main floor of the house.

Raphael looked up from the pot he was stirring and spooned the concoction into a cup, thrusting it at Gabriel. The soup was strongly herbed: nettles for stopping the flow of lifeblood, Burdock for purification, Agarbathy for healing soul scars, Dandelion for remineralizing the body, and Balm of Gilead warding against heart break.

Gabriel's head shot up from the mixture, "Balm of Gilead?"

"You know what you did was perilous. Adamina has dedicated herself to Uriel to save this island. She would never betray that pact without Uriel dismissing her from it. She is at his command, Gabriel. I know your heart. It is a fool's path you tread and you never tread lightly. You are stubborn and I know no matter what I say you will stay on this island now until you win her over or…"

"It will not come to that Raphael!" Gabriel slammed the emptied cup down on the large island in the kitchen. *I will not let her be destroyed by him.*

Father will not let you kill him, even if he falls out of favor, Raphael warned, *Father will not see you sacrifice yourself for a mortal, especially one who should have died with her kind.*

He has no sway here. He cannot see what it is I sacrifice, nor does he care about a retired Angel, Gabriel waved his hand dismissively as he turned away from Raphael, *And she is not exactly mortal, is she Raphael?*

Raphael ignored the remark, but his expression was acknowledgement enough, *Father does not care if you are retired, Gabriel. If he has need, all must answer him. There is no choice.*

As long as I live, as long as the other gods live, as long as Mother is alive, we all have choice, Raphael. It is only a matter of what we choose and how long we choose it for. I must return to Adamina.

Raphael sighed, "Wait, take this."

Raphael placed two cups, a ladle, and a small pot of soup into Gabriel's hands. Gabriel maneuvered the burden to comfortably rest on one arm.

"And do not eat it all before she wakes up and has a chance fill her own hunger," Raphael warned as Gabriel disappeared out of the kitchen and back up the stairs to Adamina's room.

Wouldn't dream of it.

12

READ AND DARKNESS WEIGHED upon her soul. She swam through the shadows, struggling to reach the surface. She was drowning. She was hollow and drowning. She gasped for air and her breath was smothered by the people of shadows. Shadows swirled and stifled, strangled, and called to her. If she gave in, the shadow would sustain her. It promised her life, it promised her rest. She would not have to suffer if she became one with the shadow. She would find a home in the shadows they told her. For a fraction of a second, she almost gave in. Suddenly white light surrounded her, no, it filled her, and it was shining from her, pulling her upwards, out of the darkness. It changed her.

She heard a voice, a gentle, loving voice filled with pain and sorrow calling to her. White and pink clouds enveloped her body, the light nearly blinding her. The clouds cradled her. She saw her hand reach up, her arm extend forward as if of its own accord. The clouds burst apart and then swirled around an impossibly bright light. A hand, then an arm, a torso, a fuzzy silhouette of someone appeared out of the light. Her heart sang and her whole being relaxed as if it had been tense, waiting for this arrival, this connection. Like lightening it coursed through her. The hand grasped hers and gently pulled. Liquid fire poured through her veins. Searing pain, then nothing, she felt nothing as it settled into her, as her heart beat loudly. The scream of Avalon, discordant and raw echoed through her, but she was a world away. His eyes, she realized. Her being sighed his name at the realization, *Gabriel.* Where she ended and he began, she had no way of knowing.

Knowing... Adamina was filled with knowing, more knowledge than she had ever possessed overwhelmed her and made her dizzy. She became aware of the feel of coarse sheets against skin. Her skin. Terror surged forward with the hollowness in her belly. Her eyes shot open.

She let out a cry and sat up. "My children, where are my children!" Panic flooded her and her hands rested on her abdomen.

"Peace, Adamina, Peace," Gabriel held her and stroked her hair.

The familiar scent of him filled her nose. The shock of his presence would be addressed later. She must know where her babies were.

"Where...!"

Gabriel cut her off and spoke quietly, "They are with the priestesses, Adamina. They are safe and healthy."

A torrent of emotions flooded her and she began crying. Gabriel reached for a bowl of Raphael's soup.

"Hush, Adamina. Hush. All is well. Eat this."

He placed the bowl in her hands and she managed to hold it, barely. Her crying quieted to silent tears at the smell of the soup. Seated behind her, supporting her weight, Gabriel began to spoon small amounts of food into her mouth. Adamina swallowed. When she could take no more food, she turned her head away and asked for her children again.

Gabriel nodded and smirked at her persistence, "Alright,

Adamina, I will have them brought here."

Raphael, please bring Adamina her children…, Gabriel didn't wait for his brother's response.

He removed the bowl from her hands and deposited it on the table beside the bed. He helped Adamina sit up and he moved out from behind her.

"I want to stand," Adamina demanded.

He knew better than to protest.

"Very well," Gabriel stepped back from her slightly, giving her enough room to maneuver down from the bed, but not so much that he couldn't reach out to her.

With great struggle, Adamina inched her body down until her feet touched the floor. She placed her weight on her feet. Her body protested and wavered. Blood rushed from her head as she stood upright and her legs gave out, unable to continue straining. Gabriel caught her before she fell. He gently hoisted her into his arms and back into bed before she could protest.

"You will rest," he commanded, careful not to express the sternness of the seasoned General of an army that he was.

He was equally careful to cover the disproportionate agony and despair for Adamina in her weakened state. His sacrifice and connection to her were already affecting him much more severely than he would have liked.

To her own surprise, Adamina did not protest. She looked at him instead, studying his features: they were as familiar to her as her own. It occurred to her that her husband was nowhere to be seen.

"Where is…" before she finished her question, Gabriel cut her off to answer.

"Uriel has left. He won't be returning for some time," he assured her.

Adamina swallowed, closed her eyes, and inhaled. Her mind raced with what he had done to her months ago. She was safe, she assured herself. She focused on her breathing, focused on calming herself, of removing the memories that scared her mind and heart. She felt the weight of her own chest with each breath and became distantly aware of Gabriel's hand resting on her own. He brushed a lock of hair away from her face.

I can help you with that, if you wish.

Adamina felt the hum and pulse of Avalon in her blood. She became one with the island. It sheltered her, protected her, and it encouraged her to accept the Angel's help. Her sense of acceptance was all Gabriel needed, no words, no nod or cue, their connection was too deep for such base responses. Gently, Gabriel entangled his energy with her own, and that of Avalon's. They flowed together as one, the three of them. Gabriel reached for the memories and braced himself. He had heard of Uriel's handy work and knew what he was about to experience would not be pleasant or kind. Gabriel wondered if his brother was ever capable of kindness.

The memory emerged. Uriel was on top of Adamina, holding her down. She asked softly, unsure of her own voice, *Uriel, please, don't do this*. Gabriel saw Uriel's eyes go black and his heart ached. Rage boiled inside of him and Gabriel tore at the memory. Details followed, the smells, tastes and sounds. Soon the memory was nothing but a black void in Adamina's mind. Adamina's gratitude and sorrow were all that contained his fury.

Her body's memory of the event was the most difficult to replace. It had to be guided away from the memory, the instant reactions, the primal urges of protection. A body retained the imprint of an attack like this to protect itself from further assaults. Like a careful gardener, Gabriel began to work out the bruises, the strain, and the terror deep inside muscle and tissue, massaging the darkness and pain out of them. He whispered and caressed her with his powers and his hands, reintroducing love and the sense of safety, tilling away the tears and tension.

He reached out with his spirit and touched the space

below her heart that extended into her stomach, that pit where agony rests and a void builds on its own accord. Gabriel knit the void shut, filling it with the heavenly light of pure, unaltered energy, straight from the source. The agony burned away, having no place in the purity and light, leaving no trace behind. Finally, her body relaxed, a tear slid down her face and Adamina blinked her eyes open.

Gabriel caught the tear and wiped it away. The knowledge of what happened remained with her, but Adamina no more felt the sting of memory or the daggers of agony. She was whole again, new, clean. She didn't feel as old, or as scared, or broken any more.

She smiled and whispered, "Thank you."

Adamina realized how close he was to her. His face nearly touched her own and a hand was cradling her jaw. Against her will, her eyes darted to Gabriel's mouth. His full, gentle lips were pulled into a subtle smirk. She fought against the urge to kiss him. She pulled away. The space between them felt immense now. She ached to close that space.

"Gabriel!" Raphael called from the stairs as he hauled the two new-borns up them, one on each arm.

Raphael's shout broke the trance Adamina was in and she blinked. Gabriel was standing beside the bed, leaving her to doubt the truth of all that transpired only moments before. She pushed away those concerns and questions with the sight of her babies bundled up. Twins... she had had twins.

"Bring them to me."

Adamina embraced the children, one in each arm. Their faces radiated as they slept. Movement beneath the child on her left arm startled her and she looked into Raphael's friendly face.

"Wings!" Adamina exclaimed, Raphael nodding affirmation.

"Both," he clarified.

The child on her left woke from her slumber and gazed up at her mother for the first time. She had bright golden hair and deep, dark inquisitive eyes.

"Hello Aera," Adamina whispered and gently nuzzled the child's perfect nose.

The infant on her right arm roused and squirmed, drawing Adamina's attention to a girl who looked very much like her father with coal colored hair and sparkling sapphire eyes.

"Hello Mora, my beautiful daughters you will always desire to have the wind beneath your wings, won't you," Adamina smiled and turned to Raphael, "I think I will need help with these ones. I lack the experience to guide them in flight. Will you be their guardian Raphael and assist me with them?"

Raphael bowed slightly, "I would be honored."

He stepped forward and Adamina placed Mora into his arms. The laughter of young girls filled the hall and the chatter of women followed.

"Mommy! Mommy! Are you okay?" Nerina raced in and tried to jump on the huge bed. Gabriel lifted her up so she could take the place of Mora at Adamina's right.

Adamina squeezed her daughter close, "Yes, Nerina, Mommy's fine."

Nerina smiled and looked at Aera, "She's going to be a handful, Mommy."

Adamina laughed and beamed at her eldest. Artemesia peaked out from behind the skirts of Palla.

"Artemesia, my dear, come see your new baby sisters," Adamina called.

Shyly, the nearly-four-year-old girl inched toward the bed. Gabriel lifted her up and sat her on the edge by Nerina. Artemesia stared up at Gabriel and nodded a silent thank you then turned to Aera. Raphael brought Mora close so the girls could get a good look at her too.

"This one's Aera and that one is Mora. They are both beautiful, just like you darlings, but they are a little different. See they have wings. You must not be jealous or cruel or mean to them dears. They are your sisters and you must support them and protect them from harm," Adamina instructed softly.

Nerina nodded, "Yes mother."

Artemesia stared at her young siblings in curiosity, "I see?" she asked softly.

Adamina nodded and gently unwrapped the blanket wrapped around Aera and a tiny feathered wing stretched out and relaxed. Artemesia's eyes grew large in wonder and she looked at her mother, then back at her baby sister. Clearly her baby sisters were special, just like her older sister who could do stuff with water and her mind. Artemesia wondered if she was special, feeling as if she was missing the special stuff that her sisters had. She altered her gaze to her little girl toes as she contemplated this special stuff, trying to figure out exactly what it was, and why she didn't have it.

Artemesia's eyes darted up to Gabriel's. Nerina had told her they spoke with their mind. She tried and tried and tried, but Gabriel couldn't seem to hear her. Then he winked at her and she lit up, maybe he had heard her. Maybe she had a different special stuff, she realized. The gardens like growing when she touched them, after all. She could tell when they needed water, when they were ripe. Maybe she was special after all, and maybe she didn't speak with minds or fly, but she could flower. With a smile she looked at her little sisters.

The priestesses gave their blessings and well-wishes to Adamina and quickly left. The mother and her children fell asleep there in that big bed. As the sun sunk into the horizon and the moon slid in to take its place, they slept deeply under the watchful eyes of Angels.

13

B RINGING LIFE INTO THE world is one of the finest expressions of the power of creation. But a re-birth, to re-create, is another thing entirely. It requires the destruction of whatever existed before. But, if the forces of destruction do not decimate everything and eliminate what was, what remains begins to grow into something greater. Lucifer understood this power thanks to his expulsion from heaven, for what, seeing things in a different light?

He stood in front of a crowd thirsting for his words. A grin slid across his face and he half expected to see Uriel in the needy mass. Short dresses swayed. Feathers floated everywhere from those boas that were oh so in. Jewels flashed along-side cameras. Men in suits stood eyeing women with short-cropped hair. All of them had purchased items of the highest fashions. Items he had capitalized on. Some of those men in the crowd were regulars at his fashionable men's clubs. Some of the women were their entertainment. All of them, right where he placed them in this economic game of power and wealth. A pass-time really, as he fleshed out the true powers he sought to build his own with.

"We are at the height of abundance!" Cheers rose around him and he quelled them with a simple gesture, "You asked for homes with electricity, water, and heat. I listened. You wanted faster motor-cars, I listened. You wanted grand parties, my friends, and here you are. Please enjoy the hor duerves and quell your thirsts on my champagne. My staff will provide for your every need."

Lucifer let a dark smirk slide across his face. The only way to gain advantage, was to put everyone else at a disadvantage and make them comfortable with that disadvantage.

"Banish me, Lord Almighty, and everything that belongs to you will suffer."

He turned away from the crowd's cheering and clapping. The band started up the music and the cheers turned into the loud hum of conversations. Whispering a few words to his butler, the best money could buy, Lucifer left the guests in the hands of money and sin. He securely locked his study and shed his clothing. He reached out into the darkness and pulled until his form no longer held the mortal masquerade and slid up to the sky.

He rewove his mortal form in midair, molding vast charcoal wings to carry him through the barrier of Avalon. Unfortunately, Uriel was just smart enough to keep the location hidden from him, but he had found a way around it. He had sent a bastard of Uriel's in, with his own darkness inside his soul, so Lucifer could track the location of this island. Lucifer congratulated his own genius and directed his flight towards the forbidden paradise. He tore through the barriers his mother erected. With a force that shook the ground, he landed and pointed his monstrous form toward the gentle, powerful Adamina.

"I think it's time I finally meet this precious gem that has gods and Angels alike in a twitter."

ADAMINA STOOD IN A clearing, face tilted up to the sky, a light rain falling. Her arms stretched upward, greeting and embracing the rain with joy. She began to sing the song of the rains. The power of Avalon thrummed through her and out of her. She was its catalyst, its guiding hand. Gabriel had taught her how to harness it, use it, find it when she required. Gabriel had also taught her more precious things. In Uriel's absence, Gabriel had taught her patience, and had given her a safe place. He had tended to her home, fixing, cooking, and helping with the children. He was so dedicated and caring to her daughters and they adored him. A smile graced Adamina's face and she took a deep breath. She guided her awareness back to her task. The clouds circled above gently then moved away and towards the priestess house. They had been suffering a slight drought and needed the rains. With the gentle moisture falling on the gardens, Adamina released her hold on the song of magic and relaxed.

She had resumed her place in the priestess house again, with Palla's continued help of course. The house was now a constant center for activity. Children and women everywhere, laughing, singing and playing. New and strange luxuries had arrived. One, sweetmeat, had enraptured many of the women for its dark bitter-sweet taste and its soothing properties. A few of the women had journeyed with new husbands to lands far away. Their words and stories reached desperate women and orphans who sought refuge.

Her coven, as Palla called it, had grown to thirty three women. Diane had passed into the next life a short while ago and Palla had taken up her duties and role as Matron of the House. Ranks, like those of the sailors, had been introduced and they called Adamina High Priestess. Adamina insisted there was no one woman above another in the house now, trying to do away with the nonsense of it all. They were a family, not a crew.

Adamina's own family had grown as well. A woman desperate and near death had appeared on her doorstep a season after the twins' birth. She begged Adamina to take her child. It had wings. She said the child, Kamiel, was Uriel's and Lucifer had told her to come to Avalon and give her to a woman called Adamina. The little boy sure looked like his father. Adamina pitied Kami, as she had come to lovingly call him, and had adopted him as her own. Adamina had felt only the slight pang of betrayal, but love chased it away. Kamiel was four now, a quiet, brilliant, sensitive boy who loved animals. Curious though, she had never met Lucifer. Why would he send the boy to her to be raised? His mother had passed away a short few days after her arrival and was given the burial of a priestess.

The Angels Ramiel and Tyrryal had also returned from their duties. Uriel had instructed them to wait on Avalon for him when they had carried out the tasks God wished of them. That was three seasons ago. Gabriel had appreciated the young novice, Ramiel, and the distraction he provided. Training him had offered an outlet for his military expertise retired life could not provide. Tyrryal assisted Adamina occasionally, but Ramiel preferred to spend his time training and honing his skill for battle.

Nerina, nearly a woman already, had grown fond of Ramiel. There was something in his strength and heart she was drawn to. She barely noticed she was being doted on herself. One of the orphan boys that lived with the priestesses, Eli, blonde and lanky, had given his heart to her already. Where ever she was, he was close behind. Adamina hoped that Nerina's heart would be strong enough to make the right choice between the two. Tutored by Raphael, the eldest daughter had learned to control her Angelic abilities as well. Nerina was skilled with bringing the rains, staving off floods, calming the water or livening it up. She had begun to master pulling it out of the air and directing it where she needed.

Normally, it would be Nerina out in this field, reaching toward the sky, calling the rains. But Adamina had given Nerina a day off, and, she needed the space herself. Relished were the moments of connection to Avalon, the moments of peace and quiet. The ground shook beneath her and Avalon shouted a warning. Adamina's balance faltered slightly.

"Hello, Adamina," a deep, menacing voice boomed behind her.

Adamina turned around and fear lodged her voice in her throat. She could only stare at this massive man with dark hair and haunting eyes. Grey wings stretched out behind him. He was a beautiful, terrible sight.

He chuckled at the scent of her fear, "I am Lucifer. I apologize for not meeting with you before now, but I was otherwise engaged."

Adamina swallowed and nodded, "A pleasure to meet you. What brings you here now?"

"I come to simply say hello. And, to ask something of you."

He took a step forward.

He placed his hand on her belly and she flinched.

"What is it you wish from me?" Adamina questioned and stepped away, covering her solar-plexus with her hands.

Gabriel had taught her this was where magic came from. That place inside of her where the wisdom of Goddess rested held all of her power. With this energy, she could bring anything into her life if she desired it. She wished desperately for the safe, comforting presence of Gabriel now. Adamina tugged on the magical tether to him that she had discovered during his training of her, calling silently.

She scowled at Lucifer. In her training with him, Gabriel had relayed Lucifer's story to her. He was an Angel too blinded by his hunger for power and goddom to care about anything. Upon this first meeting, she understood Gabriel's anger towards his brother, and the disgust. Adamina had never felt anything so dark and so angry in her life. The waves of it coming off of Lucifer made her ill. His mere presence had started to suck her magic and strength from her.

"I want Avalon. I want the magic inside of you. Will you give me your life, Adamina?"

"I will never give anything to you, Lucifer," she spat out and took another step back.

"No? But you gave yourself so willingly to two of my brothers. I had hoped you would be as accommodating to me…" Lucifer laughed.

"I gave Uriel nothing but my word. Everything else he took. Tell me how is he since he abandoned his family?"

"Abandoned is such a harsh word, dear Adamina. Uriel has simply been helping me. Why, hello Gabriel," Lucifer turned his attention to where Gabriel now stood.

"What do you want here, Shamed One?" Gabriel knew it was a risk to use this name, but he needed to draw his brother's attention away from Adamina.

Lucifer reacted in a fury of rage and in the blink of an eye was holding Gabriel's throat. Adamina gasped then called on fire, building a ball of it and aiming for Lucifer.

"Adamina, no," Gabriel choked out.

Lucifer let go of Gabriel and laughed in devilish delight, "I see you have taught her much dear Gabriel. But you didn't tell her we cannot be destroyed by any other than Mother or Father did you?"

Lucifer reached for the fire and smothered it.

Ignoring Gabriel now, he returned his attention to his original goal, "Tsk, tsk, what a way to greet family, Adamina. I simply came to let you know Uriel is on his way. And Adamina, I will have the power of Avalon. One way or another."

In wisps of gray and black, Lucifer vanished leaving behind a chill. Adamina stood frozen on the spot. Uriel was coming back. A fear and the sense of responsibility to her word caged her and her eyes filled with tears.

"Adamina, Uriel left you," Gabriel consoled.

"I gave my word, Gabriel. I have to keep that word. I am his wife after all."

She swallowed back the emotions and kept them under a tight calm.

"But…" Gabriel beseeched desperately.

He wished he had professed his true feelings to her, instead of offering his friendship. He felt trapped and angry at his own stupidity. He was going to lose her again. He should stake his claim for her heart right now and challenge his brother. He should wrap his arms around her, cover her with him. He had already marked her soul, like a fool. He had put her in a difficult position. His actions had tied her to him forever and had damned them both. *If Uriel found out…* No, he would keep her from harm, from his brother. It did not matter if she only thought of him as a friend. He could live just as friends, as long as she was safe, as long as he could be near. That was enough, he told himself. It would have to be enough. She interrupted his thoughts.

"I hope you will stay, Gabriel. The cabin will always be yours if you wish it."

"Of course," was all he could say.

She walked passed him towards the house to tell her children their father was returning.

ON THE WINGS OF a lightning storm, Uriel sailed home to Avalon. He had to reclaim his family from Gabriel and teach his wife obedience. Lucifer had told him so. How dare his brother touch what belonged to him! Uriel raged forward toward his house. He tore the front door open and stormed into the dining room, following the sound of laughter. How dare they mock him? Gabriel was nowhere in sight, but his family greeted him with joy.

"Father!" Nerina called out excitedly, remembering a man who had played with her and doted over her mother.

Uriel loomed in the doorway.

"Aren't you going to say hello to your children, Uriel?" Adamina questioned.

Uriel spotted a boy at the table. His son? Lucifer had told him he sent the woman who bore the bastard here.

"Hello children," he said passively.

They all replied in unison.

Small, deep blue eyes held the gaze of a man that barely saw him. Kamiel knew his father by the sight of him. He knew the man his father had been, was, and would be, that was his gift and his curse. He knew far too much for his young self. He knew because he saw the futures, saw the past. Another Angel, Tyrryal, had become a proxy for father, and Kamiel had no love for the type of man Uriel was and would become. Tyrryal had taught and guided the young boy and Tyrryal had loved Kamiel as if he was his own son. Kamiel had a father, this man he wanted nothing to do with.

With love in his heart, Tyrryal had developed a distaste for his former commander. There was no justice in abandoning a family like he had. Tyrryal knew that many of the Angels saw the mortals as lesser, but not he. Every being that existed held value and affected everything else. One small ripple could turn into a big wave if properly positioned. Now that Uriel had returned, Tyrryal aptly avoided him, but always stayed close by for Kamiel, and for Adamina.

Dinner had been set, and Uriel was ravenous. He feasted with them in an awkward silence. Although he searched, he did not detect Gabriel anywhere near by and believed Lucifer had been mistaken. But Uriel would stay and make sure no one interfered with his family again. Over the seasons, the silence did not improve much. Uriel barely got to know his children. He refused to let his wife attend the priestess house. He had taken Adamina to bed many times, but no children had resulted. She began resisting and refusing him, sleeping in a separate room. He had enough. Eventually, Uriel would have his male heir.

HE FELT HER HEART. Her fear. Her pain. It tore at him, ate at him, but there was nothing he could do. Gabriel wept with the knowledge that he could not help her and raged against his restraint. She had asked him to so he hid away, out of sight and reach of Uriel. Freewill was a curse, the connection to Adamina a vice, and Gabriel prayed for his absolution. Raphael could do no more. Perhaps Tyrryal, who was linked to the dark world, would have more freedom, could do something more than he could. There had to be some hope.

What are we going to do? He has already been twisted. I would recognize Lucifer's handiwork anywhere. The hope that remains is small.

He sighed, *I don't know Tyrryal. You were there when*

the Shamed One defected and you are closer to Uriel than I. We both know where this will lead.

What about Mother? What about Raphael?

Mother cannot do anything more than any of us, Father has not the care, and if he knew about Avalon, they would be lost anyway. Raphael cannot heal the sickness in Uriel now. Only returning to ether will do that. It cannot be forced on him. He clings tightly to his mortal coil. He will not let it go until he sees a male heir to suit his desires, or until she dies. What will come, will come, no matter what we do. What does the darkness whisper?

That things can always change. It will cost lives before anything can be laid to rest. There is one way you can be with her, Gabriel, but it is uncertain. And, I see a great deal of despair in that future.

I have to try now. While we still have time.

I know. I do not envy you, but I understand why. We were not prepared for the magic of love. Once it takes hold, it seems to never let us free. Is it our shackle or our joy, Gabriel?

It is our destiny.

We have never had a destiny before. I am not sure I like it.

Gabriel smirked in irony, *That was what you said about ale the first time you tasted it. Now you have chucked back half my stores.*

Aye, true enough. But I suspect the bitter-sweet taste of destiny will be harder to swallow. And much more difficult to acquire a taste for.

14

NERINA SNUCK UP BEHIND Ramiel and Eli, planning an attack. In each hand she held a cup of ice cold water that she had just retrieved from the river. She grinned like a mad woman and tried to suppress her laughter as she moved right in behind her friends without them even noticing. She held the cups over their heads and poured out the water with a satisfying splash. Nerina shrieked with laughter and jumped back as Ramiel and Eli cursed her and her icy mischief.

Eli grinned and let out a laugh.

"Nerina!" shouted Ramiel angrily, "Why would you do that?"

Nerina laughed and ran in the opposite direction, anticipating retaliation from at least one of the men. As she ran, she shouted back, "Ramiel, if you weren't so uptight, it would have been more than just a cup full!"

Eli was already on his feet.

"Eli, don't chase her, that is what she wants us to do! Don't let her get her way!"

Ignoring Ramiel's warning, Eli ran after Nerina. He had been her best friend, and she his, since they were infants. They were inseparable, even with Nerina besotted with Ramiel. He would never force Nerina to be anything other than who she was, to love anyone other than who she loved. He would never understand her affection for brooding Ramiel, but he never once judged her for her love. She deserved to be happy, but it did not appear to him that Ramiel would offer that happiness. Ramiel saw Nerina's games as a childish way for her to get attention, but she was just having fun and enjoying herself. Why could he not see the light and beauty and vibrancy of the lovely Nerina?

Eli was turning a corner in the forest that he knew hid lots of rocks and logs, so he slowed down a little. He had lost sight of her. Stopping for a moment to breathe, he was attacked from behind by a tangle of arms that wrapped around him.

"Ha!" exclaimed Nerina happily while laughing heartily, "I knew I could get you! We are so even now, it isn't even funny how even we are!"

It was true. The sneak attack had got him in return for the one he had administered several days ago. She turned around, laughter slowly fading from her eyes. Eli stopped laughing also. She was looking for Ramiel.

"Rina, don't let him ruin your fun. He is just angry that you dumped water on him. Where is that gorgeous smile of yours? Lost to a brooding brute of a man, shame."

Eli nudged Nerina playfully, trying to rouse her spirits.

She shook her head, tears in her eyes, "No, Eli, you don't understand."

He sighed in response, understanding all too well, "Rina just let it go for now."

"No, Eli, I will not let it go!"

Nerina stood abruptly with fury in her eyes and began to storm away. Eli jumped up.

"Eli, don't! I have had enough. He never wants to have

fun! I can't stand it anymore! He needs to know how I feel. He needs to open up, loosen up, or go away."

Eli just bowed his head and walked beside Nerina back to Ramiel. He could feel her fury as if it seeped from her skin. He dared not push her. He knew her all too well to push, and, perhaps a small part of him hoped for the ending of the love affair. A small, selfish part of him he rarely nurtured. When Nerina was out of the forest, she could see Ramiel lazily awaiting their return. His posturing infuriated her because she could read his smug superiority in it. If he believed he was above fun, above her, he was sorely mistaken. As she approached him from behind, she shouted to get his attention.

"Ramiel!"

He turned quickly, the anger in her voice alarming him, but it never showed on his face.

"Ramiel, we need to talk."

Nerina was standing in front of him now and the energy around her was not only tangible to him, but a vivid pulsing dark blue with flashes of silver, a storm ridden ocean. Ramiel had never seen that kind of energy surrounding Nerina before and was left to search Eli's face for some sort of indication as to what it meant. That blasted boy had his head faced down and his tail between his legs. There would be no help from him.

"Nerina, darling," he began quietly, hoping that could calm her down a little, "What is the problem?"

Eli, from behind Nerina shook his head. He knew that Ramiel's statement would just make her angrier; especially because it was evident that he genuinely didn't understand what he did that could upset her so much. Never call Nerina 'darling', it was received terribly. He had had a black eye to prove it once.

The energy around Nerina began to lash about, "You don't get it do you? You really don't."

"I don't get what, Nerina. I have done nothing wrong,

so why are you so upset with me."

Her face reddened in fury and she pulled at her hair and screeched. "Ramiel, I can't stand you sometimes! You are always so uptight and proper and annoying! I try to have some fun and you ruin it by thinking you are too important or valuable to fool around every once in a while. Would it kill you, just once, to do something fun with me? And by fun, I don't mean going for a walk. I mean like what Eli and I just did. PLAY! You are so insufferable. I don't want to talk to you. I am going back to my home and I am going to stay there. Do not come find me. I don't want to hear you or see you, let alone talk to you for the rest of the day and maybe tomorrow."

"Fine," Ramiel stated flatly, "If that is how you feel, then perhaps I will not come seek you out ever again. How does that sound, Nerina?"

Her mouth gaped. Wordlessly she turned her back and ran through the forest back to her house with tears in her eyes. She left Eli with Ramiel. She did not want his sympathy or support. She slowed as the house came into view. Her mother, Adamina, was outside gardening and her father, Uriel, was watching her and barking orders. Her sisters, at least most of them, should still be doing their chores so she wouldn't be bothered trying to get to her room. Even though she shared her room with Artemesia, she would get privacy because her sister was rarely around anymore. Every time she saw an opportunity to get away from the family, Artemesia took it.

Nerina passed by her parents without any question because she did not let them see her face. She could feel her mother's gaze lingering on her as she walked into the house through the back door. Nerina hurried down the hall and up the stairs. She threw herself into her room and onto her bed. The tears flowed freely now as she sobbed into her pillow, her anger and sadness pouring out. She let her sobs overtake her body. She really loved

Ramiel but at times he was so banal. All she wanted to do was have some fun because her mother had relieved her of chore duty for the day, allowing her to spend all day with Ramiel and Eli. She had known when she went to dump the water on them, Ramiel would be upset, but she hadn't imagined it would cost her the relationship.

I should have known better, she thought to herself through her tears, *Ramiel would never change. Why did he have to be so stoic?* The young woman beat her hands against her pillow while screaming incoherently.

Mora and Aera were playing with the other children at the priestess building. They were chatting amicably while cleaning the windows when they saw Eli coming towards the house without their older sister. They watched him as he approached, faces etched with curiosity and suspicion.

"Aera, Mora, have you seen Rina?" Eli's voice was laced with stress and anger which caught the two girls off guard.

"No, we thought she was with you," replied Aera slowly.

Aera closed her eyes, searching for her sister's presence. After a moment, Aera opened her eyes and said, "She is in her room. And she is really upset. Ramiel broke up with her!"

Mora bopped her lightly on the head for meddling too far with her gift. Aera flashed her a dirty look and rubbed her scalp.

"I am going inside to talk to her," Eli declared, and he started to head towards the house.

Aera called after him to stop him, and the two sisters rushed towards him.

"Mora will go inside to talk to her," Aera waved Mora towards the house while shushing Eli's protests. "You may be her best friend Eli, but we are her sisters."

He nodded, knowing how much Rina loved her sisters.

Perhaps it was better if they soothed her heart right now. He could wait.

"Rina?" whispered Mora as she slowly opened her sister's bedroom door, "Rina, can I come in?"

There was no reply, so she cautiously entered the room. On the bed lay Nerina sobbing quietly. She sat on the edge of the bed and smoothed her older sister's long blonde hair away from her face. She caught a glimpse of the girl's tear stained face and bloodshot eyes. The sight brought tears to her own eyes. Mora knew it must be hard on her sister to lose Ramiel like this.

"Nerina, I'm so sorry," she said quietly.

Nerina rolled over onto her side to face Mora. She wiped her eyes as Mora reached to take hold of her other hand. Mora squeezed her hand gently, bringing a small smile to Nerina's face.

"Mora," Nerina said softly, sadness evident in her voice, "Who told you?"

"Eli, well, he said you were missing, Aera found you and figured out why."

Nerina tried not to cry again. She was the eldest. She had to be strong for the others. Mora pulled her older sister into a tight hug, offering the only comfort she knew how to give. Nerina held onto Mora, and cried. After a few minutes, Aera burst through the door.

"Alright, darling sister," began Aera with a wicked grin on her face, "How badly would you like us to hurt him, and where."

Nerina burst out laughing and shook her head. At that moment, the love and caring that surrounded her was immense and she relished it. There were times when she dreaded having sisters, and a brother, but times like these made her love them even more.

"Sorry ladies, no harming of Ramiel today" Nerina replied with a grin on her face, "Although I did smell fresh pies from the priestess house. Unless of course everyone would rather we hang out on my bed all day."

"Rina, will this cheer you up?" asked Kamiel as he entered into the room carrying one of those pies and utensils. The sight of him filled her with great love. She loved her brother dearly. Loved his soft, gentle soul and strong heart. He always knew just how to calm her. She gave him a tight squeeze and removed the pies from his fumbling grasp.

"Kami, this will definitely cheer me up."

They dug into the commandeered pie with relish and chatted excitedly, chasing away most of Nerina's heavy sadness.

AT DINNER, NERINA AND her siblings quietly pushed their food around, too full to eat everything. Adamina watched them with a smile on her face. Uriel's face slowly flushed to a vibrant red. Nerina looked to her mother and quietly asked to be excused from the table. Her mother glanced to her plate, seeing she had only eaten a small amount of the vegetables and nodded. The girl began to rise when her father slammed his utensils down and ordered her to sit back down.

"You will not leave the table until you are done eating, young lady." He gestured to the rest of his children and added, "And that goes for all of you too. You will eat everything on your plates."

Adamina rose from her seat, the smile gone from her face.

"Children, you may leave the table," all of her children stood quickly and ran from the room.

Nerina had been the last to leave because she wanted to hear her parents' discussion. She knew her mother and father didn't always get along, but they had never argued in front of them before. She slid to the ground, leaning against the wall beside the door and listened to their exchange.

"Uriel, if you were any kind of father you would know what happened and why none of our children hungry enough to finish their meals. But as you are a less than adequate father on your good days, I wouldn't expect you to understand."

"Adamina, you are wrong."

Uriel's chair scratched menacingly against the floor as he stood and moved slowly towards his wife. "I am not a 'less than adequate' father, wife. I am a wonderful father and our children know that."

Adamina backed away slowly. A tremble of fear ran down her spine at the words he spat out. Uriel's voice was eerie and full of rage. She did not want to be within an arm's reach of him. She had never seen him like this before. Uriel continued towards her peaking in a low, angry tone.

"You are my wife, Adamina. They are my children. If I tell them to stay at the table until they have eaten all of their dinner, then they will stay at the table until they are finished! Even if I have to stuff it down their throats myself. Do you understand, Adamina? Do you understand that I am the head of this family?"

"Get out of my house!" Adamina shouted, angry that her husband felt that way.

Uriel lifted his hand and struck. From outside the dining room Nerina could hear his hand hit its mark, her mother's feet stumble, and the breath her mother exhaled. It was almost enough to bring Nerina out of her cover, but she knew that would only get her and her mother in more trouble. Instead, she called to Gabriel, recalling their first meeting and his offer of help.

Gabriel! It is Nerina. You need to come over now. Something is wrong with father. He hit her and he is getting angrier and angrier by the second. She is crying. Gabriel, please hurry.

She did not wait for a response before she pulled out of his mind and resumed her eavesdropping on her parent's. Her mother was crying and begging Uriel to stop. She could hear her father muttering curses. Every few seconds there was a slap followed by a yelp.

Nerina had tears flowing down her cheeks. She to hold her breath to keep herself from crying out. Then she felt the flood of her father's emotions. Wild anger, a dark pleasure at controlling and instilling fear, a joy with each slap, and a tiny quiet voice at the back of his heart helpless to stop himself: a torn man, a lost man. Her mother felt the connection and broke it before Uriel could recognize it and turn on her daughter. Adamina desperately wanted to reach out and tell her precious child to hide with the others, but doing so could put her in harm's way. Uriel would notice. She had to get out as soon as she can, lead him away from the children.

Ten minutes had passed since Nerina had tried to contact Gabriel and the situation had gotten worse. The back door squealed open and slammed shut, followed by Uriel's angry screams for Adamina to come back. Nerina was too terrified to move until she heard her father leave too. She stood shakily and ran upstairs to her siblings' bedrooms. She found them all huddling in Aera's room, on the bed. Nerina entered the room and a floorboard creaked. Her siblings looked to her with shock and fear on their faces. They had thought she was Uriel. When had she stopped thinking of him as her father, she wondered. She reached out and embraced Kamiel tightly. After a few moments of silence, they heard hurried footsteps rushing up the stairs. Gabriel stood in the doorway panting heavily.

"Nerina, where did they go?"

She shrugged and told him what she had heard, mentally,

as to not scare the others further. He nodded in response and told them to wait exactly where they were. He promised them everything would be alright and that Raphael and Michael would be up to see them in a few minutes. They only nodded, none of them having the strength to argue or comment. He insisted Nerina watch over the younger ones. Nerina hated being the oldest and wished for the luxury of a younger position in the family.

Being in charge of her younger siblings forced Nerina to always be in control of her emotions. If she was upset or worried then her siblings soon adopted those emotions as well. Kamiel dozed off just before Raphael and Michael appeared in the door way. Nerina jumped in surprise because she hadn't heard them approach. Raphael sat on the only available corner of the bed.

"How is everyone?" he asked Aera, Nerina and Mora softly, trying not to wake Kamiel.

"Gabriel wanted us to come and check up on you fine ladies and gentleman. Michael, here, brought his harp. Would you like him to play?" Raphael asked and stroked Nerina's hair and offered her a reassuring smile.

Water girl, tears are for the brave too, he soothed.

Nerina smiled a helpless smile. The comfort was too late, but she would hold the saying in her heart until she could manage the tears. The children nodded and Michael played a soothing melody until they were all curled up asleep on the bed together dreaming of beautiful peaceful worlds. Michael and Raphael exchanged nervous glances over the children, praying for Adamina's safety.

ADAMINA RAN AS FAST as she could. She heard his footsteps behind her. Her pulse raced in fear. Her chest

tightened and her lungs burned. The only thought remaining was *run*. Faster, she dodged trees. She prayed
while she ran that she would live, her face burning from
the times he had hit her. She was sure it would bruise.
Adamina paused to listen. With a sigh of relief, silence
surrounded her. She caught her breath and wiped at her
tears. Then she heard the wing beats and a chill froze her.
Those same beating wings that saved her from the river
were coming to end her. Fear gripped at her again as she
ran, this time she stumbled as the fear made her legs
week.

"Someone help me please," she beseeched in whispers
between gulping breaths.

She stumbled and landed hard onto the ground, almost
all the way in a clearing. Adamina tugged at her dress to
try and free it but it wouldn't budge having tangled itself
in a rose bush. She heard Uriel's wing beats approaching,
and scrambled as out of view as she could manage. She
tugged furiously at her dress but it would not budge or
tear. A shadow appeared on the ground in front of her
and she looked up to see Uriel's angry face.

"I shall teach you to disobey me woman," Uriel said in
a voice that was terrifying with promise. He grabbed at
her throat and closed his hand tightly.

"Goddess…" she choked out.

"You are nothing but a female mortal," he said, his
eyes burning, "I am a god compared to you!"

"Uriel!" boomed a voice from behind him.

Her heart leapt at that voice. She thanked Goddess
and let out a sob. Uriel slowly turned around and saw
Gabriel standing there, Gabriel's eyes amber-red with
anger.

"Let her go," he said calmly. Gabriel's heart tore in
two at the sound of that sob, the fear he felt for her, the
terror. He locked it away securely behind the Archangel
General, behind eons of training, of battle, of cold steel.

"This is not your concern brother. She is my wife," Uriel snapped back at him, turning back to Adamina.

"Go home, brother," Gabriel said dangerously, an insult burning his tongue.

Uriel scoffed dismissively and lifted Adamina into the air by her throat. A small choking sound escaped her lips and bruises from his fingers formed where he held her. Her dress still caught on the nearby branches stretched, the seams straining and cutting into her skin. She tried to reach for a branch or his knife, anything to use as a weapon, but her arms were too short. Tears streamed down her face. She could feel the darkness begin to take over her and she fought against it. Uriel released his grip on her slightly to face Gabriel.

Gabriel had a sword pointed at his heart and the two men stared at each other in silence. He could not destroy the Angel in front of him, but the mortal body could be destroyed. Gabriel wished desperately to be engaged in battle, to shed Uriel's form and return him to sanity. He glared daringly, daring Uriel to fill his lust for blood. After a moment, Uriel threw Adamina angrily to the ground. She held in a cry of pain, squinting her eyes tightly closed, as she landed hard on her side with a sharp clunk of bone and lied there concentrating on taking deep breaths. Uriel turned and shot a look at Adamina that threatened revenge, then disappeared into blue-gray smoke. As his figure vanished, Adamina let out a sob and a cry of pain, collapsing in a twist of fabric and limbs.

"Adamina!" Gabriel cried softly as he ran to her, sheathing his weapon. He cradled her in his arms. "Oh, Adamina…" he said quietly.

"Gabriel…" she cried weakly, shaking from fear and exhaustion, clinging onto him for dear life. Her face was bruising from the damage Uriel had done.

"Shush, you are safe now," Gabriel soothed.

"The children…" Adamina uttered half-coherently.

Her lip was bleeding and swelling, and she would surely have a black eye by tomorrow morning. He caressed the bruising on her neck, a pained expression on his face.

"Are being taken care of by Raphael and Michael," Gabriel assured.

A deep hate fueled by rage boiled beneath the surface and Gabriel silently swore revenge for her injuries. He cut her dress free and lifted her, carrying her to the cabin. He knew she could not return to the house in this state. She needed a safe place untouched by this madness and pain. He would take her to their cabin.

Adamina was a strong and hardy woman very much changed from the young girl she was when she had first set foot on Avalon. Now, she felt fragile and small as Gabriel held her in his arms. It took all his will to keep his body from shaking with the anger and concern he felt for Adamina. He loved Adamina. He had loved her from the moment he had laid eyes upon her. His promise to watch over Goddess' treasure haunted him. Well, where was Mother now? Far away, consulting with gods and abandoning Avalon to his kind. She left Adamina to Uriel's snare. No, he stopped himself, he had done that. He should have never let the hand fasting happen. He should have stopped this all before it started. He had made a promise and he had failed to keep it.

Gabriel placed Adamina upon the mattress. He lit a fire in the small hearth and set to boiling herbed water. He tore up a clean shirt and dipped the strips in the boiling water, snatching them out of the water with his bare hands as he needed. He tended to her wounds and had to re-set her dislocated hip. Their connection made it easier to urge her body and mind to rest. He guarded her as she slept, minding each wound until there was no trace.

SHE AWOKE TO THE light of day and had immediately asked about her children again. Gabriel had reassured her that they were under the care of the trusted Raphael, Michael and the other priestesses, and that Uriel had gone on one of his voyages over the seas and would not return for a while. She calmed at this news and ate a little of the stew he had prepared, and some bread. The stew was the same they had shared in the cabin the first time she had met him.

Adamina sat on the edge of the bed and slowly stretched some of her muscles. She was a little sore, but there was little to remind her of the wounds. She took a deep breath in and then looked at Gabriel. She noticed something within his eyes, glimmering for her, which she had not noticed before.

"Gabriel," she started and paused, his name was comfortable on her lips.

"Yes?" he spoke softly, avoiding her intense gaze.

"Thank you for helping me and intervening."

"It would be a fool who would not assist you after the harm you came to. A fool who cannot care for you," he spoke carefully, and quietly.

There was something in the way Gabriel had said those three words "care for you" that made her scrutinize him and ask carefully, "Gabriel, what are you saying?" Her body shivered and her heart beat quickly. She must be weaker than she thought. She lifted a hand to her heart in an unconscious gesture.

"I think it is obvious," Gabriel responded, "Your husband is a fool." He could no longer hide his feelings for her, "And I am a fool for loving you and letting him harm you."

A wave of emotions hit her with his words and she swallowed them back. A subtle warmth slowly seeped into her heart. She realized that she too loved this man in front of her. She had never loved Uriel. She wished that it had been Gabriel all those seasons ago who had pulled her from the river, not Uriel. She wished it had been, it would be, Gabriel. She was unable to speak. He crouched in front of her. Her eyes darted away from his. Gabriel gently lifted Adamina's chin and forced her to look into his eyes. What he saw in her eyes mirrored his own heart and made it burst with joy. He kissed her quickly, gently and just as he was about to pull away, re-think the whole thing, try and take back his confession, she kissed him back.

Adamina pulled him closer, deepened the kiss. Her desires taking over her. Her need to fill the emptiness that had grown in her and to chase away the pain rushed to the surface of her being. Then reason set in. She pulled away and caught her breath.

"But I gave my word," she whispered.

And he broke that agreement when he harmed you.

Adamina's mind raced with her heart. She tried to steady her breathing and clear her mind. Yes… Uriel had broken that promise. Avalon was not a safe place any-more. She looked up at Gabriel. His eyes liquid amber. A glimmer of freedom sparked in her eyes as his words broke a chain that held her to her promise.

He pulled her to him and kissed her again, being careful not to hurt her, not to push her. He let her decide how far this would go. Her need, her love for him, and her emptiness, compelled her to go further as she strug-gled against her reason. Her blood sang. Her skin nearly glowed. Avalon sighed with liberation. Their kisses deep-ened and receded like the tide. Soon their clothing no longer posed a barrier between them and their bodies became entangled. Limbs weaved like gentle vines. Their bodies nestled into each other. He covered her, protecting her, gently possessing her as he slowly joined his body with hers. She had been in his heart so deeply that it was not until this moment that he had realized the enormity of his choice so long ago. The ache inside of him burst through his hold and drove him further.

She trembled with the emotions rushing through her. She felt his hold release and the depth of his desire flash through him. She felt her own spirit respond, steering her towards shipwrecked. She could not have stopped it if she had wanted to. They became one. Gabriel paused in his rising passion to look into her eyes, her spirit. He whispered her name and became lost within her. Their spirits knitted together and their hearts exchanged whispers of endearment. The movement of her hips brought him back to their physical union and he began a slow rhythm, linking body with soul. He wanted to treasure every moment he could with her.

Gabriel's love chased away the last of her stiffness and soreness, healed her and filled her emptiness. She felt complete. She had not known love could ever feel this way. She had not truly understood passion until this moment. This glorious union that excited every part of her and made her more alive than she ever thought possible. Her spirit drifted with her mind and heart, removed themselves from her body and mingled with his as he made love to her. The rising climax within her warmed her core and slowly brought her back down to reality. Her climax built and swelled until it finally let go, racking her body with ripples and tides of pleasure, then slamming her down into ecstasy. Gabriel's release was not far behind her own.

He untangled himself from her gently and gazed down at her shaking form. His concern rose to the surface, perhaps the physical exertion had been too much for her. His senses slipped over her, checking every inch of her. The pulse beat steady beneath her perfectly formed breasts. No, just ecstatic joy made her shake, no harm. His body relaxed with relief and an assured smirk slid across his face. She drifted off into a pleasure induced sleep and he smiled and caressed her gently, muttering and mumbling soothing melodies.

Gabriel considered her form, her features and sought to memorize them all. He lay there for what felt like hours until the chill of the cool air set in and the fire in the hearth died down to a small glow. He rose from the bed as the sun began to stretch awake over the horizon and illuminate Avalon. He donned his clothing and set about making breakfast for them both. Reality could settle upon him after they ate, until then he was going to enjoy every moment of contentment he could.

"YOU LIED TO ME!"

"I did no such thing. I told you what I saw," Lucifer didn't have the patience for irrational out-bursts.

"You said you saw a son, my son, of Adamina who would rise to take my place with Father, ever at my side until I wished it no more," Uriel fumed.

He had fumed the entire voyage out of Avalon. Maybe his brother had not entirely lied. After all, Gabriel had meddled with his wife and his family. That meddling old man had interfered with a proper disciplining of his property. God knows what state of mind she would be in when he returned. Condoning disobedience was unwise, his eyes narrowed. He would deal with Gabriel one day soon.

"Uriel, why don't you join me? Holding open this veil is quite an effort, and we wouldn't want to be caught by a mortal talking over an opening through thin air would we."

Glowering, Uriel stepped through. Lucifer clucked and shook his head as he poured out a decanter into crystal goblets. Uriel had no taste for the finery of the drink, but the action would offer the impression of camaraderie and a pleasant distraction from this whining.

"Here," he handed Uriel one of the goblets, "take this for your nerves. I can't believe that woman!"

Uriel shot his brother a look and snatched the glass, downing the nectar and relishing the burn it left as it trailed down into his stomach.

"There, now, better?" Lucifer sat himself behind his desk, "What I saw still will come to pass. I told you that she would be round with pregnancy again, and that has not yet happened again, has it."

Sulking Uriel shook his head.

"Well dear brother, you can't expect a miracle in one mortal day. Relax. Enjoy the party. Soon, you will be bloated with the glory of your offspring. Can I offer a distraction to please you? I do hate to see my dear friend and brother so, upset."

"What is it you have in mind?"

A sinister grin slid across Lucifer's face, "Do you fancy a dance? Lord Wrathwell is hosting a very exclusive ball. He has personally selected the entertainment and only the finest forms will be floating across the floor. It will be in the tradition of the ancient Symposiums. I believe all sorts of services will be available to work out that anger. And what a perfect place to find something, expendable."

Uriel tipped his head, eyes gleaming as they met his brother's.

"Lead the way, brother."

15

ERINA SMILED SOFTLY AND gestured behind her to Artemesia, "Well, first of all, Artemesia came back after what, two moons Mesia?"

Artemesia nodded, "Yeah, two moons. I only came back to get some clothes. I guess I'll stay for a little while and help out with the family."

She paused for a moment. Her mother and sister stood before her. Her mother was a beacon of strength and warmth to those who knew her. Nerina shone like the light dancing off waves. She was proud and beautiful and bright. She could whisper water out from the ground, worked with Raphael, and had Eli who loved her. Artemesia felt she paled in comparison. She was a woman, without a purpose or gift.

Her hair was dark and straight. Her features were too much like the father she hardly knew. She had no magic or special place in the world. Few saw her when she stood there. Except the men. They saw her. They hungered for her and she relished in their attention. She found her power in her body, in her ability to turn a man's, or occasionally a woman's, head. She chose who she accepted. She found control, power, and a means of living. Someday, she would find a place out there, in one of the other worlds, perhaps she would apprentice to a craft, but she didn't belong here. Not forever.

"If that is okay with you."

Adamina motioned Artemesia to step forward. When she was close enough, embraced her grown child.

"Artemesia, you are welcome here for as long as you please and whenever you want to be here. No conditions."

She kissed her daughter on the head and stroked her hair. Adamina wished for the days with little girl toes and bright green eyes staring up at her. Her heart ached with the quiet knowing of a mother regarding the nature of her daughter's behaviour. If she tried to control Artemesia, the young woman would pull away and she may never see her daughter again. It went against every fiber of her being not to lock her up in a room and know she would be home and safe, but Adamina knew her daughters were women of their own and tried not to cling too tightly. Adamina sighed, she found herself far too exhausted lately. Perhaps raising her children was catching up with her.

Artemesia nodded and pulled out of the embrace, "You need rest, mother. Nerina and I can manage the children."

Adamina resigned to the fact that she needed rest, but refused to leave Artemesia without a promise.

"I will only go rest if you promise not to run off for a bit. I would like to share a meal or two with you."

Adamina found herself reminiscing again of little children as she stared at her grown daughters. Even Morgana, was almost a young woman and it felt like only yesterday she had been darting around the womb. Gabriel and Adamina both clung to their daughter's youth, understanding that they had little time left before she would blaze her own trail and steal the hearts of men everywhere. There was fire in that child for sure. Adamina made her way back to the bedroom as her daughters chattered and chided each other as they went about their chores.

So much time had passed since that fateful day when Gabriel picked her up and put the pieces back in place. Since that confession and that morning. A secret smile danced on her lips at the memory. As she passed by the looking glass on the corridor wall Gabriel had gifted her, she scrutinized her image. Her hair had begun to gray and the dark silver reminded her of the sword that had been pointed at her former husband's heart. Uriel had not shown his face in over ten years. Adamina prayed he would never come back.

She glanced into the room where Gabriel held their sleeping red-haired daughter in his arms, rocking in a chair with his eyes closed. The poor girl had been suffering a terrible affliction and Gabriel had rarely left her side. Her body had been covered in red pocks, but Raphael's cream and draughts worked and they were through the worst of it. Few of those menacing spots were left and the fever had broken a few nights ago.

Adamina shuddered with the idea of what Uriel would do if he returned to find Gabriel and Morgana. She steeled herself against the thought. If Uriel ever stepped foot back on Avalon, she would throw the storms about him and strike him with lightning. No, that was not her way.

She would tell him their deal was off. He had risked her life and Avalon. He broke his end of the bargain and by doing so she had been able to set herself free. She had been free to love, free to grow again, to live again. Free to create a family with Gabriel. In him she had found refuge, gentleness, passion, and protection. In him she had found an equal who stood by her side as they journeyed through life together.

Oh what joy she had found in the real magic of love. The power they created together, the bond they shared had grown and strengthened. It was so thick and electric she could almost touch it. Love making had become a sacred ritual, an expression of all the power in the universe, and, in themselves. Adamina had never realized the power she had held before Gabriel had entered her life. Now, she was alight with it. She felt as if she was Goddess herself, and if he, her golden consort. Those quiet intimate moments were as magnetic as the loud, children filled moments they shared together. This was love and this was family: unity, truth, and equality. And maybe, that magic, that love, would be enough to save Avalon. Maybe, Goddess was wrong and Fate had shifted. Maybe Avalon would not fall and she would grow old and die in Gabriel's arms.

It had been hard for her to understand why people in the stories she had read so long ago with Pagan had rejoiced in their unions together. Uriel had shown her nothing but coldness and left her frozen to her core. Gabriel had warmed the ice inside her soul. He had healed wounds. He had made her whole again and guided her to her own strength. He may be stubborn at times, but he was never overbearing like Uriel. How could two brothers be so very, very different? Adamina closed the door to the bedroom she and Gabriel shared. That big ominous bed she had shared with Uriel had been locked away behind a dusty door. Climbing into bed she smiled and closed her eyes to rest.

"MESIA?!" KAMIEL'S VOICE CAME from the end of the corridor.

He loved his sister so very much. They were both quiet souls. He had tried to show her that she had magic inside of her, just like mother. That she just needed to embrace it and realize she was special too. He tried so hard, but he knew she would go. The only magic she felt was in her ability to turn a man's head and lure him to her bed. So she would go and lose herself there. His heart echoed the ache in his mother's for Artemesia. She would be leaving them soon. Not for another few seasons, but soon she wouldn't return home for clothing or food or warmth. Soon, she would find a mortal who would take her with him. One day, she would just be gone.

He embraced her tightly, "Please don't leave."

Artemesia looked up at her now tall little brother. His wings were pulled close to his body. He was practically a man. He had no need for her care.

"I'll stay as long as I can, Kami."

He nodded his response with the quiet gaze of knowing.

"Come, let us prepare supper. Nerina, would you please get the others?" Adamina asked gently.

With a nod, Nerina left her siblings and mother to locate the rest of her sisters.

"SHE'LL NEVER BUY IT."

"What do you mean she'll never buy it? I worked for four seasons for it."

"Eli, she has given herself to no man, ever. And she has dedicated herself to the priestesshood. She's meant to take mama's place there. That is the last thing on her mind."

Aera bit into a piece of fruit and looked at Eli nonchalantly. Mora smirked and continued harvesting from the garden. She stretched her glorious wings out and shook the dirt off them. Raphael was tending to his medicinal herbs a distance away in a separate garden. She waved and smiled at him. He inclined his head in greeting and returned to his herbs. Mora turned around to face Aera and tuned back into their conversation.

"Aera, if she doesn't accept it, with or without her, I am leaving."

"You are leaving?" Nerina's voice interrupted, "Why Eli, where, when?!"

She stood there in shock. He smiled nervously and swallowed. The sunlight caught her golden hair as it began to set behind the trees, giving her a halo. Her dress was silver and blue, flowing around her legs in the breeze. She blinked and pushed a renegade strand of hair out of her eyes. Eli glanced at Mora.

"Uh, we'll give you two privacy. We have to go wash up these vegetables for supper," Mora grabbed Aera's arm and dragged her away before she could protest.

"I am not leaving. Well, I might leave. What I mean is," he fumbled in his pocket.

Eli pulled out a small wooden box and held it in front of him, "Come with me, Nerina. Be my partner and journey with me. Start a family, and a life away from here."

He opened the box to reveal a deep blue stone set in silver metal. A ring meant for her finger. Nerina recoiled from the shock and took a step back. Eli stared at her, pleading with his eyes.

"I can't. Why would you want to leave Avalon? Avalon is my home."

"There is nothing here for me, Rina. I don't belong here. I can take a ship to another land and start my life there. Start a family of my own. I can write for the theatres I hear about from the other sailors. Come with me," he pleaded.

"Avalon is my home, Eli. I can't leave. I won't leave it."

"I am leaving, Rina. With or without you. I would prefer if you came with," Eli started to get upset.

"I cannot follow you Eli. I will miss you dearly, but my place is here. I wish you well."

He sighed and nodded, upset but resigned. When Nerina made up her mind, there was no changing it. He knew that. But this time he had finally made up his mind for himself, and he wasn't going to change it for the world. He would create a name himself.

"You might as well take this then," Eli handed the ring to her, "It was made for you and won't do on anyone else."

He pushed the box into her hands and turned and left. Her heart ached a little for the loss of her dear friend. She struggled to swallow as tears threatened to fall. She shook her head and let out a breath. She was a priestess now. The others all looked to her for strength and guidance. If he wanted to go somewhere else with these theatres, well he could darn well do so. Her place was here, on Avalon. She watched his silhouette fade into the sunset as he headed towards the pier and out of her life forever.

"Have you gone soft on me, Uriel?"

Lucifer would have the power of Avalon, and then he would demand his place beside the Others. Worlds would be his to command and control and his armies would ravage and rage. He would revel in the spoils of war. He would saturate himself with the suffering of others. He would reign, and Father would cower before him. *Throw me out! I will take everything you hold dear, Lord.*

Lucifer sighed, "Are you willing to give up your son? Your family?"

"Maybe they are better off without me."

Lucifer kept his anger in check, "Uriel, brother, but your son. Now is the time to return and conceive that son you have always dreamed about. Now is the time to return."

"And you are sure Luc? You are certain I will conceive a son with Adamina?"

"Oh yes, Uriel, you will. And he shall be glorious in his purpose. He will rise up and rule over a vast army," Lucifer coughed and kept his joy in check.

"Very well. I shall return. But what about Gabriel?"

"Oh, let me take care of Gabriel. He will be on the next ship out of Avalon and you will have two seasons changes worth of time before he returns."

"Good. Um, how will I get back to Avalon?"

It took all of Lucifer's strength not to strangle his brother. Uriel could be so daft sometimes. Soon, he reminded himself, he could get rid of this pawn. Lucifer clutched at the strands that divided the world and time and pulled the weakened veils open to Avalon, "After you."

"YOU'RE LEAVING?"

Artemesia nodded.

"Why? You just got here! Why is everyone leaving?"

"What do you mean 'everyone'?"

Nerina sighed, "Eli left too. He asked me to come with him as he pursued a new life somewhere else. I couldn't go with him."

Artemesia finished her though for her, "No, your place has always been here, Rina. I am sorry, this must be difficult for you. I have to go, Nerina. I cannot stay where I do not belong."

Nerina tried to reply, but Artemesia cut her off.

"You know I don't belong here. I never have. I am leaving and you can't stop me."

Nerina chocked on her tears, "At least let me hug you before you go, Artemesia. And let me tell you a few small things."

Artemesia remained silent and did not move from where she was standing, so Nerina took it as a sign to continue.

"First of all, you will be missed, dear Artemesia. No matter what the circumstances may be you are always welcome back here. We will welcome you with open arms." Nerina waved off Artemesia's protests. "Shush, let me finish. Secondly, you always have and always will belong here. But more importantly, you will always belong where your heart seeks great pleasure in being. I understand that I can do nothing more to convince you to stay so remember this. From now until eternity, in this life and all lives after this, you will always be my sister, my friend, our family. There will always be love and comfort for you her. Mother would say so and you know it."

Artemesia nodded with her face remaining emotionless. Nerina pulled her into a tight hug.

"Mesia be safe in your journeys."

"Nerina, I will be fine."

She pulled out of the hug and took a few steps backwards, staring into Nerina's eyes before turning abruptly and walking out of the house. Nerina almost chased after her, but Kamiel came up behind her to place a hand on her shoulder.

"You knew this day would come, didn't you," Nerina said without turning around.

Without waiting for an answer she continued, "We better tell mother."

"Wait until the ship leaves, Rina, please," Artemesia begged, turning around.

Reluctantly Nerina nodded. Artemesia shouldered her bag and left for the pier. She went out through the kitchen and paused. It was empty, the day-stew simmering quietly over a slow burning fire. She imagined her mother preparing that stew with love, ensuring the flavours were balanced and the meal hearty. That was her mother, so caring, so thoughtful. She loved Gabriel immensely. She would miss them all. Tears threated to escape and she swallowed them back.

She didn't belong here, no matter what they said. Her sisters, even bright-eyed Kamiel, all of them had gifts, they could see the future, control the elements, hold off or welcome changes in weather. Mora and Aera worked with Michael and Tyrryal to develop their gifts. And Raphael flew the skies with her winged sisters and brother. No, she didn't belong here. She took one last look over the island as the ship departed, then she set her eyes on the horizon of a new life.

"WHAT DO YOU MEAN she is gone forever?" Adamina demanded. "Gabriel, please you have to go bring her back. She could get hurt. She could get killed!"

"Nerina, who did she go with?" Gabriel commanded gently.

"She said his name was Braxis," Nerina replied softly.

Kamiel hung his head and stood silently in the corner. At the name Gabriel paled.

"What, what is it?" Adamina asked seeing the look on his face.

"Braxis is no man, he is a loose cannon of a fallen

Angel," Gabriel replied solemnly, "I must go after her, Adamina. I don't know how long I will be."

Adamina nodded, "Yes of course, go. Kamiel, go with him. Be safe, my love. My son. And take Tyrryal with you, I believe he arrived back today and is staying at the harbour inn."

Gabriel nodded, but inside he held reservations. He did not trust his kindred completely, but he could, he admitted reluctantly, use his expertise. Adamina kissed Gabriel softly goodbye and embraced her son. Kamiel silently nodded and followed Gabriel's hastened steps to the pier. Kamiel knew he left his mother vulnerable by taking Tyrryal and Gabriel to help Artemesia. Kamiel knew, but he could not tell Gabriel. Gabriel would choose Adamina. Without Gabriel, Braxis was going to kill Artemesia. He couldn't let his sister die. He hoped that his mother would fare alright should Uriel return before they got back. They left to the pier and Kamiel tried to hide his guilt behind his determination to save Artemesia.

16

P LEASE.

It had been three moons since Gabriel left. Adamina had thrown herself into the work of taking care of her family. Nerina had done much the same, managing the priestess house and preparing for the Autumnal Equinox when the harvests would begin. She paced in front of the house, thought about going down to the pier herself. She had sent the boys from the priestess house to check every hour if the ships arriving had ferried Gabriel and Kamiel home.

A great restlessness grew in her and there seemed no way to calm her nerves. Avalon hummed and warned that something was coming. But with the turmoil in her own heart, she ignored the warning. She had to keep her emotions under control, for if she let them reign free, she may cause a thunderstorm or change the winds and keep Gabriel away longer. Working magic had taught her that the intensity of her own emotions could influence Avalon's temperament or could manifest unwanted things in her life. She needed to stay in control.

To try and ease the restlessness, she ran. She ran to

the cliffs and stood there, gazing over the waters, willing her lover, son, and daughter home safely. She took a deep breath of salty air and a gull called above her. The sky was grayed with light clouds. Rain would be coming soon. She listened to the beat of the waves and let it calm her own heart. She would steal only a few more moments of peace and then she had to return home and prepare supper for hungry ones. Her smile stretched across her face, warming her at the thought of her family. Indulging in happy memories, she took a few more breaths than decided to head back. Adamina turned, coming face-to-face with terror.

"You do not belong here," she managed.

"I see you have been busy betraying me, Adamina. I am your husband. How dare you!" He raised his hand to strike.

Nerina, gather the children and keep them safe in the priestess house, please, hurry. Your father has returned.

Adamina closed her mind, the way Gabriel had taught her, shutting Uriel out, shielding the message to Nerina from Uriel, then shutting her mind off completely. It cut her off from Nerina and Gabriel himself, but it also prevented Uriel or Lucifer from invading her thoughts. Gabriel had trained her for exactly this. She grounded herself and stared him down, built walls and barriers.

She called to Avalon and felt the power rise. She pulled at the magic in her, pulled up through the ground beneath her bare feet. She sent the blast of hot air, a warning, towards Uriel. It knocked him off balance enough for her to bolt towards the house. Uriel was shocked at first. Then the anger grew in him and he turned around and quickly closed the distance between them. He grabbed a handful of her hair and yanked. Adamina cried out in pain and swung her arms at Uriel, sending an electric shock through him, forcing him away.

Silently she prayed her children would not see, that they were safe. The clouds above rolled and building a storm, darkened.

"I will have my son Adamina. I will have you."

"You have a son Uriel, his name is Kamiel and he is wonderful. If you would only see…"

He cut her off, "He is not our son. He is a bastard I refuse to claim as my own."

"You should be ashamed of yourself."

"I am not the whore, Adamina," he narrowed his eyes and he clutched her arm, the pain freezing her in place as he caged her in a magical boundary.

"There, that is better, isn't it? If you try anything," he spun her around and held her by the hair, "You'll kill yourself instead of me."

Adamina spit and struggled against him and he wrapped his free arm around her waist, locking her against him in a terrible embrace.

"You aren't half the man Gabriel is," Adamina growled and fought him every step of the way, trying to tear down the dark energy around her. His barrier would not budge.

A dark smirk passed across his face, "I have learned things from Lucifer that may change your mind."

With a thought he transported them into the master bedroom. Dust covered every surface and choked her. Adamina began to struggle and howled in frustration and despair. Tears fell down her cheeks against her will as she twisted and turned, trying to break free.

"You have aged wife, and with your age you lose strength," he spun her around to face him, "I will always be eternally stronger than you. I wouldn't fight if I were you. I will have you. It would be easier for you if you didn't resist."

"I will always resist you, in this and every life Uriel. That I swear to Goddess. I will always fight you and your brother Lucifer. Gabriel told me all about him, about you. I will never give you anything willingly. Never."

He threw her against the bed, "I don't need you to be willing."

She tried to scramble away and he grabbed her legs, dragging her to him. He hiked up her skirt with one hand and locked her legs against the edge of the bed and his knees. The pressure made her cry out as lightning shot up her thighs and down through her knees. He was crushing her. She was sure the bones in her legs were going to break with his weight. Then terror filled her again with the sound of him loosening his trousers. This was not love. This was not what she wanted. She tried to pull away again and he yanked on her hair, wrenching her back and into him.

The force of him tore her, searing hot from the inside and she cried out. Unable to escape, unable to fight. Her arms gave out from beneath her and she silently cried. Then she glimpsed the carvings on the bed posts, *Gabriel*. Drifting into Gabriel, safe, she imagined him wrapping his arms around her, stretching out glorious and beautiful wings. He carried her away. Cradled in Gabriel's arms, she fell asleep.

SILENTLY SOBBING NERINA COVERED her mouth. The others were safe. Aera and Mora watched over Morgana. She had turned to fight for her mother, to use what Raphael had taught her, but Avalon had stopped her and sent her to her knees. The vision of what her mother had experienced had been forced upon her by Avalon. That terrible, horrible vision had filled her with anger, but Avalon would not release her. The sensation of her mother leaving her body, then nothing but darkness. Only then would the island let her stand again, not that she could at the moment with her legs numb.

Mother, mother!

No response came and Nerina had feared the worst. Through tears and trauma, Nerina called the others.

Raphael, Michael, Gabriel, Kamiel, Tyr, Ramiel, anyone please. Please help us.

Nerina's body was racked with sobs. She clutched at the grass, trying to ground herself. There was nothing anywhere in the world that could ease the raw pain in her heart that cut to her soul. Helpless to stop him, she had never felt like such a failure. She stood up and wiped the tears from her face. She would return to the priestess house and watch the others. She stopped at the door and faced outward. She could do this. Raising her hands, she called the water under the ground and sunk a trench around the house, urging it full. She begged the water to protect them from Uriel, and it answered with a sharp hum of assurance. She could do this. Nerina shut the door and locked it tightly behind her.

RAPHAEL'S HEAD SHOT UP. He had just finished wrapping a soldier's broken leg. He did what he could to heal and help the mortals of all worlds. He was currently masquerading as a surgeon in some war. He wasn't sure which one. Mortals had so many wars. Nerina's call had echoed to him. She should not have been able to reach him here. Something terrible, soul tearing must have happened for a call like that to reach him. He packed up and gave instructions to the nurses, the soldiers, and the other surgeon. Raphael hastened to seclude himself behind a hill then rent a tear through the worlds to Avalon, cringing as he felt Avalon's pain at the wound.

Stepping through, Raphael pulled the hole shut behind him, healing what damage he could. Avalon's wards were weakening, where was Goddess? No time to find her, he sped off towards where he sensed Nerina was. He saw the magnificent barrier she had raised, the moat of water and he felt pride. She had ensured the safety of the priestess' house, and the magic was strong. The ward was impressive. He passed through the barrier safely and found her in the sitting room by the fire, hugging herself and kneeling on the floor. Her head shot up and she grappled for him. He caught her arms and she sent the images and knowledge of what she saw to him violently as she sobbed. In his mind, Uriel's force played for him. Oh dear sweet Adamina, please be safe. He reached out toward the house and was snapped back by the boundaries of Uriel's darkened magic. It was too late, Lucifer had turned him. Raphael mourned. He could protect the children or save Adamina. He chose the one his friend would have asked of him.

"Nerina, where are your sisters and brother?"

Nerina pointed upstairs.

"Okay, alright sweet heart," Raphael helped Nerina up and half carried her as she composed herself the best she could.

He would care for the scars on her heart as soon as he could. He would dull that pain and chase away that memory, but not completely. He foresaw what it could make her into. Nerina would have to choose to be darkened by it or shine brighter and freer than she ever imagined. He could not take that away from her, but he could heal the wound. They were greeted by Palla at the top of the stairs. Worry and relief at the sight of him and Nerina passed over her face.

"Palla, my dear, you must lock down the house. No

one is to enter or leave. I trust you have enough stores and water for a while?" She nodded and he continued, "Good."

Raphael gently handed Nerina off to Palla, "Calm her down dear with a strong cup of tea. I am going to check on the others."

He raced down the hall to check on the girls and figure out where the hell Gabriel had gotten himself.

THE SHIP SWAYED AND creaked as the wind and waves moved the massive vessel towards Rubar Bay. Each day wore on them all. Kamiel sat silent, or whispered conversation with Tyrryal. He avoided Gabriel's eyes with shame Gabriel did not understand. Tyrryal's motivations were still unclear to Gabriel. More so, Tyrryal's connection to the boy was unnerving. Perhaps it was Gabriel's fault. He had kept Kamiel at arm's length. Kamiel was a reflection of his father and perhaps Gabriel considered the boy a threat as a result.

A cry let him know they were close to the harbour and Gabriel paced furiously. Tyrryal helped the crew bring the ship to dock. Thirty one days Gabriel had measured, if time moved the same in Avalon as it did here. When they finally had anchored and docked, Tyrryal and Gabriel had to restrain Kamiel from bolting ahead.

They stood on the pier surveying the crumbling destitute that was Rubar.

"I don't think the lad needs to be present when we deal with Braxis," Tyrryal offered.

"I agree," Gabriel turned to Kamiel, "you can find Artemesia. If you run into trouble, call for us. The last thing we need is hot headed antics getting you killed."

Kamiel nodded, looked at Tyrryal, and then ran to find Artemesia as fast as he could.

"Let's deal with Braxis quickly," Gabriel insisted.

"We find a place, first. We sup, then we try and locate him quietly so we don't tip the beast off, causing him to harm the young miss and Kamiel."

Gabriel glowered at Tyrryal.

"Don't go changing back to ether either, it'll tip the network of them here off."

"Network?" Gabriel raised an eyebrow.

"Aye, there is a whole lot of the fallen here."

"And how can you sense them without drawing notice?"

"I walk the Shadow lands."

Gabriel eyed him suspiciously. The Shadow lands were a twisted mess of grey territory between all worlds. The Crone ruled there and she answered to no one.

Tyrryal headed confidently up a street. Gabriel's skin crawled. Rubar smelled of rotting fish and mold with decrepit buildings and crumbling cobblestone. It would not have been hard to guess it was a centre for the fallen without Tyrryal's demon radar. They had little care of anything but themselves. Gabriel bet the mayor of Rubar he saw on posters covering horse ties and buildings was fallen himself, judging by the slogans. He had to find the beast and get the hell out of here.

The inn Tyrryal found was not much better than the rest of the town but at least it wasn't dank and rotting. Gabriel appreciated the dry cot and a few hours rest, having slept poorly on the voyage here. He doubted sleep would return to him until he was back in Avalon with Adamina. He tried to reach for her and found silence. The distance from Avalon must have strained their connection, he reasoned. He sighed, frustrated.

Gabriel sat up, feverish with restlessness. Tyrryal was where he had been, sitting by the fire at a small table.

"Don't you sleep?"

"I don't need sleep, old timer."

Gabriel shot a deadly look at the bulky Angel.

"My sources tell me he will be in the alleys on the west-side. Kamiel let me know he is safe, as is the young miss. They are lodged to the north, overlooking the harbour."

Gabriel studied Tyrryal with distrust. Tyrryal figured he had better clear up this mess of seething suspicion or they would never find Braxis. He couldn't get the bloody bastard without Gabriel's help. Besides the man's brooding was giving him a blasted headache.

"My loyalties lie with no one but myself. I am not reporting back to Uriel or God, so you can rest easy, be sure. I am here to ensure the safety of Kamiel and Adamina's young miss. She is a friend and has been kind to me, I owe her much. Avalon isn't just a refuge for you, old man. I call it home too now. I was wanted by her bane husband for disobeying. She kept me alive last time he was around, said I had Uriel's best interests at heart by defending his family from harm. He let me alone because of her. I owe her much."

Tyrryal sighed at the expression on Gabriel's face and continued, "If we can't trust each other, you and I, Braxis will surely escape. You have my word no harm will come to Adamina or her ilk by my hand. Now stop your bloody brooding and scrutinizing me. I'm going to fill my stomach on the inn keep's stew, then head out hunting the fallen. You are either with me or in my way."

Tyrryal left the room and stomped down the stairs towards the commons, more from his bulk than his mood. Gabriel wasn't far behind. They sat downing mead and stew in silence. After the last morsel was finished and the fare settled, the two men slipped into the night to find their target.

It was dead silent, a near ghost town around the inn. They kept to the shadows of the streets, mud and muck squelching beneath their boots. It took them nearly an hour to reach west-side and half that to find the general area Tyrryal's contacts had indicated. There were pubs and brothels packing every square block in this section. The noise emanating from them would be good cover. Tyrryal leaned against a lamp post, looking comfortable while Gabriel stood on edge nearby. They waited for another hour before Braxis showed his face. Tyrryal had been right. Half a dozen fallen had ambled past the Angels as they waited. Finally, their quarry strolled out of a brothel and turned into an alley.

Gabriel cursed and Tyrryal's hand shot out, holding him back.

"This is good for us. A quiet spot, secluded from view. You go in the same way he went. I will come around back."

Gabriel pushed Tyrryal's hand away and followed Braxis up the alley. They had already wasted too much time here. It was three hours to sun rise and he was going to deal with this devil swiftly. Tyrryal's assistance not required. Tyrryal shook his head and sunk into shadow, moving himself into position.

Braxis was at the end of the alley, about to turn out of sight so Gabriel drew his attention.

"Hey, fallen. I've got a message for you," Gabriel rolled up the sleeves of his shirt as he stalked forward.

Braxis turned around, his dark eyes making his grin all the more sinister. He was twice the size of Gabriel, all muscle and menace. He laughed a low roiling laugh.

"God has a message for me, boy?"

Gabriel swung, putting all his pent up frustration behind it and plunged his fist into Braxis' abdomen, "He has nothing to do with it."

Braxis recovered quickly. Gabriel almost wasn't fast enough as he dodged the retaliation.

"Alright, fine. You don't want to play nice?"

Gabriel wrenched at his power and with an electric snap through the air pushed it towards Braxis. It hit the beast square in the chest and crackled around his body. It drew into Braxis' abdomen and disappeared. Braxis stood unaffected.

"Well then…"

Braxis took a step forward then froze. A sword sliced through the air and Braxis flew backwards, vanishing into darkness. The darkness closed in on itself and disappeared. Tyrryal stood their holding a sword. With a flick of his wrist the sword evaporated away.

"You could have told me," Gabriel snapped.

"I needed you to distract him. Which you did."

Gabriel harrumphed at Tyrryal, prepping a retaliation.

"Let's get going, something's wrong on Avalon."

Tyrryal pushed past Gabriel and raced toward the harbour, hailing the captain boarding a boat ready to sail. Gabriel kept pace close behind. He had not been paying attention to the way they had come and had no idea how to get from here back to Avalon. His senses were strained. Even if he returned to ether, there was no guarantee he would return in time.

"What about Kamiel?"

"He's staying with the young miss, I fear."

Gabriel hesitated.

"Come on! They'll be fine. I'll come back and check on them later."

The boat had already pulled away from the dock and Tyrryal clutched at Gabriel's arm, hoisting him up on deck. The entire voyage home Gabriel paced, wearing the planks smooth, when he was not working to keep his hands busy. Terror gripped his heart and he hoped to find Adamina safe and at home with the children. Tyrryal said he did not know what, but something was wrong. Tyrryal would not elaborate how he knew this. He would never betray Kamiel's confidence in him.

Gabriel's lack of connection to Adamina nearly drove him mad. The voyage had taken twice as long as it should have due to rough winds and cargo drops. The shores of Avalon finally appeared on the horizon one dawn. The hour it took to reach the harbour nearly killed him.

"ARTEMESIA, I WILL NOT leave you. I will not return unless you do," Kamiel insisted.

"Your place is in Avalon, just leave me be!" Artemesia whirled away from her brother.

Gabriel and Tyrryal had dealt with Braxis. What that actually meant, Artemesia did not want to speculate. Artemesia had known he was dangerous, but she did not discover how dangerous until Kamiel had explained the truth of the man's nature to her. It sent chills down her spine as Kamiel described his particular specialty. Braxis was skilled at collecting souls and consuming them for their powers. She had been next on the list. If his muscular brutish form had attempted such a feat, however, he would surely be disappointed. She held no special powers. The best she could do was a bit of basic herb work, just like any of the other women on Avalon.

Artemesia sighed as she stared out the upper floor window of a small apartment they had rented. This place was so different from Avalon. Tall skinny houses adorned with decorative colors and fixtures, people running through cobblestone streets, even the occasional carriage hurried by. Life, this place thrived with it, and convenience and fashion. She loved the unique hats of the olive colored people that lived here. The hats would hide her slightly pointed ears and make a great statement with a new wardrobe. Braxis had left a considerable sum in her control. She smiled at her freedom.

She never cared for Braxis. He was a means to an end. She would never admit it, but she was grateful Gabriel, Tyrryal and Kamiel had shown up. The man, fallen Angel she corrected herself, had become brutish. The bruises from their last encounter were secured under a bodice and ample skirts. She would be more careful next time. Her bare feet were cold on smooth wooden flooring. She moved about to return warmth into her extremities.

Kamiel stood by the door, steadfast like a soldier. His dark hair very much like her own. In fact, much of Kamiel's features mirrored hers. Like her's, his cheekbones were high and his face was wide. His nose was less slight then her own and his eyes were amethyst, but even a passer-by could tell they were kin. He did not, however, have her pointed ears and she envied him for that. They had their purpose, when luring clients. Many thought she was of fantastical race, a treasure, and they would pay higher prices for exotic tastes. The last thing she needed was a brother chasing away clients.

"Go back to where you belong, Kamiel," she insisted.

"I belong there no more than you do, sister, and you know it," Kamiel returned.

She did know. She knew that he had always stayed to the edges of the family, grateful to Adamina for taking him in, but always, like herself, feeling not quite at home. No, she could not send him back. If their roles were reversed, he never would have sent her back. Gabriel had promised not to force her to return, but advised that mother was worried sick about her. It may lessen her mother's worry to know her and Kamiel were together.

"Very well, but you earn your keep. I won't be supporting the both of us."

He nodded with a slight smile, "I knew you would say that. I have secured employment, sister, on the passage here. A lord asked me to his service and I accepted. He also offered that he required a new gardener and herb-woman."

Artemesia hid her indignation. She calmed her emotions. This was a new start for her. She would not carry the past forward with her. She was, however, still very upset that he had secured tempting work that ensured her safety. He had played on her weakness for working the soil, growing plants, and healing and cooking. She would have a solid job doing what she loved. She would probably get grand quarters and could secure fine clothing. Not to mention the Lord's estate could be brimming with eligible knights and workmen. Maybe a nobleman or two would take notice. Suddenly her future seemed full of brighter possibilities. She nodded at her brother and they left together to secure a table at the pub below her apartment.

"I am starving, and you are buying."

Kamiel nodded with a smile and summoned the server to take their orders. Tyrryal and Gabriel were already on their way back and he had told them he would stay with his sister and ensure her safety. He hoped mother was alright.

THREE LONG MOONS. HE swore to himself. Raphael, for the first time in his existence, had wished he had chosen to be a warrior instead of a healer. It wasn't as if he could have chosen that path for himself. If he had Gabriel's strength and training, he would have stormed into the house and removed Uriel from Avalon permanently. Blasted brothers, they were more trouble than they were worth. He paced the main floor hall in a foul mood. They were running out of stores. Where the hell was Gabriel? As if in answer, the water whispered loudly in his ears and Raphael's head shot up.

"Stay here, do not let anyone in," Raphael insisted to Palla and raced out the door.

Where the hell have you been?

In Rubar Bay, eliminating Braxis to save little Mesia. The seas did not cooperate on the return home. Where is Adamina? What happened, I can't find her. I can't sense her anywhere.

Is Mesia safe now? At Gabriel's nod Raphael continued, *Adamina is…. Uriel is back, he has been here since shortly after you left. Bastard took advantage of the opening I guess. And worse, Lucifer has gotten to him, Gabriel. You have to help her. I think she is still alive, he wants that blasted son after all. I've had the children and others holed up in the priestess house. Gabriel, I can't reach her. She's either closed her mind off, or she's…*

She has to be alive or he wouldn't still be there.

Panic pulsed through him. Gabriel raced towards the house where Uriel held Adamina captive. He prayed she was still alive. He scolded himself for ever leaving her. This was all his fault. He would end Uriel's mortal coil this time. If he came back, he would kill him again and again until they could find another way to be rid of the damned Archangel. He pushed against the ethereal barriers. They tore like barbed wire but he didn't care. He kicked in the front door. Uriel had been sitting down to dinner in the dining room for his evening meal.

"You," Uriel stood up.

Gabriel shot out a hand and magically held his brother in place. An Angel never used his powers against another. But Gabriel would make the exception. If Angelichood meant allowing his kind to use other living creatures, other mortals as play things, violating their freewill and increasing suffering, Gabriel wanted nothing to do with it. Had the world gone to the Hells?

"Where is she?"

Uriel only smirked and stared at Gabriel. A small whimper he wasn't sure he had actually heard came from a large chest at the end of the room.

"Dear God."

He could not believe it, did not want to believe. Was Uriel truly that depraved and far gone? Gabriel raised his hand higher and commanded the air not to release Uriel, then turned his attention to freeing Adamina. Uriel's wards broken, the chest began to glow and hum with the power of Avalon. Gabriel tore at the iron lock, crushing it and wrenching it free with one hand. He threw the lid open. A greatly emaciated and pregnant Adamina lay in the fetal position. The children inside of her suffocated her slowly as they pushed against her lungs. Gabriel gently lifted Adamina out of the chest and sat her in a nearby chair. She took in a deep breath and coughed, but she was so weak she was unable to open her eyes or keep herself up.

Tyrryal burst through the door. He had lingered behind at the pier to take care of some business with the blacksmith.

"What the hell is going on?"

At the sight of Adamina in Gabriel's arms and Uriel held in place by Gabriel's magic, Tyrryal raged. Tyrryal was a big man in mortal form. Larger than all his kindred, it was a terrifying sight to see him angry. Tyrryal ignored the smirk on Uriel's face as he pulled a sword of swirling shadow from thin air, and cut. He cut through Avalon into a world of darkness and torment. This was his gift, justice dealt to those who deserved it. There were worlds like this just for his use that no one else could access. Worlds that Darkness and Agony and God had gifted him. He could not kill Uriel, but he could seal him there for a very long time. The floor gaped open and swallowed Uriel up, sealing behind him. After a long silence, Tyrryal tuned into Gabriel's utterances.

"Adamina, please. Adamina, please look at me darling," Gabriel begged her.

She was not responding and her breathing had stopped. He could feel the children, another set of twins, slowly losing oxygen as well.

"Tyrryal, get Raphael, now!" Gabriel commanded and Tyrryal obeyed for once, carrying his bulk swiftly out the door to get the healer.

He was losing her. He could feel her life slip away. He was not sure he could save her this time. Raphael burst through the doors. Tears streamed down Gabriel's face as his amber eyes begged Raphael to save her if what he was about to do didn't work. He would not be here to help her if it failed. He stood up tall and nodded to Raphael then his body began to dissolve into Amber light until Gabriel returned to ether.

Floating there, looking down at her, Gabriel merged himself completely with Adamina. Angels did not die, could not be killed. They were pure energy. But they could fracture apart, or, their energy could be used up until there was nothing left. Gabriel did not care if this risked his existence. He would save Adamina or end his existence. He would not live without her.

Raphael rushed to Adamina's side. He pushed down his feelings of guilt and anger and set to work. Four lives now hanged in the balance and Raphael was damned if he would lose even one of them.

17

*Y*OUR SON HAS BECOME *a force of destruction, I can't keep up. The rifts are growing!* Time sat with the Others. His robes billowed around him, although there was no wind to stir them.

You think you have problems? Try maintaining balance in the universe when all sorts of creatures and energies are being twisted, turned, and released to cause chaos. I don't even think Chaos could keep up with him! Balance protested. Her shadowed side had become stronger, and her light had begun to fade, *not to mention what it has done to my hair!*

Chaos himself had been unable to attend this gathering due to a sudden increase in godly duties. He never passed up the opportunity to stir up the council of gods.

The Fates rolled their eyes, if they could be said to have any eyes, *Bala you don't actually have hair.*

Balance narrowed her eyes at The Fates. Today they decided that a purple, glowing, translucent mass with black orb-like ocular spheres best represented them. She curled her delicate nose in disgust and the Fates glared at her. They were constantly scheming and making her life difficult.

If there is any more darkness bred in the universe, I fear I may explode! Darkness lumbered in, much unlike his usual flowing self. His belly was round and swollen.

Light whispered, words were barely audible and everyone had to strain to hear its complaints and fears as it shifted and shimmered, unstable. Lucifer's antics had affected light as well, and not for the better. Light gave up trying to be heard and wondered what Physics would think, if Physics could just pull themselves together. All of the gods broke out shouting protests except Agony who had been having a quiet discussion off to one corner with the honorable Justice. Agony wanted more control over wars now that Lucifer's injustices were keeping Justice too busy to keep up. Agony rejoiced trying to convince the Others that this was a good thing. He was the only one, it seemed, to benefit from the renegade Angel's antics and his optimism did not go over well. They all began to turn on him.

Hush all, peace, murmured Goddess and the room fell silent. *Well, what do you have to say, my consort?* She stood there, a vision of moonlight and peace, waiting and silently praying for a break in this session to check on Avalon and fix the weakening wards. The meeting had been continuing for too long, but if she slipped away now, God would suspect and he would surly find Avalon then. In her opinion, the apple did not fall far from the father tree. She gazed at him and felt sadness at his pride. It was his turn to chair the debates, however, so she had deferred the room back to him. The Others stood gazing in expectation. God sat for a long time in a throne of gold, his form was that of a great tree with a face. He shifted form to a bi-pedal clad in armor of dragon scales, magnificent and intimidating, and, stepped down from his throne. It dissolved into mist behind him as he trod the room in circles with authority.

My friends, it is one fallen Angel throwing a tantrum.

How could he possibly cause so much damage? Surely you can prevent him from such tantrums in each of your domains? Fates, what say you of Lucifer.

Lucifer is the son of gods, his spirit, however is at odds. He shall troll the worlds and fill them with hate, the force of Destruction of himself he makes.

Balance rolled her eyes at the dramatics of the Fates then turned her attention to God. If she did not know better, she would say he had gone pale. He waved his hand in a dismissive fashion.

An Angel can be nothing more than an Angel.

Tell that to Time, he will have to run linear for centuries just to get everything straightened out!

They started up again, voices filling the space with a great raucous.

Enough! Enough! God shouted shaking the auditorium, *I will sort it out one way or another. Leave it to me.*

Glances of skepticism passed between a few of the Others, but most nodded. Everyone returned to their duties, leaving Goddess in a quiet contemplation alone. If she was mortal, she was sure she would have a headache with it all. She sighed softly. Lucifer was not her responsibility since God had taken over the Angels. She could not return to Avalon just yet, God was still suspicious of her, so she reached to the farthest worlds in the universe and decided to watch over them for a while. She needed the stretch.

HE WAS HUMMING, JOYFUL despite the walk through a grey covered world. A sinister grin playing across his lips. Clouds floated above and covered the world in grey; threatening rain, but never delivering, keeping the city in that dreary, oppressive, in-between state. He tipped his hat at a pair of gorgeous birds in luscious cloth and was rewarded by cooing and shy-clucking behind fans. He was at his most dandy: clean, crisp and well dressed.

His coal black, double-breasted frockcoat was tailored to his tall, gorgeous physique. His blood-red cravat was impeccably knotted. The high collared shirt boasted a tone of grey more vibrant and lush than seemed possible. His trousers clung to the muscles that graced his powerful legs. The gloom and doom he had been dealing was running smoothly, but it wasn't enough for him to unleash half-Angel brats, twist existing creatures to make them more, and release the hellish hounds. It was never enough.

He needed more. More power, more strength. Father had stripped his powers as much as he could. What little remained, Lucifer fed and grew on darker powers. Unfortunately, forming a body without Angelic mastery over the basic physical elements made it much more difficult. Instead he opted for the illusion of a form that had substance from the sheer density of the darkness he had accumulated. And what a grand glamour it was.

But it was not enough. He wanted his mastery of the elements back. He wanted a magnificent body at his command, wanted to pour acids from the skies of worlds, ignite fires with a thought, drown and suffocate with a flick of his hand. With Avalon, that would be possible. In Avalon, he did not have to strain, the place practically created a form for him. It was saturated with raw, untouched elements. It vibrated with raw magic. And he had met the key to unlocking it all.

She was a gorgeous woman. The last of her kind Uriel, had advised him. Lucifer was a collector of unique objects. It was a shame that taking Avalon required her to be tortured so unskillfully at the hands of his bumbling brother. A simple sacrifice for something much greater.

Perhaps he could resurrect her and make her queen of his dark world, he mused to himself. Twist her into a glory of a dark goddess, if he had time. He just had to bide his time a little longer and Avalon would be his.

"PLEASE COME WITH ME."

"Don't ask me that again. I can't, you know I can't."

At the look on his face and the taste of his emotions, she sighed and fought against the tears.

"I can take you from here. We can go where he won't ever find you, or the children," Gabriel pleaded with Adamina.

"You said he was locked away somewhere, didn't you?"

Gabriel pursed his lips and remained silent.

"If Uriel is locked away in some other place," Adamina continued, "then I do not see what the problem is!"

She was scrubbing at the dishes furiously. A strong, gentle hand caressed her arm and gentle lips kissed up her neck. He would get nowhere trying to convince her in fear, perhaps his love would do the trick.

"I can't ensure he will stay there forever my love," Gabriel explained softly and rested his head on her shoulders, wrapping his arms around her protectively.

"Who would release him from there? Surely not Tyrryal or yourself, nor Raphael."

Gabriel stayed silent. He was darn sure that Lucifer would do just that. Gabriel was afraid Avalon, and Adamina, would fall into the wrong hands. He did not think her weak or unable to protect herself. She had power she could not even imagine. He wasn't even sure of its limits, if there were any. But a body was fragile and Lucifer relished an easy fix.

Realizing he had been raising his voice in his emotion, he softened his tone, "Uriel will return, Mina. Lucifer will see to that. You know he is not well and he refuses to return to ether and help himself."

She paused her scrubbing of dishes, "I know Gabriel," she sighed, "please do not ask me to leave my home. Even with you, I cannot."

"At least let me train you to protect yourself."

Adamina turned and looked at him questioningly.

"You have gifts, like your children. Your people were born with magic in their veins, but you only have touched the surface. You can use these gifts to protect yourself and the children. He will return, Mina. I could not forgive myself if he harmed you again."

"Alright, when do we start?"

He pulled her away from the chores she was doing, "You should be resting my dear. It has been a long day. We will start tomorrow."

Turning her to face him, he planted a gentle kiss on her luxurious lips. He felt her melt and relax into him. He murmured her name and she kissed him back. Her smile interrupted the moment and she leaned away from him. That smile said all that needed to be said, ever. He would give up everything to grow old and die with her. She was a grace he had never fathomed could exist. He got lost in her eyes. They were the most complex swirling of greens and browns. Through her eyes he plunged down the connection he had forged that fateful night, and glimpsed her soul. Goddess had put a divine spark in her. The training would prepare her, but he knew it would not ease the worry in his heart. Losing her would destroy him. A cacophony of screaming youth rolled into the kitchen, breaking their reverie.

"Sh-Rah, give back!" Sheehan demanded with tears in his eyes. He was several inches shorter than his twin sister. His twin sister, the near replica of Artemesia with amethyst eyes, was hanging his blanket in the air away from him. Big brown little-boy eyes filled with impending water-works complimented by a little-boy lip quiver.

"Shira honey, it's not nice to tease your brother. Please give him his blanket back," Adamina asked, walking over to the two toddlers.

The little girl returned the blanket to her brother with a sigh.

"Bad Shra," Sheehan said and snatched it from her with a glare.

"I sawry Sha-an," Shira hugged her twin, "Don cry."

She poked her brother in his side to tickle him and he stopped sucking his thumb to giggle. They began a game of tag, racing through the house. Adamina smiled after them. Aside from a strong streak of trickster and their dark hair, the twins had nothing of the darkness of their father in them. She wondered if staying on Avalon was the right decision. Maybe she should tell Gabriel they would go to another land and live there safely, where Uriel could never find them again. Avalon hummed below her like a purring cat soothing a distressed owner. No, she had to stay here. This was her home.

Leaving Avalon meant abandoning the priestesses. It meant giving up Pagan's house and the only home she had ever known. She could not do that, but she could fight for it. She yawned and a strand fell out of the thong tying her hair back. She brushed it out of her face and Gabriel placed a hand on her lower-back.

"To bed with you," he urged with a smile.

As the twins barreled near them again, Adamina scooped up Shira, who was in the lead, and Gabriel snatched Sheehan up.

"Time for bed everyone," Gabriel called out, his voice booming love through the house.

Several protests and mumbles followed.

"Do we haf to mama?" Sheehan asked.

"Yes dear," she kissed him on the cheek, "don't worry, you'll be safe from the darkness."

Sheehan had terrible nightmares about creatures in the darkness making him do bad things. He would run down the hall screaming on several occasions over the past couple months. Leaving the lamp lit in his room seemed to calm the nightmares, as did Gabriel's wards and dream walks. Morgana stormed up the stairs in moody protest, flaming red hair trailing out behind her. Gabriel and Adamina exchanged looks.

"She's your daughter," Adamina teased.

Gabriel narrowed his eyes with a smirk on his lips, "I distinctly remember you being there for the moment of her creation as well."

Adamina blushed slightly, but returned the knowing smirk back. She followed in her daughters footsteps, without the stomping and emotions.

"Gana!" Shira called, stretching her arms out towards her older sister.

Morgana's foul mood lightened and she scooped her sister out of Adamina's arms to tuck her in bed. Gabriel went about making sure Sheehan was snug in his own bed. Adamina wondered down the hall to check on the others. Aera and Mora decided they were sleeping at the priestess house now. They were young women and Adamina knew she could not force them to stay here. She paused at the doorway of the empty room and her heart ached for them. Doubts about how she had raised them slithered in. If she had made mistakes that would cost them less than the best in the world…

"Not a chance," Nerina's soft voice interjected her thoughts.

Adamina turned around and they embraced each other. She was so indebted to her daughter for the care and attention Nerina had put into the family and the priestess house. She had come such a long way and Raphael's teaching had left her in control of her gifts. Nerina could bring or stave off the rains, raise water from the ground, even cause the river to slow or hurry. If it wasn't for Nerina, they may have starved last summer. The drought on Avalon had been so terrible that she had to draw mists around the island up into rain for the land.

"Oh my dear water-girl, if there is anything I can do to ease your pain…"

"I know mother," Nerina stepped out of the embrace. But there wasn't anything to ease that kind of pain. Only love and time would heal the wound.

"I wonder if I made the right decision about Eli. And how can I forgive father for what he did to you?"

"I can't answer those questions for you Nerina," Adamina steered Nerina to her bedroom.

"But I can tell you that clinging on to anger can help us cope, but if we cling too long, it can destroy the good inside of us. You my dear have a lot of good. I would hate to see it smothered by anger," Adamina rubbed Nerina's back.

Nerina smiled sadly back at her mother, "Goodnight."

"Goodnight."

The door clicked quietly shut behind Nerina. Mother and daughter sighed softly. Nerina would spend another fitful night trying to rest as her mind and heart did battle.

"I wish I could ease her pain," Adamina said softly to Gabriel who had come up behind her.

"You do all that you can and that helps," Gabriel kissed her on the cheek.

It was her turn to be steered towards the bedroom. Adamina smiled. It astounded her how she could find joy after such horrors had happened in her life. She was sure the man with the hand slowly sliding further down her back was the big reason for that. She swatted his hand away and shook her head at him with a smile.

"What? I can't appreciate the love of my life?" Gabriel

whined as he closed their bedroom door.

She smiled and wrapped her arms around him, curling close and connecting their bodies in that pleasant puzzle that fit just right. He caressed her hair and held her to him. This room, their room, their home, he observed silently. He had converted the extra bedroom into their new master suite over twelve moons ago. The memories of Uriel clung to the old one, which was locked and shut up again. He had begun the plans for building a new home for them, where their cabin was, and would surprise Adamina with it as soon as he had completed it. Then he would burn this house and the terrible memories it held to the ground the second he could.

They were making new memories. Joyful ones that shone brightly and chased away the shadows. He playfully chased his wife into the bed, rolling her in kisses and caresses, wrapping her up in the quilt and blankets. His wife he thought with a smile. They did not need a ceremony to tell them that. They had quietly committed their lives to each other in the night. The light of a moon had glared above and the soft grass of a meadow had lay below them. Oh yes, they were making memories. He would make one tonight with her. A memory of love so strong it would chase away that pain that always lurked under the surface of her gaze. He could feel the echo of her heart beat as if it was in his own chest.

He could hear the soft inhalations and exhalations. Her skin tasted like ocean air and honey. She smelled of wildflowers and soil. He rememorized every curve of her body: the way she felt, her scent, how she tasted. He reveled in how her body had changed over time. He would sear those memories into him and clutch them to his heart forever. Tonight, and every night, he would reaffirm their love, their commitment for as long as he had with her. The time would have to be enough.

He had taken to cursing mortality, wishing it for

himself. As she aged and her hair became silver, he became more aware of time's toll, and how he could not go with her when her time was up. He pushed the thought away and reveled in the moment with her. She made him weak. She made him. Together they climbed to the clouds, and together they fell, wrapped in each other's arms. They tumbled softly into the bed and pillows again, the satisfaction sucking them down into a deep slumber together. Safe, loved, and complete they sailed the world of dreams and into the break of a new day in paradise.

"WE WILL MOVE TO something more difficult. Block me out of your mind," Gabriel instructed.

They stood in the meadow at mid-day. Adamina had been a quick study. Gabriel had taught her some hand to hand defenses and she liked knowing she could do something to protect herself.

You're daydreaming, Mina. Focus.

I can't block you out. You are always there at the back of my mind. I don't want to block you out.

Focus! He forced his energy on her, forced himself into her mind, becoming the General of an Army he was.

You're scaring me!

Uriel will not be kind. Now block me out.

He started berating her mind with thoughts and words and images and noise. She built the barriers like he had instructed, pulled them tight around her and solidified them. The discordance ceased.

"Well done."

He plunged forward, furiously trying to tear at her barrier. She gasped and stepped back from the force of it and he wrenched a hole.

"Keep it up against me!" He shouted furiously.

She struggled to build what he tore at, build a second barrier, but her emotions ran away with her and she lost control, falling to her knees sobbing. He dropped his assault and fought within himself. General or lover. Sternness or compassion. He had been driving her hard and she had done better than most in his squadron had. This was a side of him he had not wanted to resurrect with her, it could be ruthless. He inhaled and pushed the General away and reached for his woman.

"Forgive me Mina. I have pushed too hard for fear of losing you to him."

He sat beside her, cradling her and caressing her hair. Slowly, she regained her composure and steadied her breathing.

"Again."

"What?"

She pushed him away and stood, "Again. I asked you to treat me like those Angels you trained. You would not show compassion to them during training. I will not fail again." She stared at him determined.

He nodded and flung out a hand as he stood, pushing her backwards. She stood up right and slid some distance away, then stopped as she deflected his force away from her. He felt the barriers go up and he attacked again, tearing at the defenses of her mind. He was relentless and they did not stop until dusk slid the sun away behind the horizon. She was soaked in sweat and her muscles were shaking from the effort she had expended.

"You did well, love," he reached for her and she pushed him away, her mind still guarded against him, her eyes cold. He feared he had turned her into one of his soldiers and he grasped at her tightly, whispering her name over and over. She struggled at first but the coldness slowly left her eyes and the battle–ready walls came down again. Soon she was his Mina, weak and shaky, but he could hear her and feel her inside of him again. He held her a while longer until she regained her strength and they returned home for the evening. She stumbled twice and he resisted the urge to catch her. She needed to be aware of her own strength even in this weakened state. From what he saw, she rivaled any Angel he knew.

He bathed her carefully after supper and carried her to bed, pulling the covers tight around her before he went to check on the children. Sleep took her quickly.

"Is there a limit to her?" Raphael asked softly.

Gabriel closed the door behind him to muffle their conversation, "If there is, I haven't found it yet."

"Aside from mortality."

Gabriel winced at that, "How are the children?"

"Fed and most are in bed, the ones that should be anyway. Mora and Aera are training with Michael tonight. Their abilities are more up his alley. Sheehan and Shira should be having their lessons in about a year, as you know. Nerina is at the priestess house ensuring everything is in order. Morgana is helping her. Any word from Kamiel and Artemesia?"

Gabriel shook his head, "I'm going to work on the house."

He turned and left, a war inside himself and Raphael shook his head. It was a fool Angel that tied himself to a mortal. He had learned that the hard way himself. Some wounds never heal no matter what you do with them. Raphael settled himself on the couch for an evening doze. He would be in the kitchen bright and early the next morning to feed the never ending hunger of children. Adamina deserved a break and he would be surprised if she woke before mid-day.

18

A *DAMINA…*
She became aware of a voice calling her and opened one eye. Odd, Gabriel wasn't there beside her. The house was quiet and the sun was hidden behind clouds. She wasn't sure how far the day had progressed yet. She yawned and stretched, rolling back up in blankets and closing her eyes again. She began to drift down into sleep once more, slowly falling into its resting embrace.

Adamina!

She sat up alert.

Hello?

Adamina, Adamina, Adamina!

She tore out of bed and got dressed. She raced down the stairs and out the door. No one was around. Gabriel must have taken the children to the priestess house.

Adamina, come here, the voice whispered in her mind again.

Gabriel?

Hurry.

Where?

Hurry, hurry, hurry.

Adamina dashed off in the direction she felt the voice calling from.

Hurry, hurry, hurry! The voice urged.

She ran. Her legs carried her through the trees, past the brook, nearer and nearer the harbor. The splash of the ocean against the cliffs roared in her ears. She was near the edge of the island. She burst through the trees into a clearing and froze. This was where she had first met Lucifer. She had not realized she was avoiding it until now. She looked around frantically, spinning in a circle.

"Gabriel?" she called out.

"Try again."

Fear clutched her in its grasp. She knew that voice all too well. She turned in its direction.

"Hello," he stood there with a smirk on his face.

"Oh God," she stepped back quickly.

"Nay, not God, my dear," joy and threat danced in Uriel eyes.

"Gabr…"

Uriel cut off her scream with a lightning fast move. He covered her mouth with his hand and held her back to his chest, locking his arm around her waist. She called out with her mind.

Gabriel!

"Stay silent."

"Thank you for containing her, Uriel."

Lucifer stepped from the shadows of the trees. Adamina's eyes narrowed with loathing and anger.

"Hello Adamina! How nice it is to meet you again."

Lucifer nodded and waved his hand at Uriel. He let her go. She stumbled forward in between the two Angels. She searched for a way to escape them.

"I come to ask you again, Adamina," Lucifer cooed, "Give me the power of Avalon."

"I wouldn't even if I could," Adamina spat back.

In the blink of an eye he stood a breath away from

her, "Don't say I didn't ask."

Lucifer placed his hand in the center of her torso and yanked at the energy there. Adamina tried to fight and pull away, but Uriel had moved to hold her in place again.

"I will have Avalon."

Pain seared through her and her eyes grew wide. Uriel clamped a hand around her mouth to muffle her screams. Lucifer pulled and sucked her magic, her energy, her life out of her body into one glowing green orb of power. It was a long process taking several minutes, but he could wait. He had all the time in the universe.

PAIN. HIS HEAD SHOT up and looked in her direction. Across the island Gabriel ceased his building and paused to listen. The frame for their new home was almost completed. With a whisper on the wind of his name, he raced across the island in a panic. He felt the life slowly draining from her. He felt Avalon scream. *No, no, no,* his mind raced. He ran as fast as he could and burst through into that fateful clearing.

She lay on the grass. Her hand was folded across her chest in a futile protective gesture. She wasn't breathing. Gabriel couldn't sense her soul anymore.

Uriel was crouched over her and Lucifer stood holding a green orb in his palm.

"Gabriel, I am glad you could join us," Lucifer greeted him.

Shock forced him to stay silent, unable to process his surroundings. Then it hit him full force and Gabriel screamed, lashing out. Uriel caught Gabriel and tried forcing him back. They grappled. Gabriel won the struggle, pushing Uriel away and to the ground with a boot to his head. Before Gabriel could plunge the heavenly sword he had conjured in his hand into Uriel's chest, the coward disappeared into a mist and floated away.

"What a greeting for your dear brother, Gabriel," Lucifer gave him a look of mock disappointment.

Gabriel stood there seething and mourning, looking for the opening. Battle took hold and he stepped forward, sword ablaze with holy fire and ready. Gabriel's eyes were aflame with fury. Wings stretched out of his back, black with promise. Lucifer clenched his hand around Adamina's life-force and began absorbing it into himself. Gabriel could not attack for fear of fracturing her essence. Helpless, he stood there the tears burning up in heavenly fire before they had a chance to fall.

"Lucifer, no!" Gabriel reached out toward the Shamed One, beseeching.

Lucifer's physical body tingled and shivered at the warmth and the sensation of the power sinking past the surface to his core. And then it was gone.

"What!" Lucifer looked about him.

The power had just disappeared. Her life and the magic of Avalon had just disappeared.

"That's impossible!" Lucifer yelled, he looked to his brother and then looked below him, taking a step back.

The grass beneath his feet died off, the death spread outwards quickly. Lightning snapped above them and thunder roared and moaned. A fire started in the woods behind him, racing towards Lucifer. Rage swelled inside Lucifer. He should have the power over the elements. He should have control over Avalon. He should be a god! Instead, the woman's essence had just vanished and the blasted island turned on him. He narrowed his eyes at Gabriel and then shimmered away. Gabriel screamed and lunged, missing his brother as he fled. Tears and smoke burned his eyes and he threw the sword away in anger. The flame disappeared the second it left his hands. He plummeted to Adamina's side.

"Adamina," Gabriel gently lifted her head, wings sagged behind him.

"Adamina, please, Adamina," Gabriel sobbed and shook her, "wake up. It's time to go home now."

But no response would come again. He hugged her tightly to him and wrapped his wings over her. *Adamina!* Around him Avalon stormed and burned, died and dried up. Inside, Gabriel wished for death. He looked to the heavens as tears fell down his face. Then an idea slid into his head. He gently placed Adamina's body back on the ground and stood up. With a beat of his wings he soared up into the clouds wracked with lightning. He dissolved away the mortal coil and returned to the realm of the gods one last time.

I AM SORRY.

He fell. He clutched her to his heart. He would find her. He had to. The memories slipped away a little and he clung on harder.

I cannot bring her back. Instead, I can, however, make you mortal, my son. You will be born again. I cannot guarantee the form, or when, or where, or even if you will ever find her again. Will you take that risk for a mortal? Would you give up everything?

Yes, he would. He must find her again. A life without her would be joyless, cold, and empty.

For her, I will.

So be it, Goddess whispered and with a kiss set him free.

Goddess mourned the loss of Avalon, but there was

hope. She let it rest and rebuilt it again. God had not found it. None of the Others cared to look for it any more. It was still her own. She had seen the glory of Avalon, the priestesses, the mists and Camelot. Yes, Avalon would rise and live and thrive. She had created without God, and done it well, and it had been an Angel that destroyed it.

A GREAT GREEN ORB floated toward her. She was in the gardens, alone. Nerina stood up to face the orb. It hovered for a moment a few feet in front of her, and then it revealed the translucent figure of her mother.

Do not be alarmed, my dear water-girl, Adamina smiled.

Nerina's eyes filled with tears.

Avalon is dying, I will stay here and keep it alive until you can take the others to safety. You must leave Avalon, my daughter. You must leave and grow and live. You will never be alone. I promise. I love you, Nerina.

Her mother's image and the green orb had disappeared. Lightning and thunder raged above her. She had no time to mourn. Avalon was dying. She ran. She yelled out to the others. Priestesses hurried, packing and herding young ones. Nerina sent others to the harbor. Children were ushered in a long line down to the coast. Boats were raising their anchors already.

Nerina looked toward the horizon and saw trees burning and bending. Life slinked out of Avalon, her home. Out of the forests walked many animals. She met the eyes of a stag.

"Bring the larger supplies here, strap it to the stag, the does, the larger animals," Nerina shouted.

Even as it was dying, Avalon provided for them.

Blessed Be Goddess, Nerina praised.

Children and women alike carried smaller animals. Birds perched on antlers and shoulders or flew above. The fish and deep sea-creatures had left the sea of Avalon already and slid into other worlds. In a hasty procession, animals and priestesses and children made their way to meet the men in the harbor, to load on to boats and to sail away. Away from Avalon.

"Nerina!"

She turned at the familiar voice calling her name.

"Eli?" Her heart leapt, "What are you doing here?"

"I came back for you. I couldn't live without you. What's going on?"

"I will explain later, come help me with the twins," Shira and Sheehan were huddling in the arms of Palla.

Nerina would take them with her and raise them, for mama, for Avalon. She would start another priestess house with Palla's help. With Eli, with Shira and Sheehan, she would build a family and a new kind of paradise. She stood at the bow of the ship, gazing over a dying island. Her heart ached for her home, for her mother. A tall looming figure stepped out of the smoke and Nerina strained to make it out.

"Gabriel!"

No, not Gabriel, but Tyrryal. His features became clear as he stepped onto the dock and pulled the plank up behind him.

"Nay, dear Nerina. Gabriel will be no more in your life. He has left to find your mother." At Nerina's quizzical look he elaborated, "They are to be reborn. He gave up heaven for her, lass. And once you lot are seen safely 'way, I'd be betting he started a bit of a trend."

Tyrryal smiled and winked, "Cast off!" he ordered the crew.

Tyrryal inclined his head towards the crew-men, "New recruits." Tyrryal began shouting orders and seeing that this lot got this hulking mass of wood out into the open waters and safely away from this world. Last out, Tyrryal sealed the mists of Avalon shut to let it destroy itself. He whispered a prayer on the wind for his dear friends, then set himself to the safe delivery of the cargo and crew to the nearest suitable port. He would follow his brother's footsteps just as soon as he saw the twins grown to handle the world themselves.

19

DARKNESS CLOSED IN. ASSURED that all of Adamina's children had escaped the island, Gabriel prepared for the final step on this part of his journey. Gabriel had to die. He burned with Avalon, in the cabin where they had first met. He felt his immortality stripped from him. If he could have screamed, he would have. But nothing was as bad as the agony he had felt at losing her.

Just as Gabriel believed he could bear no more, the agony lifted and he drifted in darkness for a while. He felt warmth blossom through his being. A fixed body, what would it be like? Unable to shift form, unable to exist as … as what? He couldn't quite remember. Panic rose in him, the need to escape. No, not escape he had to find something. He reached for a memory that wasn't within his grasp. Something was pounding in his head and heart and he focused on the beating. Heart beats, echoing heart beats, calmed him. He could hear murmurs, music, and laughter. Slowly, he lost all sense of self. He only knew warmth, safety of the mother.

A child with a vague sense of purpose fought his way into the world. He let out a bellow at the shock of cold and breath. Oh it was painful, but the needs of a young body quickly chased away the discomfort and scraps of memory. His mind a jumble of thoughts that no longer sounded like thoughts. All he could do was suckle greedily, stretch, kick, grow, until he could remember and search again. Memories lurked in the unconscious, quietly whispering to him until the body and mind were ready to hear the soul again.

Part 2

H E AWOKE WITH A start, sweat streaming down his back. Suspending his weight upon his arms, he lifted his face toward the sunlight. Blinking away the haze of sleep, he stood. The straw made him itch from head to toe and his rump ached. Still, it was good to sleep away from the cushions and silk once in a while. He had told his father it built strength into the body. The Duke had harrumphed at him, but pressed Gabriel no further. The joys of youth and freedom would soon come to an end for his son after all.

Gabriel rubbed life back into his limbs and began the chore of tending to his stallion. Gabriel would allow no one near Shadow Whisper if he could prevent it. Gabriel owed Shadow a debt. The magnificent stallion had appeared out of nowhere, shouldering a fallen tree off a young Gabriel. Shadow kept the wolves away and led Gabriel back to safety. Since that day, they were never witnessed apart. They grew together and played together. They had won many a college hippomachie, Shadow truly was a war horse in spirit. Gabriel would ensure the life-debt repaid if it was in his power.

After a thorough grooming, Gabriel mounted the horse without a saddle. The countryside was beautiful, what was not farmland or town was meadow, moor, and forest. Acremen tipped their broad rimmed hats as he passed. Birds chittered over his head and about the trees. Gabriel's regular journeys to the stream had left a path trampled to the dirt. He doubted anyone else knew of the stream. Too many were afraid of the superstitious stories about the forest being enchanted and filled with arborous men. Shaking his head at the nonsense of it all, Gabriel dismounted, letting the reigns hang.

Peeling off his clothing and queere-peepers, he slid into the stream with his eyes closed. He kept walking until the water was at its deepest, a head taller than he. When he opened his eyes, the ripples of light and the gentle flow of the stream soothed him. He would stay as long as he could, letting the current wash away tension. Gabriel was blessed with a gift, his father believed. Weathering the elements longer than most was a sign from God that they were chosen to be royal, according to his father.

Gabriel was not sure what he believed about his supposed gift. He was a man of science and reason. He neither dismissed nor believed anything he did not experience or measure for himself. However, there was no denying water its due credit, it was a peculiar element. Gabriel had experienced its unusual properties and mystery both in the labs at Oxford and here in this stream. Water held some power of the universe. But he was also a man drawn to creativity as much as science and, so, he dismissed neither the musings of research nor the melodies of the world. If he waited long enough, allowed his mind freedom to imagine, water whispered to him. He was never able to make out the words, but he could feel it, as if he had once understood what it was telling him. It was alive, roaring through river beds, trickling down brooks, and falling from clouds, that much he knew for sure.

His body finally forced him up for air. Gabriel inhaled, regulated his breathing, and stretched. After a few more moments, he climbed out of the stream. He had brought a sack of fresh clothes and his coin purse. He wanted to make it to the smithy before the market became crowded. Shadow's bridal needed repair. Gabriel would never hear the end of it if the Duke found a servant had not been put to use through a London crier. Mind, his father could not do much about it anymore. Gabriel closed his eyes and pictured his father. The Duke was lying in the master chambers big four post bed. He was nearing death. Gabriel dreaded the day when the Dukedom fell upon his shoulders.

The smithy went about repairing the bridal. Gabriel

opted to wait out the repair, internally cringing at the "your grace" the smithy offered. His father was not yet dead and people already addressed him as Duke. Was this whole bloody town out to shackle his neck in gilded iron? Did they understand that it meant his freedom? He was more a slave to titles than the servants themselves. What he would not give for a simpler life. He left Shadow standing beside the iron, overseeing the job. Gabriel smirked at the unease the smithy felt by the gaze of his horse. Like himself, Shadow set the peasants at slight ill-ease. It would ensure a good job.

"Alexander!" a woman's scorning voice pierced through his thoughts and sent Gabriel's heart racing.

There was something in that voice. Gabriel looked down to see a small boy had his hand around an apple.

"Put that down right now!"

The merchant glared at the boy and moved toward him. Gabriel's gaze followed the woman's voice to a ruggedly dressed lady with a babe on her hip and one in her belly as well. Protectiveness ignited in Gabriel, and slowly he felt his soul come alive. *Who is this woman that has me so moved?* Instinctually Gabriel caught the merchant's raised hand. Gabriel quietly offered to pay for Alexander's prize and the merchant withdrew with a nod. The woman's eyes grew wide at the scene. They swirled with an odd greenish hue that he had never seen on any other woman. And he had gazed into a fair number of women's eyes.

"Your lordship! Apologies for my son's behavior. He's a wild one and hard to contain."

She curtsied as best as she could. The added weight of children made her feel awkward. The merchant saved Gabriel a response by explaining the offer of payment.

"Thank you my lord," the woman curtsied again, "How am I to repay you?"

"Your name will be payment enough," he managed to reply.

"My name is missus Godfry Woodville," she blinked at him.

Anger hurled itself forward. How could a minor nobleman keep his wife so ill? But, he reminded himself, this was London, and much of luxury had been burned to ash all too recently. It was a slow start to rebuilding. Still, a Justice of the Peace could assuredly keep his wife and children in better state. The peasantry would call him a shamocrat. Gabriel contained a smirk at the thought.

"No Madam, not your husband's name, if you will please, your name," Gabriel insisted.

She blushed at his request of familiarity, "Adamina, my Lord."

The sound of her name sent his head spinning and sparking into fantastical tales of lost worlds and witchcraft and angels. Joy pulsed through him instead of blood. He wrestled to contain himself. He considered the last time he had brought a woman to bed. It had not been over-long to be responding like such. After all, she was no harlot. Not a harlot in the least, his mind cooed ridiculously infatuated. She was a nobleman's wife. He restrained the urge to pass a hand through his hair and betray his emotions. Instead he bowed low.

Taking her hand and placing a gentle kiss on it, he addressed her, "Pleased to meet your acquaintance, Madam Adamina."

Her scent was spiced and familiar. The kitchen was upon her from sage to soot and he could all but touch the image that formed of her stirring the pot of day-stew. He imagined she would whisper thanks and be saddened by the death of the animals that were to sustain them. He imagined she handled each herb and vegetable with the utmost reverence and care. And then he saw himself wrapping arms around her babe-filled waist and felt himself nuzzle into her neck. His soul let out a breath he had not realized it was holding all his life.

He hardly remembered how she left his sight. Nor did he recall fully that he pulled the coins from his pouch and offered to pay for anything Madam Adamina and her children wished for. He had been struck. Dazed he floated through the day. Unable to sleep for thoughts of her, Gabriel stared at the ceiling all night and into the morning. He allowed servants to dress him and carry out the chore of Shadow's care. He all but forgot Shadow over the days to come. He held no appetite. There was only the woman who haunted him. There was only Adamina.

IT HAPPENED AT PRIME on a ghastful day. The world had fallen to his shoulders and knocked him back to earth. The funeral bells tolled out the death of his father as Gabriel and the other bearers carried the fine ebony casket to the grave. In London fashion, they sloshed and stomped through cantankerous levels of culch. Gabriel was grateful that the graveyard was atop a hill and would not be so damaged by the flooding. The whole district followed in the procession and watched and wailed as they laid his father to eternal rest. Gabriel looked up and saw her. It was as if the whole world stood still. The wind held her hair in hand, taunting him with its softness. It shone in the sunlight, dancing colors everywhere. She was an angel here for him, an apparition of comfort. He felt warm against the chill of the rain. He yearned to reach out for her. Her eyes met his in sympathy and then she was gone. They all were gone, and he was alone at the foot of a marked grave. His joy turned backwarding.

Her heart ached for him. She could not explain why she felt so deeply for this man she had met but once. She

owed him a debt that could never be repaid. He had provided food to her and her children when her own husband spent his fortune recklessly. Gabriel had sent her
rich fabrics and seamstresses to supply her with appro-
priate dresses for her position. Adamina was overjoyed
with the treatment and gifts, moved to tears. The Duke
had even given her a maid and a lady-in-waiting. His
note had stated they were in need of someone to attend,
'there was too much idle help at his manor'. The Duke
had a reputation for being generous to his friends and so
his gifts were never met with suspicion. Adamina assumed that the Duke's interested lied in keeping the
support of her husband. She sent polite thanks when due
and never used more of the credits that the Duke offered
through merchants than needed.

As he predicted, the responsibilities of his rank consumed him. Gabriel all but forgot Adamina. In the
throes of his new title and duties, she slipped to the back
of his consciousness with the last of his joy. News of her
death reached him several years later. His stable-hand
had taken some of the tack to the smithy for reworking
and had barely escaped the disaster himself. London was
in poor repair and he cursed himself for not doing more
about it. He was Duke. Surely he could contribute to the
town's state. A massive building had fallen, taking her
and many others with it in the market place.

He found himself again standing at the foot of a
grave staring into nothingness. His heart drawing closed
and burning with a frigid fire. He cursed himself, cursed
the building, cursed and raged. The once-kind-Duke is
what they called him. He became brash and maddened.
Ill moods would strike suddenly leaving him throwing
the furniture at the slightest disturbance.

The servants left him in his study, a battlefield of broken bodied chairs and lamps. He knelt, head in hands, a
distain for God and heaven took over his rational mind.

His only outings were to take his hounds on the moor. He rode Shadow hard, a baker's dozen of these large, black hounds silently heeling close. On occasion, folk would trek out to see Gabriel and his hounds like apparitions through the heavy fogs and mists. They were a mournful sight that would fuel the fire of superstition for centuries to come.

She watched unseen as he turned, donned his hat and headed off into a life of bachelorhood, responsibility, and sorrowful rage. Her husband had drunk himself into a stupor a week later and fallen into the river to drown. Godfrey Woodville's remaining fortune had gone to an ornate grave too large for his position in a private cemetery, far from his wife's own grave. Adamina had a pauper's grave save for a small head stone anonymously commissioned in a public graveyard. Gabriel managed to pull himself out of his sullen rage enough to take on her children as wards. He never saw them for fear they would remind him of her, but their needs and desires were provided for. Her daughters were married off well. Her sons inherited his fortunes.

In death he figured he could finally have what he wanted and damned the scandal. He had arranged to have his body buried beside Adamina's. That a bachelor Duke should be buried in a dishonoring fashion beside another man's wife was indeed peculiar. His headstone mirrored her own, simple, like the life he had longed for. And people talked until the next political scandal or civil uprising erased it from their minds. His spirit would wait for her there. He remembered now, completely, each life, each near miss, or her absence. He remembered Avalon again. He had waited so long. He had found her and he had let her slide through his fingers.

He remained there at the foot of their graves for a long time, invisible and waiting in grief. Perhaps she would come to him if he waited. Decades later, a young girl carrying the look of Adamina about her approached their graves, whispering hopes about a future love match. He watched her place flowers at their graves: the lily-of-the-valley, white against the mossy stone. The gentle flowers caused something inside of him to finally let go. He realized she would not come to him here. He was wasting time. Adamina probably chose to live again. He floated away and into darkness, heartbeats in his ears and clinging to the memories. His mind echoed her name.

20

"DADDY!"

The four year old girl with dirty blonde hair in a dress covered in mud raced towards her father. He was a lean man, with narrow features and a kind face, suffering from minor jet lag. This business trip had been longer than the others. Little Elizabeth wasn't sure what he did exactly, not that it mattered, she was proud of him. He was her Daddy after all. And business sounded like an unfavorable mystery. He scooped her up into his arms and planted a kiss atop her head.

"Hello sweet pea," he said squishing her to him. The backyard was her playground where her imagination roamed free and large. Victor could almost see it, the mystical worlds and characters she built. She was her mother's daughter in that sense, keener than a hawk. He smiled.

"Tell me all about this prince of yours. What has he done now? Saved you from a dragon?"

"He's not a prince, daddy. He's an *Angel*. And I don't need saving from dragons, they are good people. No, daddy, he came to me in dreams again and he saved me from the bad man. We flew through clouds!"

As Elizabeth told her fantastical tales, Victor carried his daughter into the house. Tyra was already standing by the backdoor, listening intently to her daughter's stories. She had heard and witnessed the arrival of her husband from the dining room table where she was working from her laptop. The table provided a view through glass sliding doors where she could keep an eye on Elizabeth. Illustrations sprawled across the table for her selection. The artist was amazing, bringing the tales she wrote to life. But her selection had been interrupted by a client's needs. Tyra worked part-time as a bookkeeper for a couple of small businesses. Numbers weren't her passion, but her passion didn't pay the bills. The control over her schedule allowed the McAllistars to avoid the pains of finding childcare in a difficult market.

"Look at you my little heathen! Covered in mud from head to toe!" Tyra pet Elizabeth's hair and kissed her husband with subtle earnest. He had been gone too long this time.

"Let's get you washed up."

Tyra removed the little girl from her father's arms and carried her to the bathroom. The time spent scrubbing and washing and soaking out clay from the girl's hair and skin and clothes allowed Victor to unpack. Her daughter glowed with mythical ethereal light and Tyra muttered a soft word to hide it from other eyes. Elizabeth was a little witch already, and she was barely five. But the burdens and responsibilities of magic could wait for her daughter to grow. Tyra wasn't about to force a burden on such a light to the world just yet.

"Mommy?"

"Yes dear?" Tyra finished scrubbing the last of the mud out of her daughter's hair, pulled the plug and set Elizabeth down on the bathmat.

"The Angels say you shouldn't go to the party tonight. You shouldn't leave me."

Tyra toweled Elizabeth dry and smiled, "Why do the Angels say this dear?"

"I shouldn't be alone," Elizabeth replied and held her arms up for the dress Tyra held.

"You won't be alone sweet-heart, Grandma will be here."

Elizabeth stayed silent, eyes down cast.

"Oh honey," Tyra embraced her little girl as they sat on the bathroom floor together, "You won't ever be alone, no matter what I will always be with you and daddy too." She gave Elizabeth a squeeze and then set the little girl down, "Go see your father!"

A few hours later, Elizabeth fed and dressed for bed, cuddled in Grandma Tabetha's arms. The McAllistars went out for the dinner party. Tyra placed a kiss on her little girl's cheek and Victor tipped his bowler in thanks and respect at Tabetha. With a click of the door, the McAllistars were gone, their lives cut short by fate.

ELIZABETH WAS LEFT ALONE like the Angels said. She did have Grandma Tabetha, but it wasn't the same. She missed her parents dearly. Tabetha did the best she could to teach Elizabeth about magic and witchcraft, to keep her believing in Angels and dragons and fairies, but Elizabeth's heart wasn't in it. Elizabeth was angry with the divine, the Angels, the magical and mystical for not saving her parents. Instead, Elizabeth chased out childhood fantasy, grew up too fast, and dove into school to ignore her pain, her lineage and her gifts. Tabetha wished with all her heart that Tyra could have passed down their legacy to Elizabeth, but all Tabetha could do was offer and guide and hope. And practice the craft of course.

A whisper on the night air drifted toward the new moon, stars the only illumination in the night.

"By sea and land and fire still, by wind and spirit Goddess seal. Hide Elizabeth from darkened sight, conceal your daughter on this night."

Tabetha's arms stretched toward the sky, her bare feet planted firmly as a breeze rustled her robe about her legs. The fire pit in the back yard crackled and wood snapped under heat, sending embers to the sky. Under normal circumstances, Tabetha would be surrounded by twelve other women to help her, but this was personal. She would not ask her coven as the debates about consequences would endlessly trail on and Tabetha no longer had that kind of time. She drew in a breath, feeling the pulse of energy around her. The spell was ready to be released.

"As it harm none, so mote it be."

She swirled the colorful light around the pot over the fire, poured it into the brew and then guided the light and magic up to the moon. Under the watchful eyes of an owl, Tabetha released the spell, thanked the spirits and silenced the fire. She would mix the brew, simple edible herbs, into Elizabeth's breakfast eggs the next morning. She had no doubt it would conceal the girl. She had considered binding Elizabeth's gifts, but the consequences were too great. Tabetha was not the type of witch to mess with free will like that. But, she could hide Elizabeth's light from prying eyes and hungry greedy fingers. Elizabeth's power was pure, strong, and of the Earth so it was abundant. Tabetha had never seen the like of it in her fifty-some years.

The power-hungry did not understand about the cost of using that type of magic, nor did they care for the consequences. Tabetha was unsure which was worse, ignorance or duplicitousness. So she ensured her granddaughter was raised to be neither in the event that someday, Elizabeth would embrace the craft. Tabetha knew too well the call of the gifts passed through her line. One could not run from it forever. When Elizabeth was ready, the spell would break itself.

IT HAD BEEN A long day. The young boy with jet-black hair and honey colored eyes had accompanied his father to the jewelry store again. It always amazed him, the care and attention that his father paid to each of his creations. His father talked, explaining the smelting of precious metals. How each had a life of its own, and each batch had a unique personality to it. If you listened close enough they would all tell you how they wanted to be made. It was pure magic. The cold smooth metals with delicate, intricate designs created a harmony with the stones set into them. Rings, pendants, bracelets, broaches, little jeweled boxes, his father was the best in the city, even the famous and wealthy demanded custom pieces for their collections. Someday, his father reminded him, the store would be his and he must take care and attention.

His father was right, the jewels and precious metals did sing. The young boy could hear it. The more beautiful and complex the creation, the louder and more exquisite the song. But he had never heard any compare to the sound his mother's ring made. His father had made it especially for her. He loved hearing the tale of how Papa almost lost Mama because it had taken so long, five years, for him to complete it and propose. Mama thought his heart was closed to her and almost gave up. Almost. But she had hung on just long enough.

Mama had made a hearty meal that left him feeling so full he could roll over into sleep right there at the table. Papa picked him up and carried him up the stairs to his room, tucked him in, and turned to leave.

"Will you read to me Papa?"

"Alright, what will it be tonight my hard working boy? Perhaps something different than last night?"

Gabriel reached under the pillow and held out his favorite book.

"I need to hear it again, Papa. I need to dream of her again. To remember."

Gabriel's father nodded and gently took the book from his son. He had been raised on stories of fairies and magic all his life, and his work proved magic existed. Who was he to negate his son's dreams of finding his woman? If the tale was true, and the dreams and stories helped him remember her, then he would support his boy. Passionate love between souls that extended across lifetimes was very powerful magic indeed. He slid the book open and began the tale he could probably have recited from memory.

"Once upon a time there was a young girl named Elizabeth."

"No Papa! Her name was Adamina, my Mina."

Gabriel's father cleared his throat, "Right, of course my son, please forgive me." He began again, "Once upon a time there was a young girl named Adamina. She had a rainbow for hair and eyes of jade and sapphire. Mina had a magical garden…"

21

HE SHOULDERED HIS BACKPACK and headed out the door a man. That orphanage would soon be nothing but a terrible memory. Roger began to walk to his best friend's house. They had met in the year of high school before Roger flunked out. Roger had a job and a couch to sleep on. Soon he would have his own apartment and everything he could ever dream of. And he wouldn't have to work very hard at all for any of it.

Roger had found magic. It was the answer, the cure to his nightmares and key to his dreams. He would manifest all the wealth, women and wonder he wanted. Then, he would find her and manifest whatever it was she wanted. His dark, magical woman. Last year, he had begun dreaming about her. Adamina, with her soft skin and powerful magic. A mysterious figure had brought him the dreams of a young family, a man with wings and power, and Adamina. This shadow had told him that he was an Angel, fallen to earth to find the woman. Adamina would bring him great power and happiness. A burning desire to possess this woman drove him mad at night.

Roger had taken to the clubs and streets to pick up

women and ease his madness, but found that those women came with a price. There were plenty women he could access right here for free. Women willing to fall at his knees. It was just a matter of sorting through them to find the right one. Roger pushed the door open of the internet café he frequented. He needed a warm body and Brody wouldn't be home tonight. The singles chat room filled his screen as he huddled in a corner nursing a bottle of soda. He narrowed his search to locals, sent out a reply and waited.

It didn't take long for an answer. Nor did it take long to realize the woman who had answered was a beautiful young woman at the other end of the café as luck would have it. She closed her computer and walked over, sitting across from him. He hung on every single word that dripped from her mouth and soon they were heading back to his place. She asked if they could stop off at her school, and if he could wait outside for her while she reported to the last class of the day. He didn't mind so he leaned against the wall outside the main entrance, trying to look like he belonged. The school bell rang and teenagers bled out of the building with a loud haze of emotive conversations.

He spotted her as she walked by, chatting with two other girls. Her eyes glanced at him, held and darted away. Could it really have worked? The spell he cast to find her, could it really have worked this quickly? He had only cast a "Come to Me" spell last night, but here she was. Adamina. He couldn't let her get away.

"Excuse me!" He reached out and grabbed her arm.

The girl turned and glanced down at his hand, then back up to meet his eyes.

"I'm Roger. I couldn't help but notice you, and I was wondering if you'd like to grab a coffee sometime?"

"Elizabeth, is everything alright?" A dark haired girl she had been chatting with asked.

The girl took her gaze away from him and he felt anger and jealousy well up. Elizabeth nodded once to her friend, then directed her attention back at him. The jealousy and anger quieted.

"Um, sure I guess. Have we met before? You seem familiar."

"I don't believe so. Must just be that our souls recognize each other from another life," he grinned at her.

He let go of her arm so she could text her phone number him.

"See you later," he said as she walked back to her friends and out of sight.

He had found her. Tomorrow night he would call and arrange to pick her up and take her out. She wouldn't be easy, the shadow had told him to take it slow with her.

"Okay!"

The young woman returned, bag slung on her shoulder.

"Won't your parents worry about you?" Roger wondered.

"Nah, just me and my mom, and she works all the time."

Roger nodded and led young the young woman back to his place. He would have his easy access now, and his magical woman later. Who ever said you couldn't have it all?

"DO NOT TAKE THAT tone with me, my dear!" Tabetha waved her hand, bangles jingling on her wrist.

Today she was dressed in a vibrant red pant suit, thinning hair curled and face primed and primped to perfection. She was nearing seventy, but you would never have guessed it by the fire in her eyes and the passion in her step. Lately, Tabetha's steps had slowed a little and she had been savoring the moments more. The other day she had spent near an hour simply marveling at her garden flowers and appreciating each bee, lady bug, spider, and butterfly that passed by her gaze. She had marveled at the delicacy in these integral creatures, marveled how a world without them would grow no life. And yet, these fragile creatures could be so easily snuffed out by a frightened hand or careless boot. Life was such a paradox. You were more fragile than you realized and stronger than you were aware.

A seventeen year old Elizabeth glared angrily at her grandmother. She was clad in jean shorts and a t-shirt. Her hair was a vibrant blaze of summer straw. Her aura danced and blazed with the passion inside of her. To eyes that could see, she was a vibrant jewel of magic and life ready to fight for what she believed in, and that she got from her grandmother. When McAllistar women clashed, roofs fell in and birds stayed clear of the skies, according to Tabetha's mother Serena. And right now McAllistar women were clashing over what they often clashed about, a man.

Tabetha knew her granddaughter was vulnerable at this time in her life, untrained and filled with hormones and emotions. This Roger character was up to no good, she could smell it. She would chase that mongrel away if it was the last thing she did! Tabetha took a deep breath as her chest tightened and she was filled with shooting pain. It very well may be the last thing she would do.

Tabetha ached to the bone. The cancer. Elizabeth had no idea. Tabetha would not tell her granddaughter that she was about to lose another loved one. Her parents' death had devastated the poor girl enough already. Tabetha McAllistar was a fighter, that was certain, and she would fight this disease every step of the way, for Elizabeth. Tabetha would cast and beseech the gods, go through treatment, take whatever they told her until the last moment to keep herself alive as long as possible. She would be gloriously defiant to the end and ignore the visions and knowledge that her time would soon come. She had tried everything: taking trips to tropical islands for relaxation and unconventional treatments, consulting witches and doctors alike across the globe, but nothing had worked.

It had occurred to her, being a witch and knowing there were multiple sides to any dice you rolled, that she could take a different path and delve darker. It would probably assure the time she needed indeed, but Tabetha would never go there, never try her luck there. Just because death came knocking did not mean you compromised your morals. Tabetha did not fear death, but she dear fear for Elizabeth's life without her. Trust the Goddess, yes, of course she did, but the Goddess did not take mortal concerns into her hands like this. It was the responsibility of Tabetha to act as guardian and parent to her granddaughter and that meant chasing away terrible suitors. Tabetha could not leave this world knowing Elizabeth was caught in this Roger's snare. In the least, she would not allow him one step past the threshold of her door.

Elizabeth had wanted that boy to park his behind in her carefully selected sofa for a visit. Absolutely not. There was no way, as long as she drew breath in this body that she allow that young man in this house. Her gaze shifted from the sofa to Elizabeth and her anger ebbed as her heart softened. Elizabeth was nearly a grown woman and all Tabetha saw was the little girl with a broken heart, ignorant of her own power. *I should have taught you better, Mon chérie.* Tabetha sighed and shook her head. She had to keep Elizabeth safe.

"Elizabeth, find a constructive way to work through that anger and pain. I can't save you from yourself, only you can do that. I do not like Roger. I will never approve of him. I am here for you if you need me dear," Tabetha sat down in the kitchen chair with a soft thud and reached for her cup of tea, "It is your life, so mote it be. I just pray for your safety."

Elizabeth swallowed back the well of emotion that threatened to burst from her. She thought she would strangle in the pain of it all. She did not understand. She was drowning and choking in a torrent of emotion. She couldn't take this, this suffocation of her life. She turned on her heels and slammed the front door on her way out. She sped away in the old boat of a car she shared with her grandmother to spend the night in her best friend Madison's basement. There was no greater cure for the woes of life then sleepovers and late night conversations at your best friend's place. Madison and Elizabeth had been nearly inseparable since they met in school. As young women do, they talked of the world until mid-night where excited exhaustion pulled them into sleep.

SHE STOOD TALL, DRAWING down the sky. They called her White Owl, if they dared, or just elder or shaman. Her long black hair streaked with silver shooting stars danced on the gentle breeze. She was not as old as her hair betrayed and not as young as her face portrayed. She seemed eternal, caught between youth and wisdom. Part of her gift some said. Her lean body did not fill out as others had, but had grown strong with labour. She had never had children, for she knew her soul and heart lay far away.

The air was cold, but part of her gift was that she did not feel it. A hawk called in the distance, summoning her out of her reverie. Her heart weighed heavy. Their end was coming. Her tribe would be without one like her soon and they would be scattered. Their paleness set them apart from the others, as did their speech and ways. Some would survive, like the boy who would have taken her place as shaman when he was older. He would become shaman of a new tribe, she knew. But the winds had changed and the earth was restless beneath her feet.

The Spirit had told her she was to die this morning. The sun was not yet full in the sky and she would leave this world behind with the last breath drawn as it reached its mid-day peak. Her sacrifice would buy time for the others to escape. This was the way it would be, she knew. A familiar friend watched from the trees with wide, silent eyes and ruffled feathers. Mourning held his breast for what was coming, but he had a young one to raise and he would live on after her. So long ago he had promised the Angel he would act as messenger. As long as it took, but things had changed. He was her guide across the worlds and he could never leave her, promise or no. Their spirits were one as all things were. He calmed his feathers and focused on an early morning field mouse. There was time for this kill.

White Owl woke her successor's mother. It was time. The mother and father, returned from the hunt last night, gathered their things and left quickly. Others who still honored and heeded White Owl had fled already or joined the boy's family. She blessed them on their journey, and then took her place a distance from the village. The chief believed her mad. But her sacrifice would save a dozen others. That was all. But every life was worth it in the end. The Earth Mother had asked this of her. Their heavy feet on the earth resounded through her. They appeared on the horizon. Shouts, angry loud and filled with self-importance. She breathed, in and out, in and out. They laughed when they saw her standing there.

A woman. She felt their hate for her and wondered at it.

The loudest approached and grabbed at her. She stood still, staring at him coldly in his eyes. Her gifts made him let go, but the others fought, and then turned as she knew they would. She resisted them. The deadly voice of the Dark One whispered in the mind filled with greed and lust and he struck out. The opening of her flesh with that glinting weapon burned with the touch of ice and fire. But it too was of the earth, honed for killing as their hunting weapons were. She was now the prey. He pushed her to the ground. The last few fled away from the village without being seen as the men fought around her. Her gaze at the sky found peace as the sun reached its mid-day peak.

One man, tall with auburn hair and honey colored eyes fought his way to the front and demanded the attention of his men. An owl, heavy and silent flew past them and he urged the men to be silent. Honey eyes followed the decent as the owl passed by the woman's body and turned back into the woods and out of sight. But the honey colored eyes did not follow the owl to the forest. Instead they rested on the body of the woman his men had fought over. His gaze darted over the bloody wound. And his soul responded.

"No…" he whispered as he wearily approached her.

"No…" he choked out and fell to his knees.

"Adamina…"

He traced her face as if he had known it all his life. He felt the last of her slip away as he cradled her body. He had found her, but again was too late. Gabriel swallowed back the tears he would later shed in the silence of night as he held vigil for her in the forest. He could turn back most of the men, but there were eight he knew would not listen. They would pillage and burn and take, as they had taken her from him. He would find his end in this life, in battle or old age, and seek her again. Too many life-times hung over him where they had watched each other die or been promised to others or never found each other; or, perhaps most painfully, when one remembered and the other had forgotten until it was too late. He escaped into women, into many women, who would take his mind off his pain and loss more and more often. He wondered if there was a woman out there who could erase this tortured curse he carried with him, but he knew only Adamina could do that. Only her love could complete him. She was his other half, but maybe, just maybe, there was something else for him.

THE ALARM WENT OFF at six am, shattering her dream. Elizabeth was grateful for the interruption. She had thought dreams of Angels had ended a long time ago. Madison was already up. Elizabeth could hear the shower running. Madison's parents were either gone or still sleeping. To try and center herself, Elizabeth took a deep breath and relaxed into the exhale. It was almost natural to take a small moment and turn it into a meditation. Grandma had taught her that each breath was to be treasured and each moment considered when the mind allowed, and even when it didn't. There was peace in the little things that could be found with a breath and a bit of stillness. This morning, it didn't seem to be helping much. The weight of the fight from the night before with her grandmother left her groggy, like an emotional hangover.

She was weak with hunger and there was no way she was going to get through the morning without sustenance. Elizabeth rooted about until she found some passable handfuls of sugary cereal to eat dry and get her through until she could find something more substantial.

Tabetha would need the car back to get out and about for the day. No matter how angry she was, Elizabeth could never leave her grandmother trapped in their house alone. Those walls echoed with the loss of her parents. Elizabeth shut her eyes tightly against the memories of her Dad and mom walking out of the door.

Elizabeth had tried so hard to warn them. Grandma Tabetha holding her tight as she cried in bed, awoken by a terrible vision. Her dreams of Angels had been interrupted by the horrific scene of shattered glass, torn metal and blood she knew belonged to her parents. At night when the house grew still, she could still hear the terrible squeal of tires and crash of metal. Elizabeth opened her eyes and breathed, grounding herself again.

Elizabeth knocked on the bathroom door, "Madi, I'm heading back home. See you at school."

"Okay!" Madison's too-cheerful-for-the-morning voice chimed.

She ditched the car, leaving the keys on the entrance table, ran up to her room and switched clothing as fast as she could. Elizabeth relished the walk to school in the summer time. The peace, the joy, the bright sun, the birds, the lack of traffic on her route let her savor every moment. Soon her day would be filled with high-school lectures, dramas, and then her job at the gift shop surrounded by beautiful trinkets. She relished the quiet of a weekday evening in a small city mall. Like every other Wednesday, she would be home and in bed by 10. Why couldn't everyday be like quiet in between Wednesdays?

ROGER LURKED. HE SAT in his car as he watched Elizabeth glide into the front doors of her high school. He had hated high school himself, dropping out at the first chance. His rust-bucket of a car sputtered and he shut off the engine. He would sit out here, waiting, watching her until she got off from school. He would drop her off at her job and watch her daydream and dust shelves from a parking lot or bench. She was captivating and alluring and all his. He had found her. A sinister grin slid across his face. She was his and he had found her, circumstances had actually played out in his favor. Someone knocked on his passenger window, snapping him out of his joyous reverie. Annoyed, Roger shifted his gaze to the interruption. The intruder was a senior from the high school. Roger had witnessed him shamelessly flirting with a group of girls an hour ago. The kid pulled open the passenger door and plunked himself down into the seat.

"Can I help you?" Roger glared.

"Oh Uriel, don't look so cross. Aren't you happy to see me?"

Roger's eyes grew wide.

"Oh, that's right, you probably don't recognize me in this form," he held out his hands, "Lucifer, brother from a past life. You do remember don't you? No? Well, no matter. Have I got an offer for you."

Roger blinked dumbfounded.

"She in there?"

"Huh?"

"Adamina, is she in there? Did you actually find her on your own, before dear Gabriel?"

Roger nodded.

"How far are you getting with her?"

Roger's eyes narrowed, "Far enough."

"Hmm," Lucifer scrutinized Roger.

He worked out the state of things for himself. Uriel had always been a little slower and a lot more transparent. More so now that Uriel was, Lucifer resisted the urge to wince, human. The essence of Uriel was there and that was enough. Adamina's power had escaped him once. Uriel was the key to that dormant power now.

"Here is your problem. She has no idea what or who she is. If you call her Adamina, you will break the weak hold you have on her. So keep your mouth shut and you will be a very happy," Lucifer paused then emphasized his next word with slight disgust, "man."

"What's in it for you?" Roger quickly asked. No one in this world did something for nothing.

"What is always in it for me? Power, dear brother. Glad to see you haven't completely forgotten me," Lucifer patted Roger on the shoulder.

"I'm listening."

22

A TAN DIRT ROAD STRETCHED before him. The world was washed in greys. The Shadow Realm. Stripped of worldly things, his body alight with Nordic runes, Tyrryal stepped forward. His bare feet felt no pain in this world. He walked past ever changing stops, a saloon, a gypsy camp, a crippled demon with a ragged dog. All color was drained from this world and those in it. One stop along the long road never changed. She would always be seated at the table with a grey cloth, a large crystal globe and an empty seat across from her. The Crone would offer glimpses into the future and answers through the tarot. But, there was always a price. She looked at him, cards ready to be dealt. No expression crossed her face although Tyrryal swore he saw recognition in those ancient eyes. Then again, the Crone knew all.

He sat before her and with a nod she dealt, laying three cards before him.

What you seek I know.

The Moon, the Lovers, the World lay before him and she pulled him into a vision, her voice echoed in his mind.

Ten years' time, on the blood harvest, you will find the one your brothers seek. Haunted by the shadow of obsession, her end will near if she cannot see.

He awoke in his bed and blinked away the haze. Candle light danced in the midnight light on walls in his bedroom. He gave himself as much time as it took to feel mortal again. He got used to the sensations of a body again: heat, weight, sound. It took him a long while before he stretched and put away the tools of his spell. It was comforting to know, in this life, he could still reach the worlds he knew. Tyrryal still had power. He could still stop Lucifer, he would find them all, Gabriel and Adamina, Kamiel, Sheehan, all of them. It was the only way the Crone had told him he would find her again. A memory flashed, a young man held back from stopping the death that tore his heart. He still had no idea how long ago that life had happened. He only knew he had to find her again. A half smile of irony twitched on his face. He was following Gabriel's footsteps all too closely. Shaking his head to ground himself, he blew out the candle and sat in the dark until morning came.

IT HAD BEEN WEEKS since their fight about Roger. They both had silently agreed not to talk about Roger. Instead they talked about how to properly take tea, which new sweet or creamy substance to layer Tabetha's famous lemon cake with, and Kevin Klein movies. Their days had been filled with laughter and love. Now Elizabeth wiped away the tears that fell down her face. Death had taken Tabetha from her. Cancer, the doctors had told her. That devastating call, rushing in a cab to the hospital. Now here she stood at the funeral staring at a locked black box. Why hadn't grandma told her? Perhaps she would not have left that night, weeks ago. She could have stayed and mended their rift. Tabetha had been right. That was what bothered Elizabeth. Somewhere deep beneath the surface, Elizabeth knew something was off about Roger. She did not love Roger. He just paid attention to her like no one else had. He was bad news. She knew it. She knew it from the moment she met him. But Elizabeth had needed a way out, an escape from the abyss inside of her that threatened to take hold. Roger was a distraction from that.

She had called him to confide in him. He had been pleased at the news. Pleased at her grandmother's death.

"You are finally and completely mine, Adamina!"

The name from her dreams had cleared whatever haze she had been under and something finally snapped inside of her. It blazed forward like dragon fire. The anger and grief hit her and the absurdity of her relationship with this man so far beneath her slapped an icy hand at her. Cold realization and bitterness laced her voice, "We're done, Roger." She hung up. He tried to call back, but she ignored it until she had to change her number. Death had a way of putting life into perspective.

Without her grandmother flitting around, humming, baking, without the constant chatter of women every full moon, chanting and dancing and following Tabetha's lead, the empty rooms echoed despair. So she packed up and left the house, unable to bring herself to sell, and found an apartment downtown that she could call her own. She had brought with her a small cabinet filled with ancient books and strange objects that her grandmother had treasured. The cabinet was beautifully crafted, arches and spirals twisted around like vines. She gingerly fingered the delicate handles. It summoned to her the memory of Tabetha urging her to accept Angels and magic into her life again.

Tabetha had mooned about their legacy, they were

witches. She was a witch. The last one in her family. Elizabeth had been angry, too angry to hear her, but full to the brim, her anger and tears had overflowed until she was empty. Emptied of her pain, Elizabeth was ready to fill that void with light and magic. She had a calling she could ignore no longer. She cast the circle about her, using white chalk on the hardwood to draw the outline. She called on the elements like Grandma had taught her, Earth, Air, Fire, and Water in a soft voice. Incense danced lightly on the air and the flicker of candle light drew her eyes closed. She lay in the circle, drifting into sleep and letting the gods lead her into dreams.

MADAM ADAMINA... MADAMINA... ADAMINA...

Her eyes flew open and quickly closed against the glaring light of the sun. She blinked, letting the morning chase away the dreams. She had been having the same ones for a great long while. Bits and pieces knitting together in a disjointed tapestry of Gabriel, Angels, Avalon, and her own past lives where she was known as Adamina where she had been caught up in wars and love and magic. She breathed through the dreams and memories until they hazed into the back of her mind. Elizabeth rolled over and her face became buried in a mass of purring black fur. She smiled and nuzzled her big strong guard-cat, Lewis, then forced herself out of bed. In the universal feline sign for affection, he half-closed his gorgeous green cat eyes. Lewis squeaked out a yawn of love and appreciation as he flopped onto his side, taking over her pillow. She slid out of bed and rolled her eyes at him.

The sunlight shone through her windows onto hardwood floors, the warmth pleasant on her feet. She took a breath to center herself. She stretched her arm high above her, the other reaching for the horizon. She distributed her weight across her legs and held the pose. The translation for the position was Metal according to her instructor. From Metal she slid into the Water pose. Her mind always called it Water Warrior, for it was the same as the Yogic position Warrior. From there she grew and twisted into a Tree, one leg behind, one in front, arms opposite her legs, reaching. A flourish of movement brought her to Fire. One arm guarding her heart, the other reached for the sky. She struggled with her balance, an injury from her childhood adventures leaving the supporting leg weaker than the one that rested on her thigh. A flowing of circular movement brought her to the ground, into Earth, reaching down, she slid her focus beneath the Earth. Tendrils of light slid from her body, connecting with the pulse of the planet. Another pass through the poses, holding each, stretching energy to the sky, the soil, the trees, all life around her, and then she was ready.

She had found peace in Martial Arts. Slow moving Kung Fu challenged her to keep her discipline, to look within. Through Martial Arts, she faced herself. She moved the grief and anger through her, understood it. It helped that she had stumbled upon a Martial Art that was very much like the dance of witchcraft. It tied her body to her spirit and mind. It helped that it kept her fit and confident too.

Ten years had passed since Grandma Tabetha's death. Ten years filled with the craft, with Martial Arts, with healing. She felt a better woman for it all. But she would always miss her family dearly, though it was something she had learned to live with. After exploring the craft, Elizabeth had reached out to her grandmother's old coven. She had visited with them only a few times, the old women, chattering around her in that soothing way that felt like home. They had performed the initiation for her, all aglow in their circle, and then offered a place for her. She didn't join them. She guarded her secrets from and her gifts carefully. There was only so much you could tell people, even other witches, before you feared that quizzical look asking if you had lost your marbles. She was what they called a solitary, someone without a regular practice group. It would be difficult they said, but she was happy alone.

With a smile of contentment on her face, Elizabeth made her way to the shower. It had taken her a long time to perfect the art of morning, drooling and hap-hazard hair aside. Unfortunately, the water heater challenged her grace. She let out a cry of indignation as the water shot out an icy blast startling her awake. Fighting against the spray, she fumbled for the hot tap and twisted it up. Blessed warmth fell over her skin. She soaked, lathered, rinsed, and repeated until she had scrubbed and moisturized the last of the night away. Life's greatest luxuries were simple.

It was warm enough to let the air dry her body so she turned off the shower and walked toward the cabinet. Dust polished off, the cabinet gleamed as the morning sun bathed it in a halo of pale light. Elizabeth pulled the doors open. She had cleared a lower shelf to be her altar. Lighting a small white candle and a small black candle, Elizabeth knelt on the floor. She closed her eyes and imagined a sphere of pure, divine energy surround her apartment, and a second inside the first more closely surrounded her and her familiar. Lewis was lounging on the couch beside her. He feigned boredom with everything. She knew he was completely focused on the work though.

Going through the motions of calling the quarters, the elements, the Goddess, she formed her sacred space. With a whisper she finalized the circle, and felt that subtle vibration that she had learned to appreciate as magic course through her.

"I honor my ancestors, my grandmother, my mother and father. May their love and strength guide me, and may I carry the honor of the craft forward. Bless this day. So Mote it Be."

She closed her eyes, taking a moment to honor her gifts, and let the sun shine brightly on her face before she dressed for the day. She had explored the range of her gifts and found that she was able to help and guide others with them. She offered potions and spells when asked, but she was better at psychic work, healing, and Seeing. For a short while, Elizabeth even did a few tradeshows as psychic healer "Esmeralda", it brought in a little extra cash, but she preferred helping others for free. Her grandmother's estate allowed her the luxury. Elizabeth was able to reach for the past, glimpse the future, and heal the present. There was only one place so far her reach could not go: her family's spirits. No matter how hard she tried, Elizabeth could not reach her parents' or Tabetha's energies. At first she felt a little frustrated, helping others reach closure by connecting with family who had passed on and not being able to do the same for herself stung, but eventually she accepted it. After all, Tabetha's journals had said gifts came when the Goddess and God willed them to. No use pushing the divine.

She was an oddity, she felt, when it came to witch-craft and wished dearly to consult with her grandmother on the matter. The more difficult the working, the easier she found it, but mastering the simple was often a strug-gle. She still had not passed through the right of Air and felt she never would. She was adept with the energies of Fire and Water, and the energy of Earth came most easily to her, but Air was an evasive partner. Air came readily enough when she called, like in this circle. She could feel its power, but if she tried to cast, tried to lift her spells or intentions or breathe life into her magical workings using

the element, the air would become heavy, void or insub-
stantial, breaking the spell or causing it to collapse in on
itself. She used the other three elements and her own
spirit as a crutch to compensate, but it had the added
affect in her workings of making the results excessive.

Two months ago, for example, she had cast a spell for
an acquaintance. She did not particularly care for his arrogance and superior manner. There was just something
about him that set her on edge. He had come asking for
help to 'get rid of' his vehicle which had been taking an
awful long time selling. Knowing her dislike for him, she
made sure to emphasize the harm none aspect. Two weeks
later, instead of a gentle sale of the vehicle on the breezes
of fortune, a hulking wreck of an accident left the truck a
ball of fiery metal, and those involved walked away un-
harmed. Spells like that did nothing for her reputation,
nor her conscience. She grappled at balance but it seemed
to elude her, as if something was missing. Sometimes it
felt as if Air refused to cooperate on some unknown
principal of honor or debt.

Unfortunately, Elizabeth had larger problems than
her lack of connection with the renegade element. She
was having a dry spell, and other than the last spell for
her acquaintance, it had been months since anyone had
come into her life for her assistance, or since she had
heard the whispers of the Goddess. She would try one
last time, here in this sacred space, to reach out with her
gift to see anything, hear or feel or smell anything, or
help anyone. She took a breath and steadied her mind,
open, reaching and welcoming. Elizabeth felt the power
build and something stir, reach toward her. Excitement
filled her and she stretched her consciousness cautiously
toward it.

A psychic witch, no matter how open and eager, could
not just open up and welcome whatever came at her. It
could be a blessing, or something much darker, to be

avoided and blocked out. Negative energy and thoughts could manifest toward her and then she would be clearing away the brunt of it until she could locate a source and heal the problem. That was, if the source and problem could be located or healed at all. A blurring of colors began, sound trickled in, then silence and darkness, nothing but an empty abyss in her mind's eye: no visions, no messages, nothing. Frustration rose and she felt filled with disappointment. N*o, none of that today Elizabeth.* After calming herself, Elizabeth thanked the elements, dismantled the circle, and snuffed the candles.

Her usual morning breakfast of hot oats in coconut milk was livened by fresh summer peaches, peeled and sliced. Their cool sweet tang danced on her tongue and she savored every minute. Life needed to be experienced well. She cleaned Lewis' bowl out and refilled it with his favorite soft food, a treat from the usual. In a few minutes he would decide he was finished sun bathing and mosey down to his bowl for his meal. When the laundry had been dried and put away, or hung over her bath tub to finish air drying, that was when the real fun began. It was Saturday after all.

A familiar ping grew a smile across her face.

"Hey Madi," Elizabeth said into her headset.

"Liz! How is Lew doing?" the computer relayed Madison's response through their instant online chat module. It was substantially cheaper, and more engaging, than a phone call to meet up online in games and chat. Madison, being a student, was strapped for cash.

"Great, sunbathing as usual. How's that degree coming?"

"All too slowly for my liking," Madison Porter relayed the woes of her far-away university life and the challenges of doing a masters that was changed to doctorate track. Madison was your regular genius. Introverted, brilliant, and focused. Elizabeth wished dearly to be right beside her life-long friend. Madi was as close as Elizabeth had to family.

"How is… what is his name again?" Madison's voice interjected into Elizabeth's thoughts.

"What is his name is right. The jerk had a bet with his friend that he could sleep with me. I can't believe people actually do that! I thought that only happened in movies."

She clicked with fury as they battled through a boss on the level of the current computer game they were playing.

"Wow, Liz, I don't know what to say."

After a long pause during the muted cut-scene Madison asked softly, "They really had a bet?"

Grins spread across both their faces and they both burst out laughing. The world seems lighter in the company of good women. Elizabeth could spend hours listening to the familiarity of Madison's voice, Madison felt like home. Just through talking with her dearest friend, tension slid out of Elizabeth's muscles and her own light shined a little brighter as if someone had polished the dust off it. Her heart ached every time their gaming sessions ended and Madison had to return to studies or work. The echoing loneliness that followed an online conversation was difficult to face.

Elizabeth filled those empty hours when she wasn't working, practicing Martial Arts, or chatting and gaming with Madison, with cat cuddles, couch time, and potato crisps. She had filled that time recently with dating and had found a few cyber flings here and there, but nothing substantial. The closest she had come to a long-term relationship was Roger. Roger, in spite of the decade since they broke up, would not leave her alone. He chased her in nightmares and was a regular piece of pathetic work. She had secured a restraining order against him after he had attacked her one late night in a parking lot. The order was a relief for her. She wasn't afraid of him. Not anymore. Now he was more of a nuisance than anything.

Then there was bet-into-bed guy. She had stopped believing in love. Stopped listening to the nagging feeling that there was someone out there looking for her: someone who actually wanted her for her. She swallowed back the tears. Tonight there was no room for tears. Tonight was Mabon and she was going to celebrate. Elizabeth pulled on her Irish wool shawl and a light coat. The wind had become bitter in the evenings already. She loaded up her vehicle with goodies for the group and headed to the community centre. A local group offered open rituals for Pagans and non-Pagans alike on Wiccan holidays. The rituals were simple, inclusive and used common and casual threads of casting circles and ritual work from a number of different religious and spiritual practices. It was a place of unity and magic.

The old building brought a smile to her face. It is white trim and heavy doors echoed a time when people cared about what they built and where. The warm chatter of voices talking around one another chased away the frosty wind. Elizabeth closed the large community centre doors against the promise of winter and made her way into a brightly lit room where people huddled, sitting and standing everywhere. She slid her coat from her shoulders and left it on the coat rack with the others.

"Welcome!" A short woman that radiated light and love greeted her.

"Bekka-Lynn, you look fabulous!" Elizabeth wrapped her arms around the woman.

"Sweet Elizabeth," Bekka-Lynn gave her the once over and clucked her tongue, "you should not carry the weight of the world on your shoulders. Leave that at the door. It is a time to be thankful for the blessings and the harvests of the year."

Elizabeth smiled and nodded as Bekka-Lynn slipped off to mingle. She tried. Oh Elizabeth tried hard to fill herself with positive thoughts and the joy of the season.

A few individuals braved approaching her to engage in small talk, but small talk was not a skill she possessed. That coupled with her strong presence did nothing to put people at ease. She preferred sitting in the corner and observing others anyway.

"If we could start the ritual in about five minutes…" Bekka-Lynn's voice drifted away.

Elizabeth struggled to focus, struggled to connect, to honor the God and Goddess in this circle. There was a time, not so long ago that she could really connect with the divine. Where that quiet hum was a roaring swirl of magic and she could let it flow through her. Ashamed of her recent disconnection, she did not take her usual place in the circle, but passed up her part as the Pillar of the North for a gentle face she had no name for. She was terrible with names and was sure she should know it by now, but she did know the woman was familiar and kind. She had no stomach for the treats and drinks and merriment that followed, but to ground herself Elizabeth drank and ate a little. She had perched herself as an observer on a chair, watching the merriment from a distance. *Where is the Goddess inside of me?*

"Hello."

Elizabeth snapped out of her day dream at the sound of a soft, deep male voice. She blinked at the muscular mass of the man that sat beside her. He smiled a tense, uncomfortable smile back at her.

"I'm sorry, do I know you?"

"No, well not from this life anyway."

His reply intrigued her, but part of her warned against a potential harm. There were fanatics in every religion, but Paganism was an easy target for the unwell and unstable. If he introduced himself as John the Wiccan or Warlock or whodawhatist whose real name was Superkindafreakolicious, she was high-tailing it out of there. There was a fine line in her books and that crossed it. He seemed kind and honest enough. She resisted squinting at the feint aura around him and cursed her blocked gifts silently.

"I'm Tyrel Hanson. But you can call my Tyr."

"Elizabeth," she was tense but mustered a nod and a smile.

"A name worthy of a queen," at her flinch he continued, "Sorry that sounded like a line. Not my intent. I just meant that you have always had a noble name."

She leaned a little further away from him. He was losing her. He could not afford to lose her. It had to be her. He was sure. He had come to the festival ten years after the vision-reading in the Shadow Realm. It was the right time. He had the right place. He struggled to find her. Her aura was bound tightly around her and concealed from magical gaze. A spell, it seemed constructed a long time ago. He could tell it was restricting her magic too. Whomever constructed it wanted to ensure Elizabeth's magic stayed concealed. At first he had thought it was Uriel's work, but was relieved upon further investigation to find it had been a witch of her family in this life. That meant Adamina was safe.

"Do you believe in past lives?"

"Of course. I've performed many past-life regressions for others."

She relaxed a little. A potential client. The Goddess had another lost soul that needed a path to follow. It was a sign and meant that her gifts were needed. Elizabeth smiled more easily. She only hoped she could help him.

"Good. What I'm about to tell you may sound odd, but please hear me through before you respond."

She may be a skeptic and on-edge, but she would listen and judge for herself what he had to say. She never turned anyone away that needed someone to listen, no matter what she thought about what they came out with. He was kind and appeared to be safe enough.

At her nod he continued, "You see, in another life I had a friend who loved my brother dearly. She was lost during the war. I think you might be that friend."

She sat and looked at him for a few moments. Yep, she should run. *Oh calm down*, she scolded herself, she was in a public place and her own issues about letting people close due to grief, according to her psychologist, could be put on hold for a darned minute. Taking a breath, Elizabeth replied with careful words and openness, "Many things are possible. What leads you to believe this?"

"Your presence, your look. Souls carry similar traits and personalities through each life, ones they are fond of, things they have yet to resolve. I know you are her. I bet you find yourself drawn to the spirit of the Earth powerfully, connected to the Goddess. You feel blocked. I can tell from your aura. You feel like something is missing. You are skilled in all the elements, except Air. And the reason is because my brother never got around to instructing you fully in that element. I bet you talked to Angels as a child, or even saw them. All your life, you have felt undeniably sure that Angels exist. And I bet you have dreamed of a man, an Angel, all your life. Or am I wrong?"

"Oh my God, no offence buddy, but this is the twenty-first century. A witch needs no man to guide her in the elements. This sounds like something…" she cursed, "Did Roger put you up to this?"

Elizabeth stood up suddenly and took a step back looking around her wildly. Bekka-Lynn glanced at the sudden movement to make sure Elizabeth was alright. Elizabeth half smiled reassurance at Bekka-Lynn. Roger was the only living person who knew about her dreams. He had broken into her apartment several years ago and stolen the journal she had kept on the dreams. She said a silent thanks for restraining orders. It had to be Roger.

Elizabeth managed to get a hold on herself. No, it didn't have to be Roger. Roger had not contacted her since the order was issued. Besides, Roger was not cunning enough to send another man to do his dirty work anyway. Roger enjoyed the dirty work.

"Roger? Who is Roger? I am sorry if I have alarmed you," Tyrel stood up as well, but slowly not to startle her any further.

He knew his size could intimidate. He had not realized how on guard she was and cursed himself on his oversight. This Roger character must have done a number on her. He would have to look into Roger, and thankfully his career as a private investigator granted him access into all the right places to do just that. She headed for the door. He followed her to apologize again. She pulled her coat on. Before he could protest at her exit, she held up her hand to cut him off.

She sighed and paused for a moment, *oh what the hell, maybe he could answer some questions for her*, "You came in your own car?" At his nod, she continued, "Follow me and we'll talk more about this at my place. This is something that should be discussed in quiet company where I cannot hear the voices and minds of near fifty people."

At least that part of her power was working, even if she couldn't control it any more. The drive home gave her time to think. It was not far, only a few blocks, but the chilly breeze that had been her enemy on the way over became a sobering, grounding friend as it glided in through the window and around her body. She parked the car on the street in front of the building and saw him do the same. She took a deep breath and muttered under her breath and eyed him with her gaze. He was tall, very tall, and broadly built. His face was ancient and open, like a gentle Viking. He carried himself with uncertainty, which was odd. Elizabeth was lead to believe men of his stature could find confidence in their mere massiveness alone. Assessing no threat from him, she took one more breath and stepped out of the vehicle. Not that her sense of him was accurate as she could not trust her gifts, but she trusted her gut. She felt comfortable and at ease with him, like an old friend. He followed her up the steps in awkward silence.

Her apartment was a five-hundred square foot haven that housed a kitchen, bathroom, sitting room and small bedroom. It was cozy, tidy, and filled with her presence. He settled himself on the small modern couch that doubled as a futon. She disappeared around a corner to the kitchen. She returned several minutes later with tea and set it on the table. She poured a cup for both of them. That was when he noticed the massive black cat sitting in the middle of the room staring at him.

A warning stare. You mess with her, you mess with me, Lewis indicated. Once Tyrel had received the message, the cat flopped down on the floor. He had guessed the cat weighed about twenty pounds of pure muscle, well almost pure muscle. Not that he should be any judge mind you. Tyrel had gained quite a lot of weight recently and was in desperate need of a trip to the gym. He liked this cat and was comforted knowing that Elizabeth was protected. She would need all the protection she could get.

Tyrel could sense Uriel nearby. Uriel's fiery despair permeated the city and it was stronger outside of the apartment. Shielding from multiple techniques encased her apartment and dispelled the negative energy away from it like camouflage. Tyrel wondered at how much skill Elizabeth had manifested in this life. Judging by the work and her aura, it was a considerable amount. What was more important was how she was holding up. Her power and her pain would make her an easy target to spot. He would come back later this evening, while she slept to lay another shield over her own and conceal her more fully. Tyrel smirked. Uriel would not respond well to find another man's energy keeping his prize from him. If he was anything like he had been while an Angel. Perhaps it would draw him out and expedite Tyrel's search. Uriel had not been pleased to find out about the mass exodus of Angels started by Gabriel. He was even less pleased to discover that he had awoken mortal himself. Punished for aiding the out-cast Lucifer, Uriel was doomed to be blinded by his lust, hate, and cowardice as a mortal. Dying, being born, raging, and dying again as long as God wished it. Since God had readily accepted masses of the first-borns' exodus into mortality, Tyrel suspected that God would wish it for a very long time. It was an easy out, re-establishing the Angelic ranks with more obedience and less power. God would be pleased with servants who did not question him.

Elizabeth held the mug of steaming tea to her lips for a moment. It was a shame it was not one of her fine bone china tea cups that made tea that much more wonderful. But this was no tea savoring moment. This was a gulping mug. A mug to guzzle warm liquid repeatedly out of until the nerves and soul had been soothed. Lewis wandered over sensing her anxiety and curled up in her lap. He purred softly and she relaxed a little, relishing Lewis' warmth. He was her shield and her companion. If this Tyrel guy was a threat, Lewis would have told her by now.

"I am glad to see you are well."

Elizabeth just cut to the chase, "Back when I believed the dreams, the Goddess offered proof of its existence. She said I would know the truth with a true name revealed."

This was a world, a tale, a dream, that she was all but ready to give up. This was just a childhood fantasy. Shadows and gods did not exist like that in real life. There were no Angels, no one there to save her from Roger, from the bad men in her life. No, she did that all on her own. She was sure he would not be able to answer this question and Tyrel would be sent on his merry way.

"Madam Adamina, I once-Archangel Tyrryal am pleased to find you again. Perhaps we can find Gabriel together?"

Elizabeth didn't quite register the statement and Tyrel repeated himself.

"Friend, Adamina, I come to fulfill a debt. I need your help. In turn, I shall help you find Gabriel."

Elizabeth could only blink at the name she had heard only in dreams and used in private ritual, alone. At the sound of it, warmth filled her. She felt her body vibrate with energy, with magic again. She felt tears of joy and of sorrow well up and quickly took a breath to staunch the flow. *Enough of this childish nonsense. This was ridiculous.* Elizabeth set down her mug and stood up.

"I need you to leave now," she demanded.

"Wait, please," Tyrel pleaded as he stood, "You must find him. You must find all of them or it could be too late. Uriel has lived too long in mortal form, carried too much with him. Lucifer will start hurting people, Adamina. And without the others, there is no way Lucifer will be stopped."

Elizabeth held the door open and in defeat Tyrel slumped out the hall, down the corridor and moped all the way back home. She locked the door tight behind him and rested her back against it, still clutching the doorknob. Uriel, a cold shiver snaked up her back. That name haunted her nightmares. She gazed at the ceiling, took a deep breath and erased a world of phantoms and dreams. Elizabeth filled the night with tidying and video games, but she was restless to the core. She needed to connect with nature.

Elizabeth pulled on a sweater and locked her apartment door. The crisp air reminded her that fall, and then winter, would come all too soon. She walked three blocks to an inner-city park. It was well past the first evening patrol and well before the last patrol of the park officials.

She let her feet carry her where they willed. She slipped into a gazebo dressed in matching white, her camouflage. The moon shone bright above, so bright it chased away the stars. She lay flat against the wooden floor and listened to the sounds of nature. The water from the nearby lake lapped against the shores. A few rabbits nibbled on grass and bounced around.

The city sounds of traffic receded into the distance. She drifted in between awake and dreaming. A breath in and a breath out to find her center. Relaxing her body, Elizabeth let her mind race until it slowed, then quieted. The breeze whispered through the leaves in the trees and the frogs began to croak their night melody. She took another breath and shook the tension out from her core with a vibration of energy. Breathing and reaching, imagining roots from her core stretching into the ground and roots of light stretching above her, forming a protective circle of energy all around her.

Adamina...

A whisper in her ear jolted her back into her body. She sat up and looked around. Suddenly, the trees surrounding her offered dark concealment to fearful things. It wasn't often she feared the dark and Elizabeth was not about to risk herself to find out if her fears were warranted. Her heart and mind raced. She hastened back towards her apartment, taking the most lit route. Hurriedly, Elizabeth closed the door and locked the deadbolt, the chain, and the handle. It was only then when she finally let out her breath. The night had been cold, but her panic had chased away that awareness until she was safe inside. She smiled at Lewis as he sat there alert, welcoming her.

"I'm alright honey, just a little spooked at the dark," she said and laughed at herself.

She peeled off her shoes and put them away. Lewis escorted her to the bedroom where she turned in for the night. This was home. She was safe, cuddled up with

Lewis in her bed, in the quiet of the night. Yes, this was home. But as her eyes closed, Elizabeth could not shake the sense of being watched by something dark and terrifying.

YOU ARE MINE… HER dreams of Gabriel had been interrupted by a nightmare. A massive iron fireplace, alight with an unnatural flame loomed in her memory. A young boy, two women and two men peered into the flames. They were waiting, expecting something nervously. One of the men turned to the woman beside him. Elizabeth could not make out faces. She couldn't hear anything, but had the sense they were speaking. Then suddenly, a spirit jumped out and forced its way into the four of the people all at once, taking over them. But how was that possible? She knew of no spirit or creature that had such power. As an observer, Elizabeth could not be seen. She was safe from this thing's reach. Then, it turned and glared at her. Her mind raced, *how is that possible? It shouldn't be able to see me!* She turned her back to it and started running. Reaching out for her, it grabbed her hand. It burned. Its grasp cut through her skin, it burned! The demon-spirit spoke, *You are mine! I will have your power, Adamina. You are mine!*

Elizabeth's eyes flew open. Her heart raced and it took a moment to focus on her surroundings. Her hand, it was sore. She looked at it and realized that it was resting on a man's warm, broad back. *Help me,* she asked of him without speaking. He began to roll over to face her. *Wait, this is still a dream. Who…?* Her breath caught in anticipation, but before Elizabeth could make out his face, she woke up. She took deep breaths and sat up in bed. She was covered in sweat and filled with fleeting panic. Lewis lay beside her and she let out a sigh of relief. Home, safe, she was at home and she was safe. A burning drew her attention to her hand. A small bloody "F" with the arms facing upward glared back at her: a rune.

Ignoring the pain, Elizabeth frantically flew out of bed. She opened the tall wooden cabinet, then a second inner-door. Books of spells, ancient languages, all types of religious practices, otherworldly creatures, everything a historian or practitioner could need. She pulled out a small box that held quartz crystal runes. There was an instruction booklet that she flipped through as she sat cross legged on the floor. She lingered over its description: *Fehu, a rune for wealth, literally "cattle"*. She swallowed the fear that had lodged itself in her throat. *You are mine…* She shivered at the memory of the voice, claiming her. Cattle, someone had branded her as if she was property.

Gentle warmth wrapped itself around her. The vision of the man from her dream flashed before her eyes. She felt a deep pang of longing for him. Elizabeth struggled to remember his face. There was something different about him, something brand new, a promise all her own, something more real than her Angel. Tears filled her eyes full of grief, frustration, loneliness. She just wanted a normal life where visions didn't tell the future and cruel monsters could not touch her. She probably dreamed this mystery man up too, just like the Angels. Her mind was a cruel trickster. *But what about Tyrel's words?* Before she could answer that annoying voice in the back of her mind, the phone rang.

She pushed away irrational feelings over dreams that meant nothing. She looked at her hand, the wound had faded away. Another ring summoned her. She quickly put away the runes and locked the cabinet tight. She pressed the answer button on the phone.

"Hello?"

An automated message about some scam cruise something or other irritated her and she hung up. Shaking her head she left her fear and dreams behind as she slipped into the shower and floated through her routine. Changing into sweatpants, t-shirt, sweater, and then her runners, she headed out for a jog. The chill didn't daunt her efforts. She was too restless. The crunch of leaves beneath her feet urged her forward. Sharp cold breaths of air filled her lungs. Her heart beat thumped loudly against her ribcage. She was alive. She was grateful. The birds called and chirped around her. One flew across her path. Her feet pounded on the pavement. A familiar cluster of trees came into view. Elizabeth slowed her pace and stepped off the path.

On warm days, she would pull off her shoes and go through her forms barefoot in the grass. Her arms swinging and he body flowing into each stance with the sway of the trees and songs of birds. Today, Elizabeth needed stillness. She closed her eyes and felt the ground beneath her feet, through her shoes. She felt a sharp connection with soil, with the hum of the Earth. She let her feet carry her where the Earth drew her. She found herself touching a massive willow tree and was brought to her knees as a rush of locked away emotion assailed her.

Willow, the tree of emotions. Flashes of memories jumbled and wrought with loneliness, despair, agony, joy, triumph, passion, anger. Her parents, her grandmother, Lewis, Madison, everyone she ever met, ever walked past. All at once it assailed upon her senses, unlocking the careful hold on it all. Her amplified gifts were a wicked contrast to the dullness she had been facing. She heard squirrels dart through trees, rabbits through grass. She heard wing beats. The crunch and fall of leaves reverberated painfully. Then a hundred people in a few blocks radius, their emotions began seeping in as well. She struggled to break the connection.

"The willow is a powerful spirit," a male voice said behind her.

Her gifts, amplified by the willow, flung themselves toward him. He was guarded and she was unable to get a clear reading from him. He seemed completely calm and grounded. She clung to it, focused on him and the calm he brought. Elizabeth's power, uncontained reached for his mind. She fought against it, afraid to hurt someone, but he opened his mind to her. He knew she was prodding. She desperately immersed herself in the calm, grounded space he offered to her. Was he a friend or foe? He let his consciousness slide through her connection to the willow, and gently broke her free. She blinked and recoiled away from both the tree and the man, struggling to stand up.

"Yes it is," she managed.

Elizabeth managed to stand and turned to face him. She took a step back at the wave of familiarity she felt from his gaze.

"Who are you," Elizabeth managed to choke out. She shook her head slightly as if it would help settle the turmoil inside.

He smiled at her, "A friend, a man seeking something…"

"Men are always seeking something," Elizabeth interrupted bitingly. The experience with the willow had left her emotionally charged and irritable.

Her sarcasm caused him to smirk in amusement. He forgave her the flash of anger. The willow had turned up deep-seated pain. It had let her gift run rampant and he knew that a gift like that could take on anyone's personality or emotions within a hundred miles. He knew she would need his calm. At least he suspected she would need it, if she was who he was seeking. Even if she wasn't, she would need a guide with that much power inside of her.

Grief glinted through her eyes and then vanished as she regained control and locked all that had been released away piece by piece. Her eyes changed and the vibrant swirling green became more human, more subdued, as she regained a hold. Her eyes, yes, her eyes. It had to be her. It had to. The magic pulsed through her, the same connection, the same intensity, it had to be.

"I don't seek what other men look for," she rolled her eyes at him, but he continued, "I look for a connection to the spirit around me. I look for peace. I have been searching a long time for someone, a woman."

"Have you tried instantmatchforyou.com?" she quipped, inspiring another smirk to slide across his lips.

Those perfect, smooth, familiar lips. She felt her out-of-control emotions turn to desire. She reined them in by clinging to her irritation. She lifted her gaze to his eyes, slightly embarrassed that she had been staring at his mouth. She instantly wished she had not looked up into those eyes. They pulled her in, deep and warm, wrapping her in golden honey.

"I have tried many places, including the internet, yes, but I have not found her yet."

Elizabeth felt like a raw nerve. Electricity pulsed through her. She didn't have time for this. She needed to get home. She walked to the oak tree nearby. Unsteady on her feet, Elizabeth focused with all her effort on her destination. He followed.

Elizabeth demanded impatiently, "Who are you?"

"I am complex. I search for a woman, my wife, named Adamina…"

"Who are you?"

In a rush of anger, she flung to face him again and held out her hand. Her ritual dagger sat in it, poised six inches from his throat. Where had that come from? She had not brought it with her. Startled, she stepped back, dropping the dagger at her feet. What was wrong with her? Instead of fear or anger, he smiled at her with respect and relief. She had nearly killed him with a dagger that appeared out of nowhere and here he was grinning at her! She wanted to punch that stupid grin off his face. She felt her magic unfurl despite her attempts to contain it. She felt like she was going to burst out of her skin in a fizzle of light and float away or burn up. She stepped back and a heel rested on the oak tree. Solid, grounding, its strength seeped into her slowly.

"I am Gabriel. You remember my training, I see. But you were always shit at grounding."

Stunned, Elizabeth could only stare. Gabriel. She fought a rush of memories and dreams down with soldierly precision. Love. Love filled her and she fought against its suddenness. Thousands of years, hundreds of lifetimes. He was here. He was real and she was still in love with him. No. This was a dream. It had to be another dream. That was it. It was just a dream. Her breath was shaky and she felt ready to collapse. He lifted his hand and placed it on her shoulder. She felt his energy pour into her, through her, and felt him ground her. Her anger subsided and the intensity of her emotions dimmed.

"Adamina," he said softly.

Tears filled her eyes and she tried to pull away. *Run,* a voice whispered on the wind. She could not run, even if she wanted to. She was still too shocked for her legs to carry her that fast, that far. Anyway, she had stopped running when she had accepted she was a witch. Elizabeth shook her head again and pressed her heel harder into the oak tree.

"My name is Elizabeth," her voice cracked with emotion.

"What's in a name, you are her and you have been waiting for me."

He poured more liquid grounding magic into her. *Always out of balance, never coming up for enough air,* he thought, but that was his fault after all. He had failed to teach her about Air. Failed to guide her and protect her like he had sworn he would do, sworn to Mother so long ago. When he was satisfied that she was properly grounded and had regained control, he broke the contact and stepped back. It took all his self-control to step away from her.

She scrutinized him. Yes. Okay. Fine, she admitted there are no coincidences in life. Hell, maybe he was from a past life, but she could not be in love. *He doesn't exist. He doesn't exist!* The Angel was just a childhood fairytale. There was no way it was real. Angels didn't exist, not like that. If they did, her mother and father would be alive. She fought against the irrationality of a man claiming he was from her dreams. She must have fallen asleep against the willow and was dreaming again.

"No, you are not dreaming."

It is rude to listen to others thoughts without invitation, she snapped back intuitively.

You did invite me, Adamina.

Stunned at their mental conversation and his visible joy and amusement, she stared at him. Invite him? She realized, against her own wishes, her mind had formed the connection. She had lost the battle against herself. She felt all her walls, all her sorrow and fear melt away. She felt her body try to go into lock-down, tense and unyielding.

Why are you trying so hard not to cry?

She was not! She was. At the realization, she lost hold of her emotions. They slipped from her like sand through her fingers.

You're not real. I am going to wake up and you will be gone. You're not real.

Tears forced their way down her face. He reached out and wiped them away. He was tall, with black hair cropped short and a gentle face. He wore a black t-shirt and jeans. He didn't look like a dream. He looked real.

I am real, my dear Adamina. I am real and I am here.

More tears forced their way out and she openly sobbed. She felt her knees go weak with the force of emotion. He stepped forward and wrapped her in his warmth. He couldn't help himself. He didn't want to stop himself. He kissed her and felt her melt beneath him. He clutched at her tightly. Finally, his sacrifice, his searching had been rewarded. Finally, he had found her. Neither of them burdened by choices made for them. Neither of them promised to another in this life. Both of them remembered. He would never let her go. He took in every curve, every scent, and every sight of her. She wasn't all that different from centuries ago. More mortal, but she even looked in body a little like she had on Avalon. Exotic, beautiful, she was magic.

She returned his kiss urgently, a lifetime, many lifetimes of waiting. He was real! Her whole being burst with joy and only his arms kept her grounded. She felt like she was flying. She felt whole again. She felt peace and all her sorrows and hurts healed in his arms. She was home.

My sweet, dear Mina, how long I have searched for you.

She could not respond, but cried harder. He broke the kiss and he held her up in his arms, knowing all that was in her heart, mind, and soul. He felt her body weaken, felt her mind shut down slowly to protect itself, calling sleep around her. It was too much for her. She had expended too much energy during her encounter with the willow. She needed rest. He gathered her up in his arms as she began slipping into a recuperative half-sleep. He placed her in the car and instructed his driver to head home. The joys of good help meant they didn't question their employer's oddities. Alan was more than good help, he was a friend. He needed to ask no questions.

Elizabeth would be very hungry when she woke up

and would have dozens of questions he would have to answer for her. He saw her grief flash through her again, and he wrapped his arm around her. In her dreams, he saw the loss of her family. If he were Angel again, he would have stopped their deaths. He would have taken away her pain. But he was Angel no more. He was just a gifted mortal who could only offer a shoulder to cry on and shelter from the storm. He kissed the side of her head and whispered a vow to her.

"I will protect you, Adamina. I will always be here for you. Never again will we be apart. Never again."

ROGER SAT IN HIS apartment seething. He did not have to look out his window or go searching. He knew where she was. He knew she had found Gabriel. The fireworks of emotion and light had damn near blinded him. Any moron with an inkling of power could have seen it. He let out a roar and tossed the goblet he was holding at the scrying mirror. The mirror cracked at the force. In its reflection, he looked like a patchwork of human and fallen-angel. Coal eyes gazed back at him. His aura pulsed around him, fragments of wings, grey and glowing, showed through. Soon he would be restored to his immortality. Soon he would have his revenge. He would have her. He had to make his move now, before it was too late. He picked up the phone.

"Uriel, how good of you to call," a female voice responded.

"He found her."

"Well, that is an unfortunate turn of events."

"What the hell are we going to do Lucifer?"

She shushed him and clucked her tongue, "Careful, I

go by Lucy now you idiot. If one of the others over hears you and finds me, you'll beg for death."

Roger's eyes narrowed at the threat. The tone of Lucy's voice changed as she responded to someone's questions in the background. Roger couldn't remember the name of the corporation he, she, Roger corrected, was working for. It was some massive building that blocked out the sun somewhere in the heart of this wretched city. Roger heard a click as the receiver on the other end hung up. His blood boiled. How dare Lucifer, Lucy, hang up on him! Someone knocked on his door. Slamming down the phone Roger stormed over to his door and tore it open. A tempting blonde in a pencil skirt and white button up blouse that revealed a red bra beneath smiled back at him.

"Aren't you going to invite me in brother?"

"God damnit Lucifer, did anyone see you shimmer into the hallway?" Roger stuck his head out to check.

"Oh, tsk, tsk Uriel," Lucy swayed into the apartment and closed the door behind her, "Since when did you become so concerned with what mortals see?"

"I don't give a damn what mortals…"

"Sh," Lucy held a finger to Roger's lips and swayed her hips passed him into the living room, "You look terrible brother."

Roger's hair was a mess and he had this mad deranged look about him. He smelled as bad as his apartment. It was barely furnished with a ratty couch, a coffee table, and an entertainment center. A bachelor pad indeed, Lucy observed and withheld a sneer of disgust. Uriel always did have terrible taste. Except when it came to Adamina. Now she was a gem. A vessel full of magic he had to possess. Without the protection of Avalon, Adamina was a sitting duck. A smile slid across her lips. Uriel was a means to a profitable end. With a wave of her hand Lucy became Lucifer once more, gaining several feet and returning to his male glamour.

"That's better. As much as I like the powers of persuasion a female form can offer, I just don't quite feel myself. You know what I mean, don't you brother?"

Lucifer gave his brother the once over and sneered, "No, I guess you wouldn't know anymore would you 'Roger'?"

Roger took a step forward in fury at Lucifer's jab. Lucifer couldn't really blame Uriel for their father's scorn. Out of the two of them, Uriel had been dealt a less fortunate card with *daddy's* punishment. At least exile had allowed Lucifer access to powers. Lucifer held up his hand, stopping Uriel mid-step.

"I've got a plan to fix your problem." Lucifer didn't wait for a response but went right into the thick of things, "We know Gabriel is quite the romantic. Keep watch until he takes her out for an evening on the town. Let me know when, and I'll have a little treat ready for you. Don't screw this up like you did the last time because you're too eager to jump the prize."

Roger glared at Lucifer, the failed attempt to seduce Adamina thrown back in his face. Years ago he was so close, he almost had her. The only thing he had to do was keep calling her by her mortal name, Elizabeth, and the spell would stick. Unfortunately, he had screwed up. He called her Adamina once in his joy at the old woman's death. Just once, but it was enough to break the spell he had over her. Then, just last year, he had jumped the gun. He had gone to that parking lot to woo her, draw her in and bring her home. But she was just so bloody stubborn. He had tried to teach her a lesson, remind her that she belonged to him. That damn cop that interfered would be dead if his brother hadn't warned him against the kill. He was growing impatient with Lucifer's schemes.

"How the hell will a 'treat' help anything?" Roger hissed out.

"A beautiful blonde can always make an ex jealous,

dear brother. She'll be ready and waiting. I have just the gal in mind."

Roger's dark pupils dilated in arousal. He knew just who Lucifer meant: Jem, his go to gal at the club. It was a blessing Lucifer had kept that place running for centuries. Where else would he get his fix of flesh?

Lucifer waved his hand and returned to the female form he had donned prior.

"She'll have her instructions and play the part well. Just keep your mouth shut, Uriel. I know it'll be a challenge for you."

Lucy pinched Roger's cheek in a condescending fashion then shimmered back to her office.

23

As Lucifer predicted, Gabriel was a romantic. He couldn't help it. It was in his nature. Gabriel used every skill, every phrase, and every story he had
heard, learned and witnessed in all his lives to shower her
with his adoration. It was the little things that mattered:
the just because gifts, breakfasts in bed, candles, being a
gentleman. There wasn't a door he didn't open, a jacket
he didn't offer her. He was mesmerized. Gabriel was well
very well off and it afforded him the ability to grant her
everything she wished for. If she gazed at it, wished it, or
dreamed it, he made it hers. He used his magic, his mind,
to slip into her and know her every whim, her every hurt.
She had held on to so much grief and he would do what
he could to expel it from her. She had a weakness for
flowers and so he ensured there wasn't a day without
bright, fresh flowers surrounding her.

Days of love and romance and bliss turned into weeks.
Weeks turned into months. He was always there, at the
back of her mind, in her heart and soul. He was there in
her dreams, chasing away the darkness and nightmares.
They danced under stars, flew amongst clouds, and made

love in meadows. They dreamed entire lives over again. As they caressed each other, fingers dancing on flesh, chills of pleasure shivered through their skin right down to their core. Neither were able to tell where one ended and the other began: not in thought, nor soul, nor in body.

"I want to tell you a story my dear," Gabriel's fingers danced across the curve of her waist, over her hips.

The book, he knew, she had no idea about, or else she would have a copy herself. He had visited her place once, and while waiting for her to gather Lewis and his things, he had taken inventory of her collection. A single book-shelf full of books about mythology, science fiction, and holistic remedies littered the haphazard organization system, but nowhere had he found any signs of Tyra McAllistar's books. Gabriel wondered if she had known about them at all. The private investigator he had hired had told him she wasn't even school age when Tyra and Victor had been killed in a car accident.

The book had kept him searching for her and had given him his only clue. It was his undeniable proof that the dreams, the memories were real and that he had a chance at finding Adamina again. Now that he found her, he would restore this little bit of her life to her. He would miss the darn thing, but he had her now and no need to cling to it any longer.

"Mmm?" Her eyes fluttered open slowly.

Gabriel rolled over and tugged at the nightstand drawer. He pulled out a large children's book. It had the most mystifying illustration on the cover, but Elizabeth only got a glimpse as she rolled over to face him. He gingerly turned the first page. The book looked well-worn.

"It was a favorite bedtime story of mine in my child-hood. Once upon a time," he began softly. He didn't really need to read from the book, he knew it by heart.

"…there was a young girl named Elizabeth. She had a rainbow for hair and eyes of jade and sapphire. Elizabeth had a magical garden."

Her expression of shock stopped his soft lilting voice. His dark hair fell in front of his face. She stared in disbelief. He could feel her tremble. His gaze never left her face as he continued reciting the words from memory.

"In her magical garden, Elizabeth met trolls and fairies. She sang with the flowers, and danced with the squirrels. But the most important magical friends of all were the Angels. One Angel in particular. He was her prince. Elizabeth and the Angel would sit for hours talking, dancing among the clouds, shouting from the tops of the mountains."

"Where did you get that?" Elizabeth sat up in bed, disbelieving the story. He must be toying with her, "Stop it. This isn't funny. I told you I used to dream about you in a magical garden."

"I assure you, Adamina, this is no joke."

He closed the cover and handed the book to her. Elizabeth held the book propped against her left arm and leg, gingerly tracing the cover's art with her finger. A little girl with hair just like hers sat in the garden across from a little boy Angel. Her eyes traced the garden up to the title, *Little Elizabeth*, and then down to the author. Her breath caught and her eyes filled with tears. *Tyra McAllistar*, her mother's name in gold filigree. He smiled gently at.

"I didn't know… I had no idea…" she stammered.

"Keep it. It belongs with you."

She nodded and swallowed. He reached for her, removing the book from her grasp and setting it gently on the nightstand. He held her for a while as she shook. There was no need to speak. He knew her pain He could feel it heavy in the air. He also knew the joy behind it. When he felt she was ready, he kissed her and nipped at her skin in a trail up her chest and to her neck. Finding that spot that he knew would make her melt, he sunk his teeth to it gingerly and she shivered. He took her to the clouds and back.

LIFE WAS EVERYTHING SHE could ever want and more. Elizabeth couldn't stop grinning. She finished a long luxurious shower and paused to watch the sun slowly set, sinking below the city scape before her. She lost track of time when they were together. Lewis curled himself around her legs, purring loudly. She crouched down to scratch him behind the ears and he lifted his head in appreciation. Gabriel had showered Lewis with gifts since she had started brought him here. A ridiculous little chaise sat at the foot of their bed, just for Lewis. Expensive bowls, expensive food and treats, grooming sessions. Pampering a familiar was a sure way to its witch's heart.

Gabriel had captivated her heart completely. No, he had slid right past her feeble heart and encapsulated her soul. She could not remember a time in her life when she had smiled so much. She understood why people threw themselves at each other. She now understood soap operas, romance novels, and dancing. Things she had never before had a taste for.

Perhaps the best part was that she could share her gifts with him. She felt no shame or fear for who she was. She had found a magical partner in Gabriel. He was a pillar to lean on, someone who could channel as much energy as she need for any spell or any divination. He grounded her. He loved her. For the first time in her life, Elizabeth felt at home in her own skin. She felt limitless, strong, and magical. She grinned and restrained the urge to twirl like a little girl in a backyard of dreams. Gabriel called for her from the living room.

His place was gorgeous. Two stories of downtown elite condo heaven. Dark wood trim, rich colors, hardwood floors, quartz and slate and granite. Cashmere, velvet, and leather. He even had a small library that looked like the study of a duke. She smiled. He had been a duke once after all. More and more memories had floated to the surface with their time together. She sometimes wished she could see Avalon again. Its beauty and calm. She wished she could hear it thrum through her. She wanted to speak with the Goddess. She missed her friends, the priestesses. She longed to know what happened to her children.

"Mina my dear, I have a surprise for you."

She felt doubt pinch. Why had he never called her by her name in this life? It was always Mina or Adamina, never Elizabeth. She wasn't Adamina or Mina. Yes, she had the memories. And yes, that past was a part of her, but she was Elizabeth now. A different woman. A new life.

Her bare feet pressed against cool hardwood. Following his voice, she walked down the hall, skyclad as the day she was born. A woman of magic. A woman filled to the brim with love. A woman comfortable in her own skin. There was nothing she could not do. No evil she could not defeat with him at her side. He came into view and she stopped. He was dressed in a very expensive tuxedo. She stood staring at him in loving wonder. What a tuxedo did for a man, she marveled. He turned away from her and reached into a large bag. When had he had time to go shopping? She had not heard him leave. Maybe while she slept? That must have been it. He must have stepped out while she slept.

"Close your eyes dear."

With a smile on her face she did as he asked. She heard the muffled creak of a velvet lined box. His polished black monk strap shoes clicked on the floor behind her. Something heavy rested on her chest. She touched it and her eyes flew open. A necklace. She caught a glimpse of it in the tall mirror that leaned against the living room wall: deep, flawless emeralds and diamonds in rich gold. Her breath caught in her throat. This must have cost him a fortune.

Gabriel proceeded to shower her with a fine dress of green satin, designer shoes, trinkets and roses: deep red roses. He plucked one from its stem and pinned it in her hair. He helped her into the dress, leaving butterfly kisses all the way up to the pulse in her neck. The buzzer for the condo rang. Gabriel walked over and pressed the button.

"Car for you sir," a man's voice came over the intercom.

"Thank you Alan."

Car? It occurred to her that she had no idea where Gabriel was getting all this money. There was a lot she didn't know about him, actually. Everything she knew rested on these memories, these dreams they shared, on magic. Her cell phone rang. The call display showed Tyrel's name.

"Hello?"

"Elizabeth, I've been trying to reach you for days. I need to tell you..."

"Tyrel, I can't talk right now. I am sorry, I have to go."

"But Elizabeth!"

She hung up phone. Gabriel led her down the stairs, holding open every door except the car's. Alan held the black town car's door for them both. They drove around for an hour until she had no idea where they were. In every way he became more and more the duke of her dreams, only in a twenty-first century urban setting instead of seventeenth century London. They sipped champagne and gazed at each other silently.

Why now, she asked herself, was she so nervous, so uneasy? She had not felt this way in the past few months. It was the gifts. No one had ever offered gifts like that to her before. That must be it. The gifts made her uneasy. She did have a right to know what he did for a living. She would ask him as soon as she had the chance and he would tell her. Gabriel was honest. Completely honest with her. She trusted him. Right?

The car came to a final stop and the chauffer opened the door. Unsure of herself, Elizabeth stepped out of the car. A large gaping window offered the view of the whole restaurant. Crystal chandeliers dangled above round tables draped in white linins. Real silverware glinted on every table. She had never been to this area in the city. She avoided the luxurious in fear that she would fall in lust with it and never be able to afford it. Here she was suddenly surrounded by opulence and she was right. She was falling hopelessly in love with it all. Catching herself staring, she took a step forward to catch up with Gabriel who waited in the entrance of the restaurant. Her heels clicked on the pavement. Gabriel offered her his arm and ushered her in.

The host simply said, "Sir" with a nod and led them to a table.

Suddenly, everyone seemed to know something about Gabriel she didn't. Elizabeth felt like she was with a complete stranger and fear fluttered in her stomach. She pulled away a little, blocked him out. Elizabeth was seated by the host. She perched there, unsure of what to do next or say. Gabriel ordered for her, spoke for her, and tested the wine for her.

"Is something wrong? You feel distanced from me my dear," he asked her with concern.

She couldn't find the words to respond. She opened her mouth to ask exactly what it was he did for a living, but then she saw him behind Gabriel's shoulder.

"Roger! Oh my god," Elizabeth lifted up the dessert menu to hide behind it.

"What's the matter? Who is Roger?"

Gabriel went on alert and scanned the room. When

he recognized Uriel's presence in the room, Gabriel cursed himself for his foolishness. He had left them both unguarded in his infatuation. He had forgotten all about Uriel and allowed him to waltz right into her life again. Old wounds reopened. Ancient fears surfaced. Gabriel motioned for the check, but it couldn't come soon enough.

"Elizabeth! I'm surprised to see you here."

Roger walked over to their table. A gorgeous blonde hooked on his arm. Elizabeth put her menu down. Roger looked awkward in his suit. A cockroach masquerading as a butterfly.

"I could say the same to you, Roger. Doesn't the restraining order require you to stay so many feet away? Who's this?" Elizabeth could not hide the bitterness in her voice.

She couldn't help but feel as if Roger's mere presence had left her violated, tainted somehow. She would never understand how they had ended up dating. He was not at all her type. He couldn't keep a steady job, was prone to dark moods, and there was always something off about him that she couldn't quite put her finger on. How he had wound up in a place like this with a girl like that was beyond her imagination, and Elizabeth had quite the imagination.

"Of course, where are my manners? Elizabeth this is Jem. And don't worry. I'm not here for you."

"How do you do?" Jem shook Elizabeth's hand gently.

A shock from the blonde made Elizabeth cringe, she disliked the woman almost as much as she despised Roger. Roger faced Gabriel with a sinister gleam in his eyes.

Hello, Gabriel.

Gabriel's eyes narrowed, but he did not respond. So Uriel could still communicate this way. Pretending Gabriel couldn't hear him could become a tactical advantage.

"Roger, Jem, this is Gabriel," Elizabeth motioned as she introduced him. It occurred to her she didn't even know his last name. She didn't even know if Gabriel was his real name.

"My pleasure, Mister…?" Jem said as she shook Gabriel's hand.

"Lockwood," Gabriel replied.

"As in *the* Lockwood? Lockwood, the big gem business tycoon? Truly a pleasure," Jem batted her eyes at Gabriel and held onto his hand too long.

Elizabeth felt a stab of jealousy and was surprised. She was not a jealous person. Elizabeth mustered the courage to stand up. The shock that the man she was with was *the* Lockwood, whatever the hell that meant, made her sick to her stomach. It meant he had loads of money and plenty of secrets.

"If you'll excuse me, I need to visit the ladies room."

"Don't be long dear, we have an appointment to keep," Gabriel said in hopes that their quick departure would calm her nerves a little.

"Oh, you're leaving?" Roger asked.

"Yes…"

Their voices drifted away as Elizabeth darted off and slipped into the washroom. Black tile and mirrors made the space seem not only luxurious but also massive. The glittering chandeliers and luxury suddenly made her feel trapped and Elizabeth wished for a patch of grass to walk barefoot in. She splashed water on her face as an alternative. Giving herself a few quiet moments of peace, Elizabeth focused on her breathing. When she felt as ready as she could be, she returned to the table. Roger sat in Gabriel's place smug as a cockroach in a designer tux.

"Roger, what do you want? Where is Gabriel?"

"Nothing at all Elizabeth. Gabriel just stepped in back to check on something."

"Where's your date, Jem?"

"Oh, she goes her own way," he said dismissively. "Why don't you join me for a drink?"

"Not in a million years Roger. I thought I made that clear."

Elizabeth, exasperated, left him at the table and went to seek out Gabriel. She followed the faint pull to him, pushing back the kitchen doors. The cook gave her an odd look, and then focused on the meal he was preparing. Staff seemed sparse here. She wandered down a hall, all the way to a small office. Opening the door she found Gabriel. And Jem. Elizabeth's heart shattered into a million pieces that cut up her soul. It took every ounce of strength she had left to keep her knees from buckling. His arms around Jem. Her legs around him. His lips on her neck. Elizabeth could only manage a whisper, his name choked off by sorrow.

"Gabe…"

At the sound of her voice, his head shot up. A dazed look blurred his eyes and he paralyzed in place. *Damn it, what the hell?* Gabriel tried clearing the haze from his mind and slowly regained control. He had been at the table, Elizabeth had left to the washroom, then what? He couldn't remember. Anger at his own arousal sent a ripple through his tense muscles. He saw her there, the despair on her face, but he couldn't reach out to her. He struggled against himself to try and say her name, but his lips wouldn't move. Why had he come back here? He couldn't remember.

"Come on baby, don't stop," Jem's voice cooed on and then she turned to follow his gaze.

"Oops," she giggled, "guess we're caught aren't we? You have my number, call me."

Jem slid away from Gabriel and walked passed Elizabeth, righting her dress along the way.

"I'll see you around, darlin'," Jem slipped out of the kitchen and returned to Roger who escorted her out of the building.

Roger's eyes betrayed his dark joy at the knowledge

that his trick had worked. *Looks like I'm not the only one at a disadvantage because of mortality,* Roger mused. He had to advise Lucifer of the plan's success, but not before he enjoyed his evening treat.

Gabriel couldn't deal with the turmoil inside, so he made the biggest mistake in his life and ignored it.

"Adamina."

"That is not my name," Elizabeth said turning her pain to the only weapon she had, anger. He felt the energy in her build.

"I was just," but he couldn't find the words. He couldn't lie to her and couldn't tell her the truth. He was stunned, tongue tied. He couldn't admit his flaws, his weakness. He wouldn't admit it to anyone. Not even himself. His pride was too great, and lust tasted sweet.

"You just what?"

She grabbed his cellular phone off the desk. She flipped through numbers. Dozens of women's names and numbers, including Jem's flirtatious texts. So this was the real Gabriel. She wanted nothing to do with him. Dreams and fantasies were just that, this was real life.

"It's over," her voice went soft and dark, her eyes cold.

She threw his phone at him. Before it hit him, it exploded into a million pieces. He put up his arms to shield his face from the shrapnel. The move was unnecessary because none of the shrapnel hit him. No matter how angry, she could never bring herself to hurt him. But she could shut him out and leave him. She glowed with magic and her aura pulsed brightly, nearly blinding him. Then she was gone. She had shut herself off from him. No longer could he see her magic. No longer could he hear her thoughts. Adamina was gone and he had killed her this time. Elizabeth turned on her heels, and left him there. She hurried out the back door of the restaurant, looking straight ahead of her. He didn't stop her and she didn't turn back.

In the alley way, she broke down. Shaking, shattered to her core, she cut the last cords of energy that tied them together. Tears streamed down her face, but she would not sob. She would not give him that satisfaction. In that moment, she gave up on Angels and magic and dreams. She locked up her heart, bound her magic, and severed herself from that life forever. She wished hard for the counsel and couch of a best friend, but Madison was miles away at school. Elizabeth dug her phone out of her purse and dialed the only other number she knew.

"Tyr, can you come get me?"

The only question he asked her was where. He was there in a matter of minutes. He didn't question her tears when he picked her up. He simply asked where to.

"Anywhere, but home," Elizabeth said, her voice laced with anger.

He drove her to his place. He didn't stop her when she cleared out his stash of alcohol, but he kept her away from the balcony. There was no telling what she would do. Her heartbreak was smothering even him as it radiated out of her in a thick cloud of despair. She didn't speak for the rest of the night, just pounded back liquid poison and stared at the wall. When she finally passed out, Tyrel carried her and tucked her into bed.

Tyrel found a pass card to a condo building and assumed it was where Gabriel had whisked her off to. He cleaned out Gabriel's condo of her stuff, carefully escorting Lewis in his carrier. Gabriel was lucky he didn't show up or Tyrel would have taught him a lesson in mortality. He knew his brothers' vices too well and suspected what had transpired. When Tyrel returned home, he released Lewis into the guest bedroom. He made sure there were several tissue boxes available for her when she woke up. Tyrel's heart ached for his friend, but there was nothing more he could do for her until she was ready.

He did, however, have to look for Lucifer now. A

slight flicker of Lucifer's dark power, and Uriel's, followed Elizabeth. It was faint, but they were here, somewhere in the city and Tyrel was going to find them both. With the gods as his witness, when he did find them, Tyrel would tear the power from them and make them helpless forever.

HE RAGED. LUCIFER, THERE was no other possible solution but Lucifer. Uriel wasn't sly enough to pull something like this off on his own.

"Where is he?" Gabriel roared as he slammed Roger's body into the dingy apartment wall.

"Tsk, tsk, Gabriel, it is not healthy to let your anger run away from you," Roger sneered at his once-brother.

"Uriel, that's enough of your bullshit. Tell me where that bastard brother of ours is or I will kill you, damn the consequences."

Gabriel glowed with vengeance. The power that had slept inside of him, the powers he thought were all but lost, had been slowly awakened by Adamina. Now they erupted in a deadly rage directed at those who sought his destruction, those that had taken Adamina away from him once again. Roger hung in the air with smug triumph. Gabriel's murderous rage only sweetened the plot of his plans. Lucifer always was the genius of the family. Roger may be mortal now, but he was Angel once, and he would be something more soon. He was so close to immortality he could taste it. He sucked at the energy spiraling off of Gabriel. That is it once-brother, Roger mused, seethe and let your anger fuel me. *Soon I will have what we both desire, immortality and the woman. You will be left with nothing you self-righteous...*

"I am sorry, brother, I have no idea where Lucifer has

flitted off to," Roger said in a mocking tone.

"Liar!" Gabriel threw Roger into the coffee table which buckled under the force and dropped Roger to the ground.

Clambering out of the debris, Roger brushed himself off and stared Gabriel down. Gabriel's muscles twitched against his restraint. It would be so easy to kill this worm of a man, too easy, but Gabriel was not a man to prey on the weak. He turned around, fists clenched, and stormed out the door.

"I will find him, Uriel, and I will kill him. Then I will return for you."

Gabriel slammed the door and squealed away in some expensive car Roger didn't care to identify. Roger's eyes went dark with irritation. The smugness became a darker mood. He went into the spare bedroom that housed his altar and the mirror. Roger lifted the black veil from the scrying mirror and with a wave of his hand it rippled.

"Illumino."

When a female Lucifer appeared in the glass, Roger didn't wait for a greeting.

"Gabriel is coming for you."

"Oh, you let me worry about him, dear," Lucy's blue eyes swirled and a smile glinted on her face, "Give him a couple weeks to stew. My presence is shrouded from prying eyes. I will contact you when the next phase of the plan is ready. Sit tight Uriel. If you get antsy, visit the club before you do anything stupid."

The mirror reverted and Roger covered the glass. He turned to a large fireplace that housed a cauldron. Lifting the lid and setting it aside, Roger grabbed a knife and pricked his finger to drop a few drops of blood into the brewing potion. Then he added Gabriel's hair he had collected during their altercation. He replaced the lid on the cauldron. Roger waved his hand and the fireplace disappeared. With another wave, the room appeared like an ordinary guest room. It was ready for her.

ELIZABETH AWOKE TO PURRING, her face buried in black fur.

"Lewis!"

She began crying again. She hugged him tight and he purred louder. After hours of clinging to Lewis, drifting in and out of sleep, Elizabeth managed to pry herself out of bed. She was still wearing the gown. She tore it off of her, tore all of it off of her in a frenzied despair and threw it in the trash. Tyrel had left a suitcase of her clothes and she pulled on sweats and a t-shirt.

Opening the door, sunlight blinded her puffy eyes. Without a word, he handed her a cup of coffee. She mustered appetite for an apple, then her stomach clenched shut again. She left the coffee barely touched. She was agitated. She had to do something, had to escape from the pain that threatened to tear her in two. She stood gazing out at the view from Tyrel's balcony, not seeing anything. She took deep, struggling breaths of cool air. She focused on her breathing.

Elizabeth plunged herself into her gift, but when she reached for it, it disappeared. She called for the magic in the Earth. Feeling it hum, she visualized her spirit stretching towards the sky and then dug it deep down into the ground. But she couldn't hold a connection. It snapped and shrunk away from her like a stranger in the night.

Finally she turned to Tyrel, eyes filled with tears. Embracing her as she cried silently, Tyrel understood why his brothers could fall in love with this woman, could lose their minds over her. She was more than a woman. She was magical. She was the Earth, as much as she had been of Avalon. She was strong and vibrant. She reminded him of home. But here, now, he was worried she would shatter into a million tiny pieces, like stained glass. Tyrel's own head and heart swirled with thoughts of chasing away her loneliness, chasing away her pain. He wanted to fight for her, and rid her of this torment. He got ahold of himself.

"Sorry," she stepped back as if she had received a shock.

"Don't mention it."

He left her to herself. She needed time until she could breathe again without feeling the crushing ache inside of her. His own heart echoed that ache for one he had lost lifetimes ago. Knowing this pain, it baffled him that Gabriel could be capable of utterly destroying the person he had searched for for lifetimes. Jealousy and rage threatened to boil-up and eat him alive. Tyrel had been looking and never found the woman who had died because of him. Madigan, he winced at the thought of her name. Images of her long black hair, her skirts flowing in the wind. Like an executioner, he cut off his memory of her there. He could not relive her death again. He couldn't watch as a band of cowards killed her. All he had done was watch.

His shirt and pants clung to his muscled body. He was on a mission, after all. Elizabeth's best friend needed to be picked up from the airport. She had left a message on Elizabeth's voicemail, and her phone had converted it to text. The damn thing was buzzing on his coffee table near midnight for nearly a quarter of an hour and so he had picked it up to see what the matter was, thinking it was Gabriel groveling. Tyrel had phoned her back, filling Madison in on Elizabeth's heartbreak and he and Elizabeth's friendship. Madison insisted on flying in overnight to be there for her best-friend. He figured the surprise would life Elizabeth's spirits.

"I have to go out Elizabeth. I'll be back in an hour.

Help yourself to anything you need. I have my cell if you require."

She nodded, waving at him as he left while she curled up on the couch with Lewis. It was still early and traffic was light. He parked the car in the passenger pick-up lane and got out. Being a head taller than everyone else had its advantages. The sun rose over the edge of the building and he had to shield his eyes from the glare as he scanned the crowd for her. His eyes settled on a woman dressed in haste with long black hair and kohl eyeliner. He blinked and her image shimmered and there was Madigan again, standing in front of him. She was different, more modern of course, but her eyes, it was her. She smiled at him and moved toward him. When she was in hearing range to him, she called his name.

"Tyrel?"

His knees nearly gave out at the shock and he spoke her name before he could stop himself, "Madigan."

"Madison," she corrected him.

"Right," he coughed and pounded his chest, hoping it would knock some sense back into him, "Sorry."

She slid into the passenger seat. He fumbled with the door and then followed suit. He sat there for a while looking at her in silence.

"Is Elizabeth okay?" she asked.

"Oh, yeah, she's fine. Gabriel hasn't tried to contact her again since. But she's in a lot of pain. Gabriel doesn't deserve how much she loves him."

Tyrel scowled as he pulled the car back into the flow of traffic and onto the freeway. It took them nearly an hour to get to his apartment as Tyrel drove slow and safely, cursing every time a vehicle got near them. They sat in silence the entire way. As soon as he parked the car, Madison flew out and up the stairs to Tyrel's apartment. Elizabeth hadn't moved an inch.

"Liz?" Madison said softly and made her way to sit

beside Elizabeth.

"Madison?" Elizabeth turned her head and blinked then wrapped her arms around her best friend and started crying again.

Madison hugged her tightly, "It'll be alright."

24

I T HAD BEEN ALMOST a year. A year and Tyrel was
no closer to finding Lucifer than when he had started.
He needed an in. Someone who knew Lucifer's hiding
place. A terrible thought occurred to him. The only possible way to find Lucifer was through Uriel. Tyrel would
make Uriel believe he had grown tired of being mortal.
Uriel would accept him with open arms, lead him straight
to his target and Tyrel would end Lucifer's reign forever.
Tyrel already knew where Uriel was. With Lucifer out of
the way, his own mission would be substantially easier to
accomplish. Well, at least one of them. Controlling the
demonic population was no easy feat, especially with Lucifer creating all sorts of new and terrible creatures.

The monster under the bed routine was getting really
old. Lucifer must be pretty desperate to be robbing the
magic from children. Thankfully Tyrel had help of a few
reliable magical folk, and they had put a fair dent in the
population already. Once balance was sufficiently restored, he would be free. Tyrel dropped into the driver's
seat and headed to the rougher area of town. The cock-
roaches were most likely keeping Uriel company when

Lucifer wasn't around. Tyrel guessed he would be a welcome visitor.

VERONICA MACKENZIE DEPOSITED THEIR drinks on the table. Madison and Elizabeth muttered thanks. The Bitter Bean coffee shop was quiet and it was almost closing time, lucky for her. It was girl's night and that meant good food, good drinks and excellent company.

"So how is the apartment?"

Elizabeth took a sip of her drink and then replied, "Still not occupied."

Elizabeth had moved back into her childhood house, along with Madison who was sticking around to finish her thesis in the city. She occasionally had to fly back to discuss her progress with her supervising professor, but it was nice to have her back.

"It shouldn't be long now. I hear it is a seller's market," Madison said cheerfully.

Elizabeth nodded.

"We should hit up the comic store and see what board games we can score!" Madison exclaimed.

Veronica rolled her eyes, "You know I hate board games."

"You hate everything, Veronica," Elizabeth rolled her eyes.

"It seemed like you were enjoying yourself last-time," Madison stated.

"I don't hate everything! I like spending time with you two, hate board games," Veronica affirmed then got up to assist a customer and finish closing.

On their way out Veronica asked to stop by her place so she could get ready.

"Sure, Madison and I will hit the comic store and grab some board games. We won't be long."

"Alright."

Veronica waved them off as they pulled out of her driveway and headed into her place. She mussed with her mouse-brown hair and preened herself. She chose eye-shadow colors to accent her blue eyes and applied plumping lip-gloss that matched her purse to her thin lips. She threw on a tight-fitting top and jeans. She would have to get Elizabeth to go shopping with her and pick out some new clothes. She hadn't updated her wardrobe in almost five years. Veronica fed Cheeto, her gorgeous orange Tabby, petted him, three pets exactly, and headed to the entrance closet to choose footwear. Settling on a pair of black leather ankle boots, she zipped them up and checked herself out in the mirror.

She flipped open her phone and texted the girls to let them know she was ready. *15 min.* flashed Elizabeth's response. Veronica fussed over her appearance some more. She would never admit that she hoped to meet a nice guy while they were out on the town. But secretly, she did hope for a strong-willed man to whisk her off her feet. She just hated the awkwardness of meeting people. She couldn't understand how her friends – all introverts – were so open.

Veronica did have everything she needed: a roof above her head, a small hoard of money, Cheeto, a wicked computer with dozens of video games; oh, and television, glorious television. She didn't see the need to date. She wasn't a fool though. If the opportunity presented itself, she wouldn't refuse it. At least not intentionally. Okay, so she felt incompetent when it came to social interaction. It wasn't her fault. Ugh, where were the girls. As if to answer, her phone went off with a *Here* text. Veronica rushed out of the place ready to get her evening started.

"Can we keep the board gaming at a minimum to-night?" She asked as she slid into the back seat of Elizabeth's small magenta hatchback.

"Deal."

They had only scored one board game at the comic store anyway. Elizabeth pulled out of the drive. The city was a trail of lights. The roads in Veronica's end of town were empty and it gave the area a ghost-like feel. It wasn't until they hit the vibrant lights of downtown that traffic gave signs of life. The plan was to hit up their favorite restaurant where they would be able to hear conversation, get expertly mixed cocktails, and potentially score sophisticated dates. Their version of partying was a mash-up of nerdisms and cocktails. As usual, they became intently involved in critiquing the food, Veronica complained of the horrors of the world, and Madison and Elizabeth tried to steer the conversation other directions. Scoring a date long forgotten, they retired early in the evening back to Elizabeth's house. Madison and Veronica continued their conversation in Madison's basement suite and Elizabeth reveled in a quiet evening upstairs.

Elizabeth climbed the stairs she had darted up and down in her childhood. If the house was really quiet, she swore she could hear the voices of her parents and grandmother whispering. She had settled into bed, and just opened the book she had been eager to get back to all day when she got a text. Disgruntled, she put the sci-fi novel down and grabbed for her cell phone. Tyrel's name popped up in her alerts and she opened the text. *Need help. 1451 Burmingham. Hurry.* Why would Tyrel need her help?

He had mentioned three months prior that he had plans to seek out Lucifer, but had said he had hit a dead end. The name had sent her mind reeling and her heart racing. She remembered him, his dark eyes. As Adamina, she had stopped him from taking Avalon and her magic. With the help of the Goddess, Adamina had unleashed her connection to the elements, all her magic at once to burn Avalon out of Lucifer's reach and to save as many as she could in the process. A wave of emotions had hit her at the memory of Gabriel lying in the cabin, waiting to die. Her spirit had sat with him, forever indebted to him. He had saved her children. He had given up everything for her. *Maybe I should...* No she didn't owe him anything. Besides, Gabriel hadn't called her in over a year. He had not tried to get her back. It was clear she was not wanted. With a sigh she heaved herself out of bed, dressed and was on her way.

It took her little time to arrive at the strange building as her damned GPS system failed her by two blocks. Her headlights flashed over the place. It was three stories high. Brick. The windows were blacked out. Her nerves got the better of her so she focused on the facts. Tyrel's car was parked behind the building. There was a door propped open. She pulled her hatchback beside Tyrel's car, turned off the engine and stepped out. Her boots clicked against the pavement and she softened the noise by adjusting her weight. She called softly for Tyrel and heard no answer. She closed her eyes for a quick moment to prepare her sight for the blackness of inside. She took a breath in, exhaled and opened them.

Silently and swiftly she stepped into the darkness. The darkness gave way to subtle shapes, then eventually to clearer images. She had entered through an area of the building that held ramshackle offices. Softly she moved down a hall, then another, making her way across the building. A noise caused her to stop mid-step. She gave the impression of a cat listening for its prey. Moving a little quicker, Elizabeth followed the disturbance. She found herself on the other side of a door, light streaking out from the space between it and the frame. Murmurs grew audible and she slid the door open further.

"Gabriel!"

Mid-sentence, Gabriel turned toward her voice.

"Tyrel?"

She stared at them both with a pained look on her face. She had not seen him since... She took a breath to steady herself, since that night. She built walls, armor and shielding around her heart instantly. She would remain grounded now, the rest she would deal with later. Tyrel held a guilty look on his face and avoided Elizabeth's eyes.

"I see you remembered how to approach silently..." Gabriel began.

She cut him off, "Don't even start."

He swallowed and nodded.

"What is going on? Tyr texted me, said it was urgent," she held up her phone.

"No, I didn't. I have misplaced my phone."

She sighed and closed her eyes for a moment. She had gotten out of bed for nothing. She was going to turn around, walk out of here, drive home and crawl into bed after smashing her not-so-smart-phone to get some peace and quiet. For all she knew, this was a convoluted ploy of Gabriel's to talk with her. If that was the case, he wasn't all that different from Roger after all. As far as she was concerned, they deserved each other.

"He's telling the truth," a sultry voice from the shadows cooed.

Elizabeth's eyes flashed open as a too perfect blonde appeared out of the shadows. She felt a wave of nausea and her gaze became fuzzy. Her third eye flew open and she saw him: a looming shadow of a demonic Angel hiding in a woman's body. Well, Tyrel had found Lucifer after all.

Her heart raced. She was not ready to take him on. She needed more time. She needed to get help. She may be a powerful witch, but she wasn't foolish. She couldn't take on a demonic Angel alone. She took a step back and arms wrapped around her tightly. She would recognize that stench anywhere.

"Roger," she said low, jaw tense.

She shifted her weight as best as she could, but she couldn't get her footing stable enough to manage any of the maneuvers she imagined executing. But she wasn't about to give up just yet. A swift kick as insurance that Roger's genetics weren't reproduced would be mighty satisfying.

"Hello my dear. Together again at last. No need to struggle, I've got you," he grinned and looked like a little kid who got to eat the whole cake on his birthday.

Lucy ignored Uriel and resisted an eye-roll. Every minion had their price and their use.

"Now, isn't this nice, all of us here. Together."

"Tyr, you bastard!" Gabriel's eyes flamed.

"I had no idea Gabriel!" Tyrel held his hands up defensively, anticipating a strike.

Gabriel turned his gaze to Lucifer.

"No," Lucy cut Gabriel off before he could speak. "The bastard you are looking for is that one, over there," she pointed to Uriel, "The one holding your sweet, precious Adamina."

"That is not my name!" She lunged, pulling Roger forward an inch with her rage. "How many times do I have to tell you freaks. My name is Elizabeth! I don't care who I was in the past. I don't care who you think I am now. My name is Elizabeth McAllistar!"

"Oh do shut her up Uriel," Lucy rolled her eyes and waved a hand. Lucifer shimmered and donned his usual masculine appearance.

Roger stared at Lucifer dumbfounded.

"Do I have to… yes of course I do… Get her out of here you idiot," annoyance dripped from his every word.

Roger checked the rage in lieu of his prize whom he dragged kicking and screaming and biting out the back door. He struggled with Elizabeth and nearly let go of her twice so he pulled out the chloroform and smothered her into compliance. Roger opened the back door of his four-door sedan and pushed her in. The car had a hole from rust and it was clear the suspension in the back had given way. There was no grace or skill to Roger, no cunning. And his misfortune was Elizabeth's fortune. She opened her eyes. Roger had forgot to douse the napkin in the chloroform. She slid a slender knife from the back of her belt sheath. She never went anywhere without it thanks to Roger's earlier escapades. As he was making his way around the car, Elizabeth quietly unlatched the lock and slid out of the door, slashing one of his tires as she stood up.

"Hey, numb-nuts. You'll always be too stupid for me!" She turned and ran back inside, locking the door and jamming a rather heavy piece of steal under the handle bar. That should keep him out for a while. She smirked. He was probably still standing there dumbfounded and processing what just happened.

"Lucifer!" Gabriel's voice roared.

She snapped her head toward the yell. Tyrel wrapped a hand around her mouth. She let out a muffled scream and was about to fight with bloody fury when he hushed her.

"Sh, or you'll give us away Elizabeth! We need to get to Lucifer. I brought Gabriel here to distract Lucifer while I let the others in."

He let her go and rummaged around a pile of building debris, "I figured he would come out of hiding tonight. I apologize that I left my phone at Uriel's and got you back into this mess."

Elizabeth glared at him, scolding. She had worked with Tyrel on a few of his demon hunts and knew how he operated.

"Does Gabriel know he is here as bait?" She asked.

"Not exactly."

He held out a vial, indicating she should take it. She stared at him like he was mad.

"It's a potion," he whispered.

"I know what it is!" She snapped back in a loud whisper.

"Then what's the problem?"

"The problem? The problem is I am in this mess. This, all this, is not real. It just doesn't happen!" She motioned wildly to make up for the restraint of keeping her voice down.

"Like it or not," Tyrel hissed, "Lucifer isn't human or 'normal' as you would like. If we don't take care of him, all hell will break lose. Literally!" Tyrel thrust the vial into Elizabeth's hand.

Elizabeth resigned herself to the vial, "Fine, but what am I supposed to do with it?"

Another man, this one tall and lean slid from the shadows, "Wait for my cue, and then dowse him in it."

"And just who the hell are you now!? The wicked witch of the west cross-dressing?" Elizabeth was going mad with all the testosterone around her. Chocolate, she needed chocolate, a good book, a long soak in the bath-tub and a trip to Tahiti. That's it. No, she hated tropical places. Somewhere she really wanted to go. She was tak-ing a vacation somewhere far away very soon.

"Don't be discriminatory Elizabeth. Witches can be male, and no, I am, as you once knew me, Raphael. My parents have named me something awfully unbecoming this life around so we'll stick with Raphael."

"Oh, brilliant, just brilliant," Elizabeth sulked.

"What, you thought I would come in here without a backup plan?"

"You usually don't have that much fore-thought," Elizabeth snapped back at Tyrel.

He sighed and shook his head, "Let's go."

"Are you shitting me?"

"You're a witch. Start acting like one!" Tyrel shot back.

Elizabeth glowered but remained silent. Tyrel walked forward again and the others followed. It wasn't long before a fourth set of footsteps on the pavement followed behind. Elizabeth turned to look but Raphael stopped her.

"He's a friend, that's all you need to know. By the way, if you hadn't got yourself out, one of us would have. We weren't going to let him get away with you." Raphael smiled.

She inhaled and kept moving. Gabriel's yelling had turned into muffled noises of pain. She sure wished she had a few not-so-male friends around here. She almost laughed at the absurdity of it all. But grandma Tabetha and the books said keep an open mind. Within the circle a true believer, out of the circle be as skeptical as possible. Like it or not, she was in the circle of all this. She would be a terrible witch if she didn't keep her mind open. Tyrel opened the door that she had been dragged through only moments before.

"Get the fuck off me you piece of…" Gabriel struggled against Lucifer's weight.

Lucifer was intermittently changing between male and female form toying with Gabriel. Before he knew it, Gabriel's arms were wrapped around blonde and gorgeous Lucy.

"What's the matter, Gabe, see a gem?" Lucy gleefully rubbed in. She grinned while playing with Gabriel's hair.

"Lucifer, get off of him," Tyrel yelled.

"Oops, looks like you're caught with another woman again!" Lucy disappeared, her cackle turning into a deep maniacal laugh.

Elizabeth felt the presence behind her melt into the shadows to follow Lucifer. Gabriel froze, expecting Lucifer's tricks when he saw her. Her expression spoke the truth.

"Mina," Gabriel swallowed and finished his ascension, "please forg…"

She cut him off, "Elizabeth."

She turned toward Raphael, about to say something,

but was cut off by Lucifer's reappearance.

"My, my, my, is it my birthday?"

"Oh do shut it Lucifer," Elizabeth snapped. She had had enough of this.

Startled by her outburst, he raised an eyebrow and then grinned. Right where he wanted her.

"No use hanging on to pretense," Lucifer dropped his hold on a mortal camouflage and took on the dark, twisted beauty he was. Massive wings and a muscled body stretched before them. Shadows coiled across his skin.

A voice haunting and dark echoed through the building, "Much better."

Tyrel slinked into the shadows slowly, Raphael nowhere to be seen. Gabriel stepped up to stand beside Elizabeth. Elizabeth stepped forward to the object of her mission and to get away from him.

"Lucifer!" Elizabeth yelled.

"Ah, the prize of the night, there you are. I could barely see you from all the way up here, merely a speck…"

"Blah, blah, blah," Elizabeth interrupted, irritated. Gabriel smirked.

"Remember Avalon Lucifer. Remember the fires burning. Remember the magic slipping from your grasp? That was me Lucifer. I burned Avalon to the ground to keep it from you. Avalon may have become a waste land, but without the flames, it could have served you well. The only things you truly have are those terrible fables about you, a satan, supposedly living in hellfire. That is all you have, a simple fable…"

What is she doing? Raphael desperately cried out to Tyrel and the Shadow walker.

She will die if she continues, Tyr, the shadow walker hissed.

Trust her, Tyrel cut them off with a low, bellowing chant and the ground began to shake.

She heard him calling to darkness, the words she

could not hold in her mind. She kept going, "Yes, that's right. Lucifer the great. Lucifer the fallen, a satan you may be in myth, but in reality you are a hollow specter. A shallow haunting that can be expunged with simple human-blessed water!"

She uncorked the bottle, lightning fast and splashed Lucifer's legs with the substance. Nothing happened and he laughed.

"I am still here!" Lucifer laughed.

Elizabeth muttered, "Alright then, plan B."

Elizabeth was a McAllistar and she would do what all McAllistar women did before her. She cast her circle, began her spell. The magic tingled across her skin, pulsed in her veins. She would call on every spirit, god, or ancestor she could. Focused on her spell work, she did not see when Lucifer struck out with a sweep of his arm. The shadow walker slid in front and took the battering. His body fell limp to the floor and shimmered. Shadows slid away revealing a slight, young male.

"Kamiel!"

Adamina's once-son lay lifeless on the floor. Inside, Elizabeth snapped. Set free, the emotions that had threatened to drown her that day she had met Gabriel, lashed forward. Lifetimes of pain, rage, love, broke free of the careful barriers she had erected and with them, her magic. Raw and magnificent, she targeted Lucifer. He had taken life from her once. He had taken her love from her twice. He would pay three times over.

"You all want Adamina?" Her eyes became swirling orbs of menacing green. "You can have her!"

The building shook. Elizabeth's body glowed. Her hair bled reds and browns and blacks, shone with gold and silver.

"You can have the land she walked on!" The concrete crumbled away beneath them. Gabriel stumbled back, afraid he would fall in. Tyrel kept chanting from a balcony above them and Raphael raced towards Kamiel, dragging him away from further harm.

Her voice deepened, "You can have the sorrow she drowned in."

Rain fell. As it hit Lucifer's flesh it slid over his skin like frozen knives. He stretched his wings as the concrete fell away and struggled to stay air born. He narrowed his eyes at Adamina, fighting against the pain. The first time he had felt pain since his fall from grace. Pools of frigid water bled across the exposed soil. Gabriel was focused on her. With the expense of this much power, her body would give out soon. He did the only thing there was to do. He gave up every last ounce of magic he would ever possess to help her rid the universe of Lucifer.

"You can have the fire she burned in," Elizabeth's eyes poured frigid tears and blazed red. Flames shot up towards Lucifer from the soil and grabbed at him like hands, burning his frozen skin. He opened his mouth in a terrifying scream and fought against them, calling for all his power. The shadows chattered and shifted in response.

"You can have the breath she choked on!" Lucifer's screaming stopped as he suffocated on her death, burned in Adamina's rage, and drowned in her sorrow.

Tyrel's voice reached Gabriel. At Tyrel's command, the soil beneath Lucifer began to open revealing a void. Clever, Gabriel mused, a void like that would hold Lucifer for a very long time. He may not like the man, especially since Tyrel had lured him here as bait, but Gabriel respected his gifts. He would one day repay the favor, though. And yet, Tyrel had offered an opportunity for Gabriel to see her one last time. He rested his gaze on Adamina. Here she stood again. He longed to embrace her, call her name, but the effort of sustaining her with what power he had left held him in place.

Adamina's form flickered. She needed more power. He closed his eyes and cast his sight, seeking another power source, but the very last of his power slipped away from him. Gabriel could do nothing more as he fell to his knees but pray she would not die.

Roger stormed into the scene, finally having wedged open the back door. He stared dumbfounded as Lucifer burned in a silent scream. Adamina stood before him. He had been searching for so long for her. His wife. She would be mother to the first new Angel, his son. She would bring him glory and restore him to heaven again. Uriel's Adamina. He stepped forward reaching for her. A tendril of magic flashed out toward him and tore at his soul. The darkness he had been growing inside of him slipped away. His chances of being restored to his power died with the last of the magic she pulled from him. Roger stumbled back screaming. Completely mortal and magicless, Roger passed out.

The last of Uriel's Angelhood fueled her. Sustained by Uriel's energy, she forced Lucifer into the trap, pushing him into the void Tyrel had created with every last bit of strength her spirit had. She began to feel weak, the magic leaving her quickly. The image of Adamina dissolved away. Her hold on the spell broke and the world went white.

Goddess stood in front of her, a vision of flowing silver robes and moon beams. God, a much wiser and kinder god, stood golden at her side. He had discovered Avalon ablaze at the hands of Lucifer. He had discovered Goddess' secret. He understood. And so, God had kept Goddess' secret from the Others.

You came into this world nameless and alone. I gave you a name, Adamina, I gave you a home. Now, you have become something more. You are your own. If you have need of me, if you have desire, call and I will answer in the whispers of the heart. You shall not see me again, in this life or the next, until you return to me for rest. Your past, you are free from. Move forward without the burdens of Adamina. The circle is broken and new again, Elizabeth.

White light seared her eyes. Then everything went dark.

Epilogue

HE TOOK A DEEP breath and exhaled. The winter had been frigid and it had been difficult to weather without her. More difficult than he had expected. His own pride had hid that from all but Alan. Alan was a jack-of-all-trades, keen and as resourceful as a hawk. Gabriel appreciated Alan's friendship. A bitter chill bit through his jacket, winter's remembrance on this spring day. Gabriel closed the zipper up to the collar and turned his walk in the park back to the car. In the end, Gabriel had been forced to admit the truth about his star-crossed quest. It had not been fate, Uriel, Lucifer or gods that had delivered the final blow. No, he had done a fine job of that himself.

An owl hooted at him and, catching sight of the creature, Gabriel smiled. Its black-brown eyes stared. They shared an ancient bond. It was a magnificent creature. Out of place in the city, but somehow finding its way, triumphing over the odds against it. The willow where they had met stood before him. Images of their meeting flashed in his mind; the way her rampant emotions had hit him the chest suddenly during his usual walk one afternoon; her heroic struggling against such incredible loss. He had been staggered by it all. He had thought his mind was playing tricks on him again. He had been haunted by those dreams, those memories for so long. But there she had been after all. Avalon had been real. Adamina, his dear sweet Adamina. The pang of loss threatened to take hold again.

She had managed what he had not been able to. He would never forget how she had looked: blazing bright, a vessel of the Goddess. Lucifer locked up tight with Tyrel's final charms to seal the cage. Gabriel returned to add some of his own wards a few weeks after, just in case. He had caught her before she hit the ground. Watched as Adamina disappeared, accepting a new life as Elizabeth. He had to let her go.

Raphael had lifted her from his arms. Unable to bare the sorrow, he left her there in the care of Tyrel and Raphael. He had wandered the streets until Alan had found him and returned him home to his bed where he had slept for three days. Gabriel exhaled. He walked slowly, savoring each step. Sunlight shone through the trees and caused shadows to dance along the ground. Birds sang all around him and geese lazily ambled past or slept in the grass. A squirrel scooted across his path and chittered at him, then ran away. Life thrived around him. There was so much to look forward to, so much to live for. His life was filled with uncertainties and mysteries again.

"Blessed Be, Elizabeth," he whispered to the trees and sent his love through the currents of the Earth.

The leaves rustled in a gentle breeze. He imagined she would be sitting in a coffee shop somewhere sipping a latte and visiting with friends. The image brought another smile to his lips. He bumped into a man slightly taller than he, with deep eyes and a tiny spark of magic. In those eyes he saw her future. Gabriel responded to his muttered apology with a nod and watched as the stranger walked away. Her future would be gentle, kind, and devoted. It took all his will to smother the jealousy and possessiveness that rose in him. The Fates moved all too quickly for his liking. His car came into view at the side of the road. Alan held the door open and he slid in.

Once Alan was settled in the front seat he asked for the usual direction, "Where to, sir?"

Gabriel smiled and replied, "Let's try the coast this time, something new."

"Sir," with a nod Alan pulled the car away.

Author's Note

Well, it is finally completed. It has taken ten years to get to this point. Hard work, revisions, complete restarts of the manuscript and now it is here. I can only hope, you the reader, find as much pleasure in reading as I did in writing.

It wouldn't be here today without the input and support of many folks. Firstly, my husband. Without him I would have given up a long time ago. His undying patience, dedication, and love kept me going when I lost faith in myself, the manuscript, and the magic of life. Thank you so very much love. A special thanks to J. V. for inspiring the story and for her input. Shannon, I couldn't have done it without you. You are an amazing editor and a dear friend. Without you, this would still be a rough first draft and never would be published.

L, T, and N, without your close friendships, guidance, and long talks about the characters you inspired, I'd be nowhere. I owe so much to you.

A special than you to Vivienne Gucwa for your beautiful photography that ties everything together.

Author Biography

Catherine Milos is a Canadian Author who lives with her husband and three cats. Catherine has been writing since she could hold a crayon. Aside from writing, Catherine's passions include rescuing strays, creating and appreciating art, connecting with nature, and being amazed by the magic of life. You can also find her playing the occasional video game, in a library, or traveling.

Follow her on Twitter @CatherineMilos, Facebook, or catherinemilos.com.

Photographer Biography

Vivienne Gucwa is a full-time fine art travel photographer, making a living working on commissions that take her all over the world. When not traveling, Vivienne holds a passion for taking photos of the city she grew up in and loves dearly, New York City.

Follow Vivienne on Twitter @travelinglens, Facebook or nythroughthelens.com.

Made in the USA
Columbia, SC
30 April 2017